THE SPINDRIFT FRAME

Also by Jim Accardi:

Dry Sterile Thunder
The Movie Moon (and other stories)
The Rosette Habit
Saigon Landing

THE SPINDRIFT FRAME

A Novel

Jim Accardi

iUniverse, Inc.
New York Lincoln Shanghai

The Spindrift Frame

Copyright © 2007 by James Roy Accardi

iUniverse books may be ordered through booksellers or by contacting:

iUniverse
2021 Pine Lake Road, Suite 100
Lincoln, NE 68512
www.iuniverse.com
1-800-Authors (1-800-288-4677)

ISBN-13: 978-0-595-41783-4 (pbk)
ISBN-13: 978-0-595-86127-9 (ebk)
ISBN-10: 0-595-41783-3 (pbk)
ISBN-10: 0-595-86127-X (ebk)

Printed in the United States of America

Thanks to:

John Callahan
Marian
Angie Lane
Brad English
Mike Cooper
Shirley Lee
Bettye Campbell
The publishing associates and editorial staff of iUniverse

CHAPTER 1

▼

SPINDRIFT

Friday, August 6
Hurricane Gregor
Latest position: 29.2N, 86.8W
Pressure: 912mb
Maximum Sustained Winds: 145 mph
Location: 69 mi. SE St. Bartholomew, Florida
Status: Category 4 and strengthening. Landfall imminent

Kelsoe Babb III:
Gregor was a sneaky hurricane. If I remember right, it started off kind of weak—just a puffed-up tropical storm—and supposedly headed for Texas. Quite honestly, even those of us who tracked him from his infancy were taken somewhat by surprise. It wasn't until the night before he hit that the hurricane center slid the warning area down to us. Still, the television, radio, police, and emergency management people here in St. Bart's did a fine job of putting out the word and moving people out of here.

Despite all that, as you know, we had a few fatalities. Some of those folks—those without transportation, the sick and crippled, a few dedicated public workers—were faultless victims of circumstance. As for the others, the individuals who could have fled but chose to remain, you have a harder time feeling sorry for them. I'm sure most of them didn't have the first clue what they were up against. I guess, if you really wanted to be charitable about it, you could say that the rest of us are to blame for not properly educating them. Most of them, anyway.

There was this other man, the one you've asked about. The best anyone can tell, he placed himself directly in Gregor's path. It's almost as if he wanted the storm to kill him. I guess you could call it a nature-assisted suicide. I've heard that he was super-depressed, that he'd just given up on his life. Even if that's true, it's sort of hard to feel sorry for him. One assumes he had the power to elect his fate, and he consciously chose death. One can only hope that he had no awareness of all the sadness and legal complications that would spin from it.

Sometime in the mid-morning, Tam Malonee decided he wasn't running from Gregor. This determination had begun the previous evening as a stubborn inclination. It didn't harden into an actual decision until the sec-ond-and-third-to-the-last inhabitants of the Surfsider sped out of the potholed parking lot without him. Claiming to have made previous arrangements that couldn't, at that late hour, be canceled, he declined an offer of a free ride out of St. Bart's, thereby stranding himself in harm's way. In reality, his only "arrange-ment" was a half-hearted commitment to an ill-defined notion that he "might just ride out" the strengthening storm. This particular bad idea had sputtered out of his intuition-and-alcohol-fueled thought engine (as had his crimes, his initial southern odyssey, and most of his many other life failures) in purely idealistic and metaphorical terms—quite vague, yet filled with obscure possibility. As he drained the last tall-boy, he envisioned Gregor as possibly a heaven-sent minister, the cleansing wind and rain possibly some variety of sacramental medium, and the eventual emerging sun possibly a divine guiding beacon. In that vision's dra-matic resolution, Tam had pictured himself emerging from the storm, baptized and anointed, reborn. His nebulous vision of a new identity—some manner of reclusive genius painter specializing in some yet-to-be-perfected and highly per-sonalized style of bold acrylic portraiture—had been incubating in his imagina-tion for months. He was less certain about his future working environment, although he felt confident that it would be in a distant tropical location. His pref-erence: a place where folks didn't ask a lot of personal questions.

About three hours later, shortly after the hurricane's inner bands began straf-ing St. Bart's Bay with stinging winds and sideways-flung rain bullets, Tam stood in the frightening mid-afternoon darkness and admitted to himself that his deci-sion not to flee was just another bad impulse, and one based on flawed informa-tion at that. Not really information at all; just assumptions and poorly informed generalizations. Indeed, all that Tam Malonee knew about the destructive power of hurricanes derived from a few scarcely registered images of poncho-clad television meteorologists leaning into driving rain. Hurricanes had never seemed like a big deal to him. He had, himself, leaned into blowing rain, not to mention blowing snow, ice, and sleet. He saw a hurricane as just another form of rotten weather, something to be endured until better weather arrived. When the attractive young woman on the all-day cable weather station had somberly mentioned "storm surge" (earlier that morning, just before the power went out), Tam had constructed mental images of glassy five-foot swells. Dozens of people had warned him about what might be coming; not a single word had registered. He had even ignored the patrolling police officer whose amplified voice had declared that evacuation was now "man-dan-tory."

Nor had it helped that he'd been drinking since eight o'clock the previous evening. He'd managed to stay sober for four whole days, but his will had walked out the door with Madison Monroe. As the result of a crash two-step recovery program of his own design (Step One: quit drinking; Step Two: don't start drinking again, or else), the guilt of his relapse was negating any comfort he'd hope to find in his once beloved "amber wave of grain." Sleep had not come to him, nor had respite from the impaling sense of personal failure. All the eleven beers had done for him was impair his already defective judgment.

Even so, every alcohol-driven preconception and quasi-delusional judgment disintegrated once he saw the towering palmettos bend into contorted postures that made him mindful of his own fragile skeleton. And once the area's power grid failed and he could actually *feel* the storm's fury rumbling in the walls and flooring, all thought previously given to a post-storm life or identity seemed like misspent mental energy.

He staggered to the juddering glass doors that opened onto the tiny "Gulf-view" balcony hanging vulnerably from the building's side. The phrase "Gulf-view," he now assumed, was pure realty spin for the oblique glimpse of sand and surf that one might have had but for the usurping presence of an oleander-swathed condo building a mere fifty yards away. Not just a building—a monstrous stepped tower that blotted out not only all evidence of the gulf, but of the sun itself. Of course, at ninety-five bucks a night (end-of-season rate), Tam and Madison could hardly have expected a breathtaking seaside panorama (they might have more reasonably anticipated the burnt sienna shag carpet, the broken lava lamp, and the stained sofa). But accommodation deficiencies had not been of concern to the traveling companions. They had not come to St. Bartholomew to lounge in luxury or view the gulf. They were there to "rescue" Madison's six-year-old daughter from an abusive father, an undertaking, at least to Tam's mind, more accurately defined by its ethical prerogatives than potential aesthetic rewards. The fact that things had turned out badly for most of the people concerned did not—*could* not—diminish the initial noble purpose of that mission. To this end, Tam made every effort to convince himself that the waste of time and resources, his new and oppressive solitude, and the seemingly ever-increasing risk of death or grievous bodily harm were a fitting price to pay for personal redemption.

He placed the palms of both huge hands against one of the door's glass panels, now filigreed with quivering veins of water. He realized then that it wasn't just the doors that were rattling; the entire balcony seemed to be swaying. He caught a glimpse of something metallic—he guessed it was a chunk of flashing from a disintegrating HVAC system—as it was hurled into the great condo tower's battered oleanders and palmettos. He noticed for the first time that the usual crash and roll of the waves could no longer be heard beneath the storm's fierce roar.

He backed slowly away from the balcony doors and sank into the sofa, taking care to avoid the dreaded stain. His long, denim-clad legs arched over the canvas gym bag that held most of his worldly belongings. He pressed his fingertips to his temples and shut his eyes. He commanded himself to do what he had always done: relax, reintegrate all freshly accessed data, and use his considerable intellect to come up with yet another plan. Obviously, he no longer had any use for the many strategies (and sub-strategies) that had taken form in his mind during the previous week. The only plan of interest to him now was the yet-to-materialize contrivance that might somehow allow him to survive Gregor's wrath.

Thomas Aquinas Malonee was a schemer by nature—plans, plots, and intrigues came as necessarily and easily to him as foraging to an orchid bee. As a nine-year-old living a few miles from a southern Michigan public golf course, he had made hundreds of dollars by wading knee-deep into a fetid pond on the par-three fifth hole to recover balls submerged by errant golfers. Shortly after arriving at high school, Tam learned that, by "losing" the first report card of each school term, he could manage a secret cache of easily forged original and duplicate records—an insurance policy against academic house arrest. In college, he had augmented an athletic scholarship with proceeds from a complex and multi-layered racketeering enterprise that eventually resulted in his degree-less ejection from the academy. And so on. The schemes had never stopped, even though they usually proved to be blueprints for disaster. His genius—his full-scale IQ had once been measured at 142 by a psychologist investigating his post-adolescent attraction to mischief-making—was generally neutralized by a

Hamlet-like penchant for overanalysis. Like Wile E. Coyote, he possessed an infinite capacity for half-baked schemes. And, like his cartoon counterpart, Tam—or someone close to him—often wound up trapped in the shadow of a falling anvil.

Now, however, he found himself incapable of formulating even the most ludicrous of strategies. All his anesthetized mind could think about was Madison. He found this development almost startling—in his brief time with her, he'd experienced as many infuriating as endearing moments. His relationship with her had gone from worshipfulness to frustration in a week's time; he had spent days struggling with his feelings for her. Their last hours together had been marred by extreme disagreement and discord. Her angry parting words, particularly the accusations of disloyalty, still reverberated in his head. But solitude, particularly the solitude of a drunken man facing almost-certain death, has the power to liberate trapped emotions. It might explain how Tam Malonee, facing devastation alone, finally decided on a name for what he felt for Madison. Despite the rancor and sleight of heart, despite the fact that he had betrayed her, he knew that what he felt for her was love.

His attention was suddenly seized by the desperate flutter of an object outside the glass doors. Through drooping eyelids, he focused on a piece of cardboard about the size of one of his small canvases. Flung by the pitiless wind, it pressed into the metal balusters of the balcony railing. He watched it suspended there, absorbing the almost microscopic bits of sand and sea salt embedded in the wind. *Spindrift.* He remembered that's what Roger had called the stuff. Roger, the sixties Ann Arbor radical who almost intuitively grasped the workings of the subatomic universe, but had to wrestle to comprehend ordinary human emotional needs. Tam thought about meeting with the man and listening to his latest brainstorm: matter, being particles, which were really waves, which were really pure energy, which was really, well, a cosmic freakin' concept, ought to be able to be dematerialized on demand, then reconstituted in another dimension. Quantum regeneration, he had called it. He had explained it all in physicspeak, his preferred communication medium. As Tam thought back on that lecture, he watched the cardboard warp under the relentless press of nature, warp and fold and slowly, right before his eyes … disappear. Not blow away, not rip to pieces. Just *disappear.* And, then, although he only partially understood the man's theory, an idea—one which was at once ingenious *and* stupid, the kind of notion that prompts other drunks to launch themselves from tenth-story windows in hopes of defying gravity—came to him. What if he were to lash himself, some latter-day Ahab, to the balcony railing at the moment of the storm's peak force? Would he be torn apart, or would he, like the piece of cardboard, just become disassembled? Roger had theorized that the equalization of energies, spin directions, etc. could be responsible for dematerializing various amorphous solids. He had also hypothesized (although he was still laboring at mathematical verification) that these disassembled solids might well, given the postulates of string theory, be capable of reincorporation in another dimension. He had speculated that the random occurrence of this phenomenon might account for the sudden disappearance of various inanimate solids. Of course, Roger had been talking about discrete, tiny amounts of solid matter. In Tam's mind, Roger had overlooked the theory's most significant application: an obvious explanation for the seemingly inexplicable disappearance of airplanes, ships, and other inanimate solids. He asked himself: If that were the explanation, why couldn't the same rules apply to *people*? People disappeared all the time—in explosions, in mysterious oceanic triangles, from the decks of cruise ships. People disappeared on remote country roads. People spontaneously combusted. It sounded crazy, but Tam had seen the notebooks filled with pages of impressive equations that proved, at least to his anesthetized and scientifically untrained mind, that it was at least theoretically possible. What better "equalization of energies" than to pit the potential energy of a human body against the almost incomprehensible power of this storm?

Or, in the event the experiment was a failure, perhaps his death would be regarded as a singular act of self-sacrifice, penance for a lifetime of disappointing others.

Whatever the purpose behind this impulse, one mystery had been solved for Tam. The opportunity to challenge the great storm was the reason fate had placed Roger squarely in his path.

He pulled his last canvas—a single ten-by-fourteen sheet—two brushes (a filbert and a weathered round), a folded section of waxed paper (his substitute palette), a stub of charcoal pencil, and a fistful of half-spent tubes of acrylic paint from a pocket on the side of the gym bag. Before he stepped out onto the balcony, he decided, he would conceive and execute one last artistic something-or-other. Something unique and compelling, but not too heavy. Certainly nothing that confessed the fear and uncertainty now percolating within him. He thought about painting the incoming storm as a primitive abstraction ("*L'orage sans Merci*"?), but quickly rejected that notion. He believed that, with no ill will intended toward the "modern" painters (self-educated in the history of art, Tam retained the untrained observer's lack of enthusiasm for the abstract medium), and even with his harsh working conditions and a limited palette (titanium white, cadmium yellow and red, cobalt blue, and raw sienna), he could manage something a little more imaginative than monochromatic slashes, drips, or geometric forms.

What exercise might be fitting for such a perilous moment? The idea of painting an illustrated last will and testament occurred to him. Of course, such a creation would be purely an *objet d'art* and not a functional instrument of estate management. He had, after all, no estate to manage. His childless marriage had disintegrated. His sole remaining blood relation had made it quite clear that he had other obligations. He'd been officially disenfranchised by his marriage family. All the recent objects of his affection were now gone. Not just Madison, but her daughter and the dog, as well. He had traded away his most cherished personal possession, the old Tele-yellow Fender in its original hard-shell case. The small roll of bills he'd accumulated by selling his paintings had been appropriated by Madison Monroe, as had the crazy purple car, as part of her exit drama. The very last of his money had been spent the previous day on the two six-packs of tall-boys, the final, tepid gulp of which he had just finished swallowing. He had no savings, no life insurance, no pension. No equity in anything but his haunted mansion of regret. With the exception of two canvas portraits, everything he owned was either in his sweating hand, clinging to his damp flesh, or crammed into the gym bag. Whether Roger's reincorporation theory was correct, Tam's art would be all that survived him in the earthly dimension. The one thing he did *not* wish to do was waste his last canvas on an ironic conceit that would mean nothing to anybody.

Then, like the surf pounding the disintegrating beach, another thought crashed into him. Perhaps his week with Madison was the thing most worthy of being memorialized. The fact that he possessed only one usable canvas, however, limited his options. He settled on a medley of mini-paintings—twelve square frames in all. One for each significant story in that beautiful and tortured twining of fate and design. There would be a frame for his odyssey's beginning, of course, and one for his projected demise (would he be impaled by a flying wedge of shag-carpeted floor, torn apart by the wind, or actually reincorporated in another dimension?). As for the remaining squares, he had more than enough subjects to memorialize.

He tilted the pad toward the scant remains of natural lighting and penciled in a square, the faint graphite border of what would be the first frame. *The beginning.*

He began sketching—the beautiful face he knew so well. And, of course, the attitude. He wanted it to be right: the inclination of her torso, the hand on her hip. Of course, the physical representation would be easy. The more difficult problem: how to capture the critical *mens rea*. How could he possibly hope to represent the deceptively agile and conniving mind that had made him her tractable pawn?

He lowered his pencil and stared at the blank frame. *God help him.* That was *precisely* where this story had started. Not with his stupid crimes, not with his heedless flight from an unpleasant reality, nor the fateful decision back in Middleboro to take the less-traveled road. Not even, as he had earlier assumed, when he first laid his tired eyes on her.

It had all started when she first spotted *him.*

He carefully printed the title *Madison* under the square and went to work.

CHAPTER 2

▼

MADISON

Saturday, July 31

Tropical Storm Gregor
Latest position: 17.8.3N, 80.1W
Pressure: 985mb
Winds: 65mph
Movement: WNW 9 mph
Location: Approx. 210 mi. SW Cozumel
Status: Strengthening

What Tam observed, in his first furtive glances around the dimly lit dining room, were the dozen or so male faces, mostly wrinkled and dour, all turned in his direction. He avoided meeting these stares by concentrating on the ketchup spatters on the laminated menu. He'd found the menu wedged between the glass salt and pepper shakers and the stainless steel napkin dispenser. These observers hadn't seemed hostile, exactly—Tam attributed the collective interest to resolute curiosity. The circumstances being what they were, though, he didn't want to be observed by anyone, hostile or not.

When he didn't see anything appealing on the menu, he began to wonder why he was even there. He was immediately able to rule out a number of possibilities. He'd devoured a "rhino" burger, palm fries, and a Kong-sized soft drink at a

Burger Jungle an hour earlier, so it wasn't because he was hungry. Nor had he been seduced by the diner's aesthetic allure—a simple, cinder-block building with peeling brown paint, Mac's external presentation was more body shop than restaurant. He wasn't interested in killing time; he had no doubt that he was already the object of an intense state and federal manhunt. It was almost as if the café had exuded some mysterious attractive force that had hijacked both his will and the stolen Oldsmobile's steering mechanism.

He lifted his eyes from the menu and conducted a quick security scan. The men at the nearby tables appeared to be deep in conversation about things other than him. Satisfied that he was no longer the object of general curiosity, he began to search the room for some clue to his mystery. As he suspected, there were no obvious answers to be found. What he observed was an open dining area reminiscent of a school lunchroom, with the exception of the single veneer-paneled wall bearing a signed football, mounted fish, and framed photographs. A closer look revealed that all the photos depicted uniformed athletes—Tam assumed they all hailed from the Tennessee countryside in the general vicinity of the diner—and, not surprisingly, men holding large fish. Tam took another slow, deep breath and closed his eyes. He knew from reading about psychic powers that sometimes humans could hear things that the other senses missed. He tried to let his mind go blank and let the ambient sounds slosh around in his unconscious. He couldn't stop himself from hearing the already familiar sounds—adult male voices and the clinking of tableware blended indiscriminately with the country twang leaking from overhead speakers. He opened his eyes and waited for a revelation that did not come. With a grimace he concluded that his investigation was just a further waste of time.

He made the decision to abandon the diner. The mysterious force that had pulled him in had clearly weakened in the presence of rational thought. Reason now instructed him that he could only lose by remaining there. Moreover, leaving would be a simple matter, unlike his other recent personal extrications. All he'd have to do was nod politely to the curious locals and slip out the way he'd slipped in.

It was just then, with one long, tree-trunk leg protruding into free space and both palms set in a standard push-off position on the table, that he caught his first glimpse of Madison Monroe.

She had appeared, quite suddenly and to uniform popular notice, from the swinging galley door across the room. She swept into the dining area with a large serving platter held expertly aloft and went to work.

Madison immediately captivated him. It would have been difficult *not* to have noticed her—with her orange blonde hair, neon green blouse, form-hugging red jeans, and lavender Doc Martens, she was like a fashion fire in a dowdy field of flannel, denim, and fertilizer-logo ball caps. But he went far beyond noticing her. His eyes *seized* her, so powerfully affected was he by her presence.

He studied her as she dipped and twisted in the narrow space between a booth and a table. The first jarring realization he had was that she bore a startling resemblance to his wife—or ex-wife, as she may well have been by then. He had ignored the papers drafted by her father's hot-shot lawyer and presented (a little too gleefully, in his opinion) by Lauren a week earlier. Tam wasn't sure whether Michigan judges could grant a divorce in absentia. Nor did he really care what the courts had to say about his marital status. He considered his marriage effectively terminated the day Lauren's father, Norman J. Holdsworthy, the self-proclaimed New Car Baron of Minter Lake, Michigan, decided that he'd had enough of Tam Malonee. It had all been done in a characteristically sneaky way, of course: Norman had sent him on a bus to Indianapolis to drive back an Impala "program" car and, while Tam was away, reclaimed his company car, changed the locks on the doors to his house and his newly opened portrait studio, moved Lauren into her own town house, and replaced him as finance manager of the sprawling Holdsworthy Auto Corral. The following day, after several phone calls to Lauren (for the sole purpose of requesting a simple explanation) Norman had had him served with a restraining order and a bluntly worded warning that further attempts to communicate with his daughter would result in criminal prosecution. And, true to Norman's practice of over-making his points, the two large and surly "private investigators" sent to serve the order also delivered an additional message—leave Lauren alone, or else. They had stopped short of any overt threats of physical harm, but Tam knew their reputations and interpreted their non-verbal prompts—massive arms crossed, beefy hands balled into tight fists— as laden with implied menace. He also suspected that Norman may have played a role in supplying his daughter with the new romantic interest with whom she had been publicly seen and with whom she appeared to be cohabitating, although Tam had no doubt that Lauren was fully capable of accomplishing that task without any assistance. She was, after all, beautiful. Outwardly, in any event. Spiritually (at least in his opinion), she was a late-stage leper; he, like a less benevolent Father Damien, had been rewarded for his devotion with a lethal infection of his own spirit. He had no argument with the substance of Lauren's petition—the "objects of matrimony" had clearly been "destroyed" by the potent corrosive of their shared affliction. Outwardly, at any rate, she was certainly gorgeous and, as he knew well from his own experience, one couldn't underestimate the attractive power of that singular asset.

This woman, this waitress, though, was not Lauren. The longer he studied her, the more satisfied he was that she surpassed Lauren in beauty. Hers was an unsophisticated, provincial beauty, to be sure, with her amateurishly applied makeup and preternatural hair color. The pure architecture of her face, however, the structures, angles, horizontal and vertical axes, even the defects—*especially* the defects—were most pleasurable to behold. Her dominant facial feature was her mouth—wide and sensual, with large and slightly misaligned teeth. She had dark circles under her eyes, but the eyes themselves were large and emerald. Even her vigorous gum-chewing confessed her loveliness: each grinding stroke of her strong jaw revealed deep dimples in her fleshy cheeks.

Tam watched in awe as she expertly dealt overloaded plastic plates and tumblers from the platter now balanced on her left forearm. With server and patrons focused on the food and tableware, Tam felt free, for the first time, to fully drink her in. He silently evaluated her physical attributes using an analytical program written by a lifetime of personal experience, decades of cultural indoctrination, and millennia of biological evolution. He noted that she moved fluidly, like a dancer, around the table, reaching, setting, and placing while the Bubbas slurped their iced tea. His gaze remained on her as she bent in his direction; his wide eyes lingered on the dangling gold cross and the patch of creamy flesh revealed by a momentary breach of green fabric. As she turned to distribute napkins and silverware, he followed the curve of the jeans from her rounded haunches to the substantial thigh, down the imagined shapely calf to the funky boots, and back up. She had the body of an athlete, he judged—substantial, but very solid. But his eyes returned, as they tended to of late, to the remarkable and portrait-worthy face.

Then something else occurred to Tam, a startling thought, to be sure, given her strong resemblance to Lauren: in addition to her physical charms, this woman seemed to have a *personality*. When the four men at the table hooted and jabbered at her, she good-naturedly gave it right back to them. They all knew her, and she knew all of them. *A Bob, two Jimmys, a Rex.* Her face collapsed into contrived fury when a straw wrapper flew toward her; just as quickly, she pounced on the offender and playfully swatted the hat off his head. When she laughed—as she seemed to do quite often—she exploded in a lusty, open-mouthed celebration of the moment. Unlike, Tam noted to himself, Lauren's tight-lipped "hmmm-mmm."

He decided then that he knew who she was. He prided himself on his natural ability to evaluate and classify the characters of others. He had found the ability to "size up" people was a critical skill of a good portrait artist. Capturing the way light fell on the facial structures was important, of course, but the adept application of selected colors to a canvas meant little if the artist didn't *understand* the subject. Tam found that he was usually able to arrive at the essence of most subjects in a matter of minutes. Rarely, particularly when confronted with an artful sociopath, the process might take him longer. He had stumbled upon this truth while performing the psychological post-mortem on his expired marriage. Sociopaths like Norman Holdsworthy, he determined, were able to deceive with their ready yet highly superficial charm. Lauren had fooled him, as well, concealing her true reptilian self until their first minor marital crisis. These miscalculations hadn't managed to destroy his faith in his character-judging talent. In fact, the tempering of his skills in the domestic crucible gave him great confidence that he had the waitress pegged. From her drawl and syntax, he determined that she was a true "country girl," obviously raised in the Deep South, probably in a rural area. This, if true, might indicate she had probably been spared the inevitable psychological stress that came from living urban life at near light speed. In addition, she appeared to be a happy person and seemed to enjoy her job, her customers, herself. At the same time, her hair color and unusual clothing choices told him that she wasn't obsessed by fashion trends and didn't take herself too seriously. The cross threw him a little off—he wasn't sure what significance to attach to religious regalia. He wanted to believe that a cross signified an aspiration to a Christ-like capacity for love and forgiveness. His experience map was littered with far too many hypocrites adorned with crosses, stars, scapulars, medals—even wimples and starched collars—to draw any fixed and absolute conclusions from a single dangling object. Nevertheless, this time he believed there might be some congruence between symbol and subject. He intuitively read her to be kind, decent, and probably forgiving. With a start, he realized that the qualities he had thus projected upon her coupled with her considerable physical attractiveness qualified her potentially as …

The One. His personalized, idealized, and probably utterly fictionalized major Other. Owing largely to his brief (the duration of a minor liaison with an intense and hairy-pitted Lakeland College art professor), pre-Lauren, quasi-feminist phase, Tam generally felt an undifferentiated twinge of conditioned discomfort whenever The One surfaced in his consciousness. It wasn't a constantly recurring image—he'd known only one other One in his life, Lauren included.

He'd dated Mary Elizabeth Conklin for about a month when they were college sophomores. On occasion, her Concept image, reconstituted in his damaged memory as a beatific vision (complete with nimbus), still drifted through his languid, moderately intoxicated mind. At such effusive moments, regret boiled within him as he recalled the drinking, gambling, and general boorishness that had driven the Actual Mary Elizabeth away. For that reason, he had trained himself to jettison the sole surviving image of the Actual her (teary-eyed and furrowed-browed, slouched against his about-to-be-slammed apartment door) the moment it began to impinge upon the conceptual Mary Elizabeth.

This woman seemed much more One-like than Mary Elizabeth Conklin could ever have been. For one thing, she was a woman as opposed to the mere coltish teenager he had known ten years earlier. For another, Mary Elizabeth had deserted him and was long gone, forever absorbed by her consigned destiny. That fact, alone, tended to render her status as an Actual One highly improbable. This woman, this waitress, was right there in front of him.

Suddenly their eyes met—unintentionally, he assured himself, even as he turned momentarily away. She had been reaching between Bob and Rex with a wad of napkins when her gaze had lifted fractionally to meet his gaping stare. He could tell by the way her eyes had twitched before locking on his that she had intended to look elsewhere. The only thing that mattered now, though, was that those wide, flirtatious eyes seemed to see only him. Accidentally or not, in that tiny fraction of a second, Tam Malonee became willing to accept a cosmic explanation for his dalliance in that bucolic confluence of space and time.

He fell away again from her lingering gaze, retreating back into the greasy menu now lying on the table. It had not taken long for the thrill of discovery to be throttled by the icy fingers of reality. It didn't matter if she was The One. Even though he might be once again unattached, he had repeatedly proven himself unworthy of quality women. And now he was worse off than he'd ever been. On the balance sheet of personal worth, his liabilities far exceeded his assets. He was a man on the run with no job, no home, no fixed destination. His only possessions were the clothes and toiletries in an old gym bag, his colors and painting tools, and his prized guitar. The small roll of bills in his pocket and the Olds Alero—anything but a status symbol—had been "appropriated" from the Holdsworthy Auto Corral, as had the stereo "boom-box" on the back floorboard. The six-pack that he enjoyed each evening, his greatest personal indulgence, seemed (to his great bewilderment) to affect women in a uniformly unfavorable way. By the measure of most people, he was a loser. In his experience, quality women tended not to be attracted to losers. He imagined that they would especially not be attracted to a loser who also happened to be the target of an active police dragnet. Besides, he assured himself, she must already have a man in her life. He allowed himself to conjure a mental image of this as-yet nameless, faceless lucky soul. Surely a Jimmy or a Rex, some oak-necked, blacksmith-forearmed electrician, sheriff's deputy, parcel deliverer. He tinkered subversively with the physical and character attributes of this conjured inamorato until he arrived at a suitably inferior personage: a narcissistic and insecure good ol' boy with a buzz cut, a bad-boy goatee, a shotgun mounted in the rear window of his customized GMC pickup. Tam permitted himself to savor this unflattering visual construct briefly before yanking himself back to reality. In reality, there were never any fairy tale endings. With an audible sigh, he resigned himself to a lifetime without The One, probably as penance for his myriad offenses.

So he could just up and leave Mac's, jump into the Alero and continue on his way. If he did that, of course, he'd go to his grave never having spoken to her. On the other hand, if he ordered *something*, he could die knowing he'd at least made contact, however insignificant, with someone who, under different circumstances, might've been The One. He could remember her face and paint it from memory; one day, when the portrait hung in his beachside studio/gallery, he could gaze upon it and savor the memory of their brief, pleasant interchange.

Having thus framed the available arguments for his inner judge, he made the decision to stay and order something. He ran his right index finger down the appended list of "specials," pausing at the Brunswick stew. At $3.95, it was probably his cheapest ticket out of the diner. At the same time, he had never cared for restaurant stews—he assumed they were exactly what they appeared to be: watered-down amalgams of leftovers and plate scrapings. Besides, he thought, if he was going to purchase food, he might as well be practical and get something that could be eaten on the run. Stew didn't strike him as an entrée that traveled well. He continued down the menu until he came to the "country chicken strips." His eyes darted from the listed price ($6.95) to the appended product description (*six strips of tender chicken, lightly battered and golden fried in all-vegetable oil—fantaschick!*) and back to the price again.

He was mentally performing a grease-manageability analysis when he realized the woman was heading in his direction. His stare remained glued to the menu, but he could still see her at the edge of his vision-field, still moving toward him, dance-shuffling to an upbeat country-rocker.

"Hey, there," she said.

Tam looked up at her. She was standing about four feet from his table. Working that gum, grinning.

"Hey, there," he replied. He realized that he was blocking her with one extra-long leg that still sprawled out into the open area between his booth and the next table. He did his best to make the leg fit under the table. She moved a foot or two closer.

"What can I get you today?" Her pen was poised above the order pad in her left hand.

"Well, I'm not sure," Tam answered. "I've never been here before. What's good?"

"Why everything, hon. It's all good." She brushed her hair back out of her eyes and grinned.

"I was thinking maybe about the chicken strips."

She nodded and blew a small bubble. "Cool. The chicken strips are great."

"Then that's what I'll have." Pleased with both the logical selection of an entrée, and his decisive handling of the ordering, he popped the menu back into its mooring.

"What sides you want with those?" The gum smacked and popped.

The satisfaction turned suddenly to a muted jolt of apprehension. He wasn't sure what she meant by "sides." It was obviously not a reference to the chicken strips themselves—strips had to be just, well, *strips*. If she was referring to side orders, he didn't have the first clue what items might be served at such an establishment. His eyes raced wildly around the adjacent tables, searching for some examples of standard local side-order fare.

"Um, just the strips," he said, finally.

She frowned. "You don't want any fries?"

Tam squirmed. He still felt queasy from the mega-dose of grease he'd ingested at the Burger Jungle. "I don't think so," he said. "The strips will be fine by themselves." He gave her an apologetic smile and shrugged. "I'm kinda doing that beach diet thing." He almost winced at this inexplicable and unnecessary fabrication.

"I'm not sure what that is, but that's cool. What would you like to drink?"

"You got some kind of diet pop?"

Her brow furrowed. "You mean like Diet Pepsi, something like that?"

Tam nodded.

"You're not from around here, are you?" She slid her pen and order pad back into the half-apron.

"Nope," he said.

"I didn't think so." She giggled. "Nobody around here says 'pop'."

He gave her an almost pained smile. "Just passing through."

"Passing through to where, if I'm not being too nosy?"

"Florida," he replied.

"Cool. Where at in Florida?"

Blood rushed to his face. "Uh, I'm really not sure." When he noticed her puzzled expression, he added: "Maybe Tampa, St. Pete. Somewhere along that side of the state. Or Miami. Or the Keys. I really haven't made a final decision yet."

"Just sorta wingin' it?"

"Yeah. Something like that."

"I'm sorry," she said. "I talk too much. My momma used to say that if my mouth was my feet, I'da walked twice around the world by now."

Tam nodded and tried his best to process this unusual metaphor, but it wasn't scanning. He attributed this to his state of near mental exhaustion, the general failure of the metaphor's tenor-vehicle relationship, or—more likely—to a concurrence of those two causes.

"It's okay," he said, finally. He gave her a patient smile. He knew that, if this woman hadn't been so powerfully attractive, he might have been five miles down the road at that moment. As it happened, however, she was, and he wasn't. That fact alone helped him overlook her chattiness.

"How about some unsweetened tea? We still got some made up, and it's *real* good."

Tam shrugged. "I guess that'll do."

"So, where you from?" she asked. She rested her left hand on her cocked hip and brushed her hair back with her right.

Tam hesitated. He considered inventing an intriguing home town, perhaps some rawhide-strapped settlement deep in cowboy country. After all, he thought, in an hour he'd be gone, and she'd never know the difference. Besides, he wasn't sure how she'd react to knowing he was a Yankee, and a lifelong one, at that.

"Michigan," he admitted, finally. "A little town I'm sure you never heard of."

"So you're just, like, going on a ... *vacation*, or something like that?"

Tam drew a long breath and sighed. He obviously didn't care to share the whole embarrassing truth with her—that he had just committed at least three felonies and that his "vacation" was, in reality, a rather poorly planned flight from a disordered life and the law.

"No. Not a vacation, per se—"

"Oh," she said, nodding knowingly. "It's a business trip."

Tam sagged visibly.

"You ain't in some kind of trouble, are ya'?"

He sagged even more.

"I am *so* sorry, hon," she said, her cheeks burning red. "That was just rude of me. It's really none of my business. See, like I said. I just don't know when to shut up." She touched him gently on the shoulder. "I'll just go turn this order in."

Tam felt an almost overpowering urge to grab her arm, to stop her from walking away. He knew that, once she had given his tacit admission a minute to sink in, she'd be repelled by him. That would be most unfair, he thought—she couldn't judge him without knowing his whole story. She should know that he was more than just some unshaven loser on the run from the law. That he had a genius IQ, was a talented (although not yet commercially successful) artist, and was a sensitive, creative person. But he didn't touch her, nor did he say anything. He just stared down at his hands and let the mortification swell.

Tam came by his conflicted nature honestly, that is, genetically. His maternal grandfather, Carleton "Coot" McMahon, an auto worker who labeled himself "the original pissed-off libertarian," spent his entire adult life tangling with federal bureaucrats. He believed government's only legitimate function was to provide defense against foreign enemies. He claimed that regulation of everything else—from education to interstate commerce to, quite expectedly, organized labor—ought to be the business of local government ("where I can keep my eye on the miserable bloodsuckers"). His fervent anti-federalism notwithstanding, Coot twice ran for Congress and afoul of campaign management laws. Late in his life, he amended his core political beliefs to include at least one additional function of government. Specifically, Coot wanted federal authorities to stop the New York Yankees from snagging every "free-agent whore" who had outgrown the fiscal suspenders of his beloved, perennially mediocre Detroit Tigers. His last words, spoken in a loud and clear voice in the presence of his pastor and three mortified volunteers from his parish sodality: "I'm coming back as a giant cock to break one off in Steinbrenner's ass!" Tam's mother, Maureen McMahon Malonee, a devout, old-school Catholic who attended mass and said her rosary on a daily basis, named her only son Thomas Aquinas in honor of the thirteenth-century scholastic theologian. Maureen made no secret of her consuming desire to see her son ordained a priest; she lit daily votive candles as insurance against his secular temptation. Instead, she lived to see Tam thrown out of college, oft-arrested (every variety of public drunkenness, possession of marijuana, failure to pay taxes), investigated by the FBI (suspicion of racketeering) and married in a Lutheran church to the daughter of a woman she couldn't stand. She wrote her son out of her will and died, feeling bitter and betrayed, on a bus en route to Iowa's Grotto of the Redemption. By way of contrast, Tam's father, Roger, was a devout protestant, meaning not only that he protested the infallibility of the pope and other tenets of the Roman Church, but also organized religion in any other form, especially the form that required its members to come to the front door of his home and "witness" to him. As a candidate for bachelor's and master's degrees in physics at the University of Michigan, Roger had protested U.S. involvement in Southeast Asia, nuclear power, and the holding of any job for a period exceeding one calendar year. He eventually protested life as a husband and father and, after divorcing Maureen in 1985, protested a court order requiring him to pay both alimony and child support. And, in his ultimate act of protest, Roger Malonee quietly disappeared from his son's life without excuse or explanation. Besides an old easel and a pint of mineral spirits, he left his son but a single bequest: the acronymic nickname, bestowed upon the boy to save him from "unnecessary butt-kickings." Sometime later in life, even as he struggled to grasp the distinction between necessary and unnecessary butt-kickings, Tam realized that his nickname was, itself, just another protest. Against his mother, against her religion, and, it seemed, against the faux creativity of child-naming.

"Here you go, hon."

Tam looked up from an active internal dialogue and saw that the waitress was standing next to him. Gratitude and relief washed over his face as he watched her place a plastic tumbler filled with ice tea and a plate heaped with steaming chicken strips and fries on the table in front of him. While she had been gone, the rest of the diners had finished eating, paid their bills, and slipped out into the relentless August sun. Tam had used that substantial interval to construct a couple of unpleasant scenarios. In the first, the waitress, aided and abetted by the loyal kitchen staff, slipped out the back door to safety. And who could have blamed her? She's working the tables, just trying to make a living, when suddenly she's face-to-face with, for all she knows, a dangerous fugitive from justice. For all she knew, he could be a serial rapist or a murderer or some other manner of violent sociopath. In the second scenario, Tam visualized her placing a furtive call, then waiting with the cook and busboy by the galley doors for the sheriff to arrive.

Neither of those things had taken place. Instead, she had returned to his table, bringing with her food, drink, and her warm smile—*not* large, drawling men with shotguns and handcuffs.

"Thanks," Tam said.

"Well, okay then," she replied. She swept the hanging hair behind an ear and grinned.

"Well, okay then."

"I know the menu just said six strips, but, since you didn't order any sides—and since we're about to close up—I talked Harold back in the kitchen into giving you a few extra. And we didn't want to waste the fries."

"Who's about to close up?"

"Well, we are. Mac closes up at two on Saturday."

"I sure am sorry," Tam said. "I didn't realize it was that late." He stared down at his plate for a moment, then said, "Maybe I should just get this boxed up so you guys can—"

"Oh, no," Madison protested, "you go on and eat. Harold don't mind. He's just back there cleaning up."

"What about Mac?"

Madison laughed. "Oh, he ain't even here. He goes home around noon every day."

Tam shrugged and began to unwrap his fork and spoon.

Madison lingered by the side of the table, looking uncomfortable. After a moment, she glanced quickly around the room, then blurted out, "Would you mind if I sit down here for a minute?"

Tam froze momentarily, the napkin and utensils suspended above his plate. "No," he said, at last. "I mean, no I don't mind. Absolutely not." He gestured toward the other side of the table.

She slid into the booth and reached across the table with her right hand. "Madison's my name," she declared.

Tam took her hand and shook it. "Tam."

She looked at him with a puzzled expression. "Did you say, 'Tam', as in T-a-m?"

"It's really Thomas, but—" He grimaced. "It's a long, uninteresting story. Trust me."

She nodded and stared down at her hands. "Here's the thing," she sputtered, finally. She paused, shutting her eyes and squeezing her face with both hands. When she began to speak, the words poured out in a blinding, throaty stream: "Listen, you're gonna think I'm retarded, and I probably am. I mean, not really *retarded* retarded, but stupid and dumb as a brick, and I know this is gonna sound crazy, and it probably is crazy, but—"

Tam stared, the utensils still clutched in his left hand.

"—the thing is, I need a ride. To Florida. I know this is crazy, and if you don't wanna do it, I'll *absolutely* understand, and I wouldn't even blame you in the least little bit, but, I mean, the way I see it, you're going anyway, to Florida, and if you're by yourself ... I figure, what the heck. What's one more—"

Tam raised his right hand. "Whoa," he said.

The crimson spread through her whole face. "You're right," she sputtered. "I mean, I am. Retarded. I mean, I'm really *not*, but—"

"Why do you need a ride to Florida?"

Madison stared down at the table. After a moment, she shut her eyes and slowly shook her head. "It's my little girl," she said. She sat quietly for a moment, then, with a quivering lip, said, "My baby." Mascara-stained tears began to roll down both cheeks. She apologized, plucked two napkins from the dispenser, and dabbed at her eyes.

Tam shot a quick glance out the window. He eyed the Alero, with its salt-spray quarter-panel rust-out and I'm-a-loser cachet, and the open, unobstructed road beyond. "I'm sorry," he said, returning to the woman. "I mean, I don't really understand—"

"My little girl is there, and her daddy's abusing her. I need to go get her. I need to take her somewhere safe—" She paused again, as emotion overcame her.

Tam clasped his hands together on the table. "I'm so sorry. How do you ... I mean, how do you know—"

Madison wiped her eyes and nose with the napkin. At last, she took a deep breath and continued. "My ex-husband, Mark, lives in Florida, in a small town in the Panhandle. He took our little girl, Brandy, and just went to Florida with her. His family's from there. His daddy owns a construction company, and Mark works for him." She got another napkin and wiped the mascara streams from her cheeks. When she leveled her eyes at Tam again, he judged that anger had replaced the sadness. "He's sick and violent. He beat me and Brandy when we were together up here. And worse. I can't even tell you the things he's done— him and his friends. He's a psycho."

"What I don't understand is how he—"

"He just took her one day, picked her up at her school and away they went. I got off work, went by the school, and they told me he'd checked her out early." She shrugged. "And there you have it."

"Does he have custody of her?"

"That's another sorry tale," she said. She twisted the napkin into a tight string. "He filed something down there with a judge. His daddy knows everybody in that county—judges, cops, the mayor, everyone." Her nostrils flared. "But, yes, to answer your question, he got custody. The judge gave him full custody, and I got nothing."

"You don't even get her part-time?"

Madison snorted. "I was supposed to have got her Christmas for a week. I was gonna take a bus down and get her. I don't have a car anymore, but that's another story. Then Mark called and says she's sick as a dog and can't travel. Mark lets her call me a couple of times a week, but that's about it."

"I don't know much about the law, but it seems like you're getting—"

"Screwed," she said. "Pardon my French. That's exactly what I'm getting. It ain't me I'm worried about, though. Brandy's being abused. She told me so last time I talked to her. And that's why I gotta get her out of there."

"Have you talked to a lawyer?"

She made a face. "Shoot. No lawyers up here will fool with it. Everyone I talk to says I'd just be wasting my time and money. Not that I have either."

Tam scratched his stubbled chin. "So let's say I give you a ride down to this town in Florida." He tried to visualize exactly how she was going to pull off this—what exactly *was* this? An abduction? A rescue? By herself, without a car, in a place where her ex-father-in-law knew everybody important.

"That's all you have to do," she said. "Just get me down there. Then you're completely off the hook. Free as a bird." She leaned forward and narrowed her eyes. "I actually got a plan, Tam. I got a friend that lives in Pensacola, girl I met a few years back. Her ex was stationed down there. She's got a car and knows a bunch of folks. She said she'd help me if I ever needed her. All you got to do is get me to her place."

Tam rubbed the back of his neck. He didn't really like the idea of aiding in the abduction of a child, if that's what this was. On the other hand, he thought, if the allegations of abuse were even partly accurate, the mission would be in the girl's best interest. Besides, he had been just a few minutes away from never seeing Madison again. Now he had been presented with the unexpected opportunity to spend time with her, maybe even help a few people out. It was as though fate had this meeting on its short agenda.

There were, however, a few other items to be discussed.

"I guess you figured out that I have a little, ah, problem back in Michigan."

She shrugged. "None of my business."

"What if I'm in bad trouble with the law?"

"Like I said, really none of my business."

"How do you know I'm not a rapist or a murderer? Or a dangerous escaped convict?"

She tilted her head slightly and narrowed her eyes again. "Well, I don't believe you're any kind of convict," she said. She reached out and took Tam's hands in both of hers. She examined them briefly and smiled knowingly. "Your hands are soft," she said, at last. "You're not hurting for money," she added, nodding at Tam's expensive polo shirt. "I *know* you ain't done any strenuous kind of work—"

He laughed. "That doesn't mean anything. You obviously didn't see *American Psycho*."

"—plus you got no scars, no ink."

His face contorted into a mask of non-comprehension.

"Ink. You know—tats. Tattoos. Everybody I ever met who's done time has scars and tats."

"I've been locked up," he assured her. "I'm not proud of it. I'm just being up-front with you."

She shrugged. "You ain't the cold-blooded killer type."

He snapped his fingers. "Just like that? You're absolutely sure?"

"Yeah, I'm not usually wrong about people."

"And if I'm a rapist?" He selected the longest french fry and bit it in half.

"I don't think you are, but, if you were, you'd find I don't rape easily."

Tam laughed out loud. "What if I just killed somebody in a bar fight?"

She held his hands up and shook her head. "You ain't no bar fighter, hon. I'm not saying you couldn't take care of yourself, if you had to. I'm just saying your hands ain't been in a lot of bar fights."

"You know a lot of bar fighters, do you?"

She sighed. "Honey, where I went to school, out in the country, we had at least one of everything. And a bunch of big ol', mean redneck boys that was cutting each other with knives in the fifth grade." A large, pink bubble appeared, inflated, then popped. "I don't associate with them, you understand, but I do know them when I see them."

"I'll say this for you. You aren't easily intimidated."

"Nope."

Tam glanced around the room. The diner had emptied; the only sound was a watery whoosh coming from the kitchen.

"What about this place, your job?" he asked, gesturing. "You're just gonna up and leave?"

"In a heartbeat. I mean, Mac's as good as gold, don't get me wrong, but I don't intend to work here until I die. And right now, getting Brandy outta there is the *only* thing that matters to me."

He knew he wasn't going to say no to her. He also knew what she was asking was crazy.

On the other hand, virtually everything he had done in the last twenty-four hours qualified as crazy.

He let his eyes drink her in one more time. As pitiful as her story might be, it was her looks that had persuaded him. It was this same weakness for oddly configured beauty that had overridden his good judgment on dozens of other occasions—and which now had his inner voice declaring, "Who knows—maybe this one crazy thing will end up working out for you."

CHAPTER 3

▼

THE GHOST OF JESSE BREEDLOVE

Aileen Breedlove's house crouched on an isolated cul-de-sac, improbably placed near the center of a cultivated field. Five other manufactured homes, each framed from the same prefab template and mounted on cinder-block foundations, had been wedged into the street's tight curve. All the structures had sharply sloped roofs with single gables over tiny front porches. Every house except Aileen's was swathed in horizontal sections of vinyl siding; hers had odd-looking vertical panels. Her short driveway had reached maximum capacity with a late model Crown Victoria parked behind a mid-nineties Honda and an old Ford pickup. Plastic icicle lights, a decorative vestige from the previous Christmas, hung loosely from the gutters. What really set Aileen's house apart from the others in her isolated neighborhood, however, were the many "accents" that crowded her tiny patch of lawn. Besides an impressive collection of ceramic fairies, gnomes, and angels, Aileen's fantasy tableaux featured a birdbath and a violet mirrored gazing ball.

Tam and Madison arrived shortly before three o'clock. The furious afternoon sun filtered through the peripheral canopy of pin oaks and hickories as the metallic drone of cicadas filled the superheated air. As Madison fumbled for her keys on the front porch, Tam held open the storm door and glanced around the neighborhood. He noticed four brown-skinned children, two on bicycles, watching from a driveway across the street.

The door swung open, leaving Madison bent slightly forward with a key protruding from her extended right hand. Tam's head snapped around. He found himself staring into the frowning, middle-aged face of a woman almost his equal in height. Her slate gray eyes glared at him through the huge eyeglass lenses that seemed to amplify her suspicion.

"Well, hey, Aunt Aileen," Madison said, brightly. "I thought y'all might've left out already."

"Why, no," the woman said, her eyes actively processing the tall stranger in the blue jeans and untucked polo shirt. "We've been waiting on you."

"Waiting on *me?*" Madison pushed her way past her aunt and motioned for Tam to follow.

He was making the half-step up to the threshold when he found his progress substantially impeded by Aunt Aileen's inert, six-foot frame. She stood jut-jawed, hands on her hips—a veritable Colossus of Middleboro. He retreated to the daisy-themed doormat and gave Madison a look that clearly said, "Well, I tried, now I'll just go wait in the car." Madison responded by grabbing Tam's right arm just above the elbow.

"Why, *yes,*" Aileen replied, her eyes never leaving the stranger. "I knew you wouldn't miss Jesse's funeral. Who's this?"

Madison had warned Tam about her aunt on the ride from the diner. "She comes on kind of strong," she had said. "I mean, she's good as gold, I swear, but she don't put up with any mess, and she says *exactly* what's on her mind. I've been staying with her and my cousin, Robert, for the last six months so I could save up some money."

"I should probably just wait in the car while you get your things," Tam had offered.

"Oh, no," Madison had protested. "That'd be the very *worst* thing. Aileen's one of them folks that's got to know everything that's going on—*everything*. She's my mom's older sister. You know how that goes. She's been running the show since she was six. There's no point in lying to her, not that I would."

"I'm not saying lie to her. I just said I'd wait in the car."

Madison had stared for a moment out the passenger-side window, as if evaluating the plausibility of this strategy. At last, she shook her head and said, "Nope. Won't work. She'd look out the window and see your car, then she'd see you and there we go. There wouldn't be no end to it after that. She'd spend the rest of her life trying to figure out who you were, where you come from, what have you. Nope, you're gonna have to come in and let her eyeball you. Let her satisfy that curiosity and be done with it, unless, of course, she's already left out for the funeral."

"Funeral?"

"Yeah. My Uncle Jesse. Aunt Aileen's dead husband's brother. He was sort of the black sheep of the family. Stayed drunk and in trouble a lot. Worked odd jobs around the county. Handyman in the winter, farming the rest of the year. In fact, he used to work some of that land right there." She had pointed to a huge field of towering, broad-leafed plants they were passing. "That there's part of the Millers' land." She had snorted ironically. "It's funny. Jesse, the family drunk, was the only Breedlove Mister Miller could tolerate. It goes back to our long-ago kin—some kind of argument that led to a killing." She had continued to stare out the window until the view changed from acres of clumped plants to weeds and then to dense pine-oak woods. "Anyway," she continued, "Aileen's husband, Ronald—he passed last year, which was kind of why I moved in with her—didn't much care for him on account of his relations with the Millers and the Haases. Robert felt like Jess had gone against his own family. Truth is, Jesse couldn't see no point in feudin' over something he had never been a part of. Any-*way*, Aileen never quit trying to save him. She'd clean him up, try to get him to church. Nothing she did worked, though. Every time he got paid, he'd go out with some of the Mexican guys and drink up his paycheck. We all thought it would kill him eventually."

"What Mexican guys?"

"The guys he worked with. When he worked, I mean."

"I guess I just wasn't expecting Mexicans in Tennessee."

"Heck, yeah. Shoot, they're everywhere now. I think they first come here on account of the poultry plant. Then some of them got jobs workin' the tobacco and doing construction. Everyone on Aileen's street is Mexican, except for me, Robert, and auntie. They're all right. I mean, they work hard and are pretty good neighbors. Robert's best friend is a Mexican, name of Eugenio. They work together in Middleboro. He's a pretty good dude. Works real hard, keeps to him-self. Doesn't socialize much, but he will take a drink when he gets off work."

He had given her a look. "Is taking a drink a problem?"

"It was for poor Uncle Jesse."

Tam had briefly floated her remarks through his mind. From this cursory scan, he made these determinations: Madison was neither judgmental nor big-oted, she had no blanket opposition to moderate social drinking, and she had an intuitive grasp of the complex forces contributing to poor Jesse's demise. He gave her a quick nod of agreement. "Sorry. You were saying? About Jesse—"

"Yeah, well. Jesse, I reckon the drinking finally done him in. They found him, laying dead out by the railroad tracks." She had frowned and paused, her affect seeming to sink under the weight of this grim reality. "All by himself, alone."

Tam had given the steering wheel a squeeze. "That's terrible. Still, I mean, we all die alone, when you get right down to it."

Madison had shot an annoyed glance his way but didn't reply.

"So why do I have to go in the house, again?"

"You just do. If I want to leave out with you, I mean."

Thus Tam had come face-to-face with Aileen Breedlove, who continued to examine him as one might inspect a suspicious package.

He announced his name and extended a huge hand in the woman's direction. Madison still had a hold on the arm, as though she expected him to bolt for his car at any second.

Aileen's hands remained on her hips. Her eyes narrowed. "Mal-oh-nay," she repeated. "Huh. What kind of name is that?"

Tam's ignored hand dropped back to his side. "French, I think. I'm not really sure."

"French, huh? I don't know nobody by that name." She nodded in Madison's direction. "Where do y'all know each other from?"

Tam squirmed. "The, ah, diner."

The gray eyes bit into him. "Well, thank you for giving Bit a ride home. That's very kind of you." She flashed a perfunctory smile then swiveled her head suddenly in Madison's direction. "Girl, you best be getting dressed. Service starts in fifteen minutes. It's gonna take ten minutes to get there."

Madison and Tam exchanged alarmed glances.

"Um, I was thinking maybe I better not go," Madison said. "I mean, I was planning on it, and all. But since Tam here has offered to give me a ride down—"

Aileen's eyes narrowed even more. "What do you mean, give you a *ride down*? Down to where?"

Madison took a deep breath and rubbed her face with both hands. When she finally spoke, there was a hint of quiet defiance in her voice. "Aileen, I'm going after Brandy. I told you I would one day. And Tam is on his way to Florida, so he's—"

"Maybe one day you will go after Brandy," Aileen sputtered, "but today you're changing out of those silly clothes and going to your uncle's funeral." She turned back to Tam and made a failed attempt at another smile. "Thank you again for giving Bit a ride. We appreciate all you've done. Now if you'll excuse us—" She grabbed the side of the door with her left hand and tugged slightly on it, a tacit affirmation of Tam's dismissal.

"Aileen, he is not leaving without me. When we leave, we're going to get Brandy." As if to symbolically neutralize Aileen's message, Madison pulled Tam all the way into the house.

Tam stood just inside the doorway and shrank from Aileen's reproving glare. Looking to his left, he could see two men slouched on a sofa in the living room. Both of them had buzz cuts, with dark hair clipped to a fraction of an inch in length. The man closest to him was burly and brown-skinned, dressed in blue jeans and a sleeveless shirt. *This would be Eugenio*, Tam guessed. By process of elimination, he concluded that the other man, angular and pale and wearing dark trousers, a white shirt, and a loosened black tie, was Madison's cousin, Robert. Both men were staring at the screen of a console television in the opposite corner of the room; they seemed oblivious to his presence.

"Please excuse us for a moment," Aileen Breedlove said to Tam. Her face had flooded with color; for a moment, she looked as though she might explode. She grabbed Madison by the shoulder and steered her away from the front door. Just before disappearing into the adjoining kitchen, Madison turned back toward Tam and gave him a reassuring wink.

He thrust his hands into his pockets and slumped against a wall. His eyes drifted back to the small living room. The only furniture was the sofa, an over-stuffed chair, the television console, and a wicker curio stand holding dozens of angel and gnome figurines. A framed print of Jesus hung over the sofa. A video game system was plugged into the front of the television; the compact black box, two controllers, and half a dozen discs cluttered the carpeted floor. Tam waited for some sign of acknowledgment from the two men on the sofa; their attention remained trained on the television screen. He had no trouble hearing the determined voices of both women in the next room. Cutting a quick glance out the storm door, he wondered whether he should make a run for it. He realized he had no ethical or moral obligation to fulfill his part of the agreement with Madison. And the little bit he had learned about contract law from his job with Holdsworthy Auto Corral informed him that he also had no legal obligation to her. In fact, he figured that things had become so complicated just since walking up to Aunt Aileen's door that nobody would ever blame him for running like a dog.

On the other hand, it was possible that Madison was the One, and the whole Aileen snag was about to be straightened out.

His hope for this particular outcome was dealt a serious blow when Madison marched back into the living room with a look of exasperation on her face.

"Would you mind coming back here for a second?" she asked, jerking her head in the direction of a side hallway.

Tam cast another sidelong glance at the Alero parked at the end of the driveway, then followed Madison down the hallway. She turned into the first room on the right, and he followed her in. The small bedroom had only a single bed and a compact dresser. On top of the dresser were many framed photos of a young girl, tomboy cute with shoulder-length brown hair. Tam assumed that this was Brandy.

Madison took his right hand with both of hers and looked beseechingly into his eyes. Unsure of what might be coming, Tam cringed. Based on his past experience in these kinds of situations, he anticipated the worst, meaning, generally, that someone might want something he didn't want to give. He had never regarded himself as selfish, just someone with a lot of needs of his own.

"Would you mind going to the funeral with me?"

Before his brain could fully process the full import of that request, Madison squeezed his hand and fired off a short list of reasons why his compliance might be in their individual and collective best interests. All Tam heard were the critical phrases, "less than an hour," and "owe you big time"; he was actively weighing the pluses and minuses before she even finished her pitch. The negatives were plentiful and persuasive. For starters, he despised all funerals—he regarded them as extravagant and clichéd dog-and-pony shows conducted for the exclusive economic benefit of the funeral industry. Furthermore, the longer he tarried in that provincial no-man's land, the easier it would be for the cops to catch up with him. Finally, he had never met Jesse Breedlove, and his family—he had Aileen and Robert in mind—had exhibited only hostility or ambivalence toward him.

On the other hand, there was Madison, the major plus-factor in the whole equation. Although he'd only known her for a few hours, he couldn't bear the thought now of leaving without her. His conclusion: as much as he disliked the notion of going with people he didn't know to a function he found distasteful and exploitive for the alleged benefit of someone he'd never met, he didn't want to drive off without Madison. He didn't know what might be awaiting them on that adventure, but he was willing to pay the required fee to find out.

"What about the way I'm dressed?" he asked.

"Nobody's gonna care. Besides, what about the way *I'm* dressed?"

He nodded. "I have another question."

"Okay."

"*Bit?*"

Her brow furrowed.

"That's what your aunt called you out there—Bit. What's up with that?"

"It's just a nickname. She started calling me 'Little Bit" when I was a baby. Now that I'm grown up, it's just Bit." She released Tam's hand and gave him a gesture of indifference, as if to ratify the importance of the nickname game to Southern culture. "So, are you going with me?"

Tam gave her a shrug of submission, then emitted a small sigh. Just to ensure that his noble gesture would be properly credited to his favors account.

He knew he needed all the help he could get.

*   *   *   *

The Central Cumberland Tabernacle of God was a simple brick building on an isolated, tree-studded parcel of land on the road back toward Middleboro. The church sign was a four-by-eight rent-a-sign marquee which read: "The Kingdom of God is at hand! … services every Sun. 10:00 AM."

Aileen Breedlove's delegation arrived at the church minutes before the service was scheduled to start. Robert drove his mother's Crown Victoria, with Tam in the front passenger seat and the two women in the back. As they entered the church's rear door, Tam had inquired whether, given his informal attire, he might be better off sitting in the back. Madison had whispered, "I told you it was okay," and guided him toward the front with the rest of her family. Indeed, as his group moved to the front of the sanctuary, Tam had spotted one man dressed in denim bib overalls and another wearing khaki slacks and work boots. They slid into the front left pew with Tam wedged between Robert and Madison.

"That's mostly Millers and Haases over yonder," Madison whispered to Tam, nodding at the dozen or so people on the other side of the aisle.

Tam cut his eyes in that direction and gave the group the once over. Six men—two middle-aged, four in their mid-to-late-twenties—four women and four small children. He thought they looked like fairly normal country folk. Nothing about them looked menacing. Or, at least, no more menacing than anyone else in the church. Plus, he thought, they had to be fairly decent people to attend the funeral of a dead Breedlove.

Tam's eyes rose from the rival clans and roamed about the room. The sanctuary was as unpretentious as the building's exterior, with twelve rows of wooden pews bisected by a narrow aisle. There was a single tinted window on the wall near the end of Tam's row; a rattling window air conditioner had been braced into the bottom half. The bare wood floor stopped at an elevated stage upon which had been arranged a movable pedestal lectern and three metal folding chairs. A plain particle board casket sat on the floor directly under the lectern. A framed picture of a much younger and healthier Jesse Breedlove had been placed atop the casket. Two somber-faced men dressed identically in white short-sleeved shirts, navy blue neckties and trousers, and black shoes sat on the chairs closest to right front of the stage. A woman wearing a white blouse and ankle-length navy skirt sat on the third chair.

The man seated closest to the audience—Madison had previously identified him as Pastor Noah Pangburn—rose exactly at four and shuffled to the podium with his Bible clutched in his left hand. Even though he looked to have once been a towering figure, he now suffered from an affliction that left him hunched painfully forward. He had a ruddy, creased face with sharp features that, along with his forward slump, gave him an unfortunate vulture-like presentation. His thinning white hair and bushy sideburns did nothing to disengage this image from Tam's mind.

When Pangburn arrived at the podium, he opened the Bible to one of many marked pages and began reading. His voice was thin and reedy and, had it not been amplified, Tam would have had great difficulty hearing him. The scriptural readings themselves offered little solace to Jesse's survivors; the passages from Genesis, Numbers, Ezra, and Proverbs uniformly condemned the wicked, the lazy, the drunk. When he reached the last marker, he closed the book, adjusted the microphone's goose neck, and began the official eulogy.

"There lies Jesse Breedlove," he began, gesturing down at the coffin. "I didn't know the man. Never would come to church, even though his brother and sister-in-law tried their best. But Sister Aileen there asked me to preach on him, so I said I would." He paused, his gnarled fingers fumbling with the page markers. "I talked to folks about Jesse. I prayed on what I should talk about here today. Then God spoke to me. He told me that we should look on Jesse as an example of what not to do with our life. The Bible plainly states in Proverbs that we are not to linger over wine, to look on it when it's red. And Jesse done that. Lingered *and* looked. The Bible says if you do that, the wine will hit you like a viper. Like a *viper*, y'all. And it done that to Jesse Breedlove. Hit him like a viper, poisoned him, took him down."

Tam could feel Madison stiffen next to him. He sneaked a quick look at her and saw her lips bending into a tight frown.

"Now everyone around here knows Jesse was bad to take a drink. Some folks told me that they seen him drunk on the Lord's day—on the *Lord's* day, y'all. Well, that don't cut it. And that's where it gets you." He pointed to the casket again. "Dead. Alone and dead, like that right there." He stared down at the podium, as if searching for some redemptive facet of the deceased's life. "I guess we can hope that Jesse was saved in his heart before he went on." Pastor Pangburn stood in silence for a moment, almost as if forcing himself not to comment on the likelihood of that possibility. Finally he turned to the woman on stage and said, "Sister Morgan will sing us out with a hymn."

Madison jumped to her feet.

"I have a something I'd like to say," she said, maneuvering toward the side aisle even as she spoke. Sister Morgan froze in an awkward, half-squatting posture just above her chair. Madison bounded up the steps and walked briskly to the podium.

"If y'all don't mind," she said, her voice shaking with anger, "I'd like to say a few words on behalf of Uncle Jesse." She cast a quick, reproachful glance in Pangburn's direction. "*Somebody* needs to say something on behalf of Uncle Jesse." She took a deep breath and stood there for nearly a minute with her eyes closed. When she continued, the tremor of rage was gone from her voice. "Jesse *did* have a problem. He drank too much. I think everybody in the county knows that. But there was more to him than just his drinking. He was a decent person. Sure, he drank too much, but, unlike most drunks, Jesse never hurt nobody but himself. He lived by himself, didn't have nobody depending on him. He never drove his car drunk, he never shot nobody. And all y'all know he never stole nothing from nobody. He never even cussed nobody out when he was drunk. He'd just drink until he passed out, and that was pretty much that. And, no, he wasn't setting in here on Sunday morning, but he wasn't out there judging folks or gossiping about them, neither."

A buzz of alarm spread through the church. Tam heard Aileen sigh audibly and Robert snort in apparent approval. He cut a glance up at the church functionaries and saw that both the pastor and Sister Morgan were sitting rigid and stone-faced.

Madison continued for ten more minutes. When she got through praising her uncle, she turned her attention to the "hypocrite church members" who made a living growing tobacco that "killed folks left and right."

"Y'all talk about poisons," she said. "At least Jesse didn't make a living off making or selling liquor."

"There ain't nothin' in the Bible against growing tabaccah," growled a large man on the Miller-Haas side of the church. He was turned sideways in the pew with one knee lowered, as if though he might break for the stage at any moment.

"There *is* all kind of stuff about *your* kind," said another man. "You and your family, especially your daddy."

"*All* of 'em," muttered a woman.

Robert got to his feet and glowered at the last speaker. "What exactly do you mean by that?"

"This is exactly the kind of thing I'm talking about," Madison said. She had leaned close to the microphone so her words echoed eerily throughout the room. "You call yourselves Christians, but Jesus wasn't about judging or throwing rocks. He wasn't about hating or grudges. He didn't put himself above the troubled people. No, He walked among them, loving and ministering—"

"You're the one who's startin' all the trouble," cried a female voice from the right side. "You and your Mexican-lovin' cousins."

Robert responded with a tartly phrased insult; this only encouraged a new flurry of harsh condemnations from across the aisle.

By this time, the pastor and his associate had jumped up and were standing at the edge of the stage. Pangburn commanded the belligerents to "behave like true Christians"; he waved his Bible through the air, as if to invoke a divine injunction against animosity.

But harsh words had been spoken; generations-old enmities had been unleashed. At this level of human arousal, the Christ-taught virtue of meekness was a most fragile adviser. Earth-inheriting is not usually foremost in the minds of the gravely indignant.

Tam slumped in his seat as the hostilities reached critical mass. In the space of a few minutes, he had cycled through mental states from anxiety (at being surrounded by strangers) to amusement (at Pastor Pangburn's censorious "eulogy") to quiet admiration (for Madison, in her defense of Jesse) to shock and alarm (at the ugly words hurled around the room) back to extreme anxiety. Now, as Aileen screamed and Robert broke free from the half-hearted restraint of two pallbearers, Tam wondered what might be expected of him. He had already gone far beyond anything that might reasonably be expected of a person in his position. Once again, he considered the possibility of escape, of slipping out the back door, jumping in the car, and putting as much distance as possible between himself and these deranged people.

Then, as is often the case for people caught in violent close quarters, his course was forged for him. He had reflexively risen from his seat to protect Aileen from tumbling bodies, when he found himself engaged with a combatant from the Miller-Haas side of the aisle. Before he could decide on the most beneficial course of action, he became entangled in a mass of writhing humanity. Fists, elbows, and curses flew; one blow landed on his jaw. Reacting rather than attacking, he secured a death-lock on a bull-like neck and was pulled over the pew rail. He had just managed to get his boots on the floor when the whole heaving scrum spilled backward in the direction of Jesse's coffin. Tam wound up on the floor under the press of other writhing combatants while the pallbearers did their best to protect the coffin.

But somebody collided with the insubstantial box anyway, causing it to shudder violently. As it shook, the framed photo of the recently departed rocked, then tumbled from its perch. It fell as if in slow motion, each end-over-end rotation of the black wooden frame registering in the collective mind of the still upright observers of the struggle.

And then it landed with a horrifying crash inches from Tam Malonee's head. The frame splintered and disintegrated, sending chunks and shards of glass in every direction.

The brawl stopped as suddenly as it had begun. Death grips eased and cocked fists relaxed. Everyone stared in amazement at the photograph which, now released from the frame, fell against the side of Tam Malonee's head. When Tam finally freed himself from his entanglement, he found himself, facedown, looking straight into the photograph.

Into the smiling face of Jesse Breedlove.

∗   ∗   ∗   ∗

An hour later, he was on a threadbare chair in Aileen's darkened living room. Odd images danced on the television screen. Two overmuscled characters in spandex were circling each other in a debris-cluttered wrestling ring while a referee struggled to keep two huge men in street clothes on the other side of the ropes.

"Who's the guy in purple?" Tam asked.

"Jupiter." The name tumbled awkwardly over the ice-filled washcloth Robert had pressed to his swollen lower lip.

"Excuse me?"

Robert lowered the ice pack and gave Tam a confused look. "King Jupiter Rex. He's only like the W. A. W. champ."

"Sorry," Tam said. "I haven't really kept up with it."

Robert nodded and turned back to the television.

Tam rubbed his aching jaw. He decided that it wasn't broken, but he knew he'd have trouble chewing for a while. He shot an impatient glance into the darkness of the main hallway into which Madison and Aileen had hastened some fifteen minutes earlier. Aileen had been pale and hunched over, her general magnitude diminished substantially by the episode at the church. Complaining of a severe migraine, she had disappeared into her bedroom, not to be seen again. This was not a major problem for Tam Malonee.

He was still unable to mentally reconstruct most of the church brawl. All he knew was that he had successfully locked down one enemy brawler until reason (more accurately, a less-combative hostility) had the opportunity to reassert itself. And, although he'd been stepped on, elbowed, kneed, and punched in the process, he characterized his participation in the melee as, essentially, a minor triumph. He'd never been a fighter—on brutal parochial school playgrounds and in sweat-stippled gymnasiums, he'd always relied on his size and wingspan to distance himself from most close-order pummeling. So he was proud of the way he had reacted to the unexpected attack. In his mind, he had taken on and neutralized the enemy's alpha male, all without a moment's preparation. He remained puzzled, however, by the whole business of Uncle Jesse's photograph. The way it had seemed to defy the known laws of physics and seek him out was just, well, *creepy*. Even as the writhing bodies had slowly untangled, the photo remained there, the knowing visage of dead Uncle Jesse right there in his face. Still, he told himself, deferring any analysis of fate's role in the photo episode, the main things were that he had emerged from the melee mostly uninjured and—perhaps most importantly—with the grudging respect of Robert Breedlove. He wasn't yet sure how he could parlay this into some personal benefit; several possibilities were buzzing like neon in his mind.

"Oh, hell," Robert mumbled now, to nobody in particular. "He got that boy in a Rocket Ju-plex."

"Rocket Ju-plex?"

Unable to tear his eyes from the action, Robert bolted upright with excitement and gave the visitor a quick nod. "Yeah. See what happens here."

Tam studied the two wrestlers and made an effort to predict from the intricate interplay of overmuscled limbs precisely who was about to do what to whom. The manic pronouncements from the television commentators and the agitated crowd bawl only served to confuse him more.

"Is the Ju-plex—"

"It's bad," Madison intoned. She had entered the living room with her packed suitcase in her right hand. "It's lethal. Don't nobody usually come back from it."

Suddenly another huge man dressed in a floral print shirt and holding a metal folding chair overhead appeared in the frame. One of the commentators shouted a warning to the imperiled Jupiter Rex. The referee, in apparent anticipation of pending devastation, crouched near the mat, oblivious of the lurking threat.

"Oh, hell," Robert giggled. His whole body convulsed in anticipation. "It's *on* now, sumbitch!"

Even more confused by this new plot twist, Tam watched as the ring intruder smacked Jupiter Rex across the upper back with the flattened chair. The masked purple behemoth dropped like a slaughtered bull while his imperiled opponent wriggled free. The spectators went wild. "An unprovoked chair attack," a ring commentator complained. "There's no place in professional wrestling for this kind of stunt!"

Robert howled with delight as the man in street clothes and his newly liberated confederate teamed up to entrap Jupiter Rex in some kind of choking leg lock.

Tam made a face and twisted slightly in the chair. "You've got to be kidding me. This is just … *stupid.*"

Robert froze, the rare and swollen grin slowly reverting to the standard frown. The ice pack fell to the floor.

"I mean, he hardly even touched him with that chair."

"Well, I guess we're ready to go on then," Madison offered. She picked up her suitcase and slid a step closer to the door.

Tam, sensing that he had genuinely offended Robert, now scrambled to modify his remarks. He wasn't so committed to waging war on professional wrestling to forfeit any favors he might have earned. "He deserved what he got, though," he offered brightly. "They can break his neck for all I care."

Robert's sank back into the couch and continued to glower.

"Of course all we got to go to Florida in is that old Oldsmobile out front," Madison said.

Robert stared at her, his facial expression unchanged.

"The thing is," she continued, "we'd probably be better off traveling in something else. I was thinking maybe the Honda."

"What's wrong with the Alero?" Robert asked. His eyes had drifted back to the television screen. "I mean, other than being a huge piece of crap."

"Well," she replied, "I think it has some kind of problem." She turned to Tam with a raised-eyebrow, it's-actually-your-problem-please-explain look.

"What kind of problem?" Robert asked.

"Um, it's the title. There's a, ah, bifurcated, elliptical lien on it."

Robert stared silently at the television for a moment, then asked, "What am I s'posed to drive to work?"

"What's wrong with the pickup?" Madison asked.

Robert's frown deepened.

"He did help you fight those boys back at the church," Madison offered.

Robert grimaced, as though making such a concession caused him physical pain. "I reckon y'all can take it," he muttered. "Key's hanging by the door. But I want it back."

"Of course," Madison said. She grabbed Tam by the elbow and steered him toward the door.

They sped away from Middleboro, leaving Robert slouched in front of his television, Aileen curled, prawn-like, in her bed, and the Poole County deputies standing guard over Jesse Breedlove's burial. Following Madison's directions, Tam headed southwest, negotiating the narrow roads that wound through the Tennessee countryside. At Madison's request, he pointed the car toward Interstate 65, the major north-south thoroughfare that more or less bisected the state of Alabama. The very route that Tam had spent the best part of the day avoiding.

Madison had not divulged the precise current location of her ex-husband and daughter, explaining that she didn't want Tam to become "accomplished to" the taking of Brandy. Tam had argued that the child's liberation shouldn't be regarded as criminal, but conceded that, with his luck, it would end up being the thing that finally got him locked up forever. "You don't need to get involved in this," she had countered. "All you gotta do is get me to Pensacola." Given that destination, it now seemed illogical to continue with his original day's travel plan—across the state to Chattanooga, then down through Georgia, stopping at some cheap motel south of Atlanta by sundown.

Illogical, perhaps, but probably far less stressful. Tam had a number of reasons for wanting to avoid a due-southern plunge on I-65. One area of concern stemmed indirectly from a strong conceptual aversion that he (along with many other midwesterners and easterners, for that matter) felt toward Alabama. His particular prejudice, however, had nothing to do with the bad publicity associated with marble-mouthed politicians or half-century-old racial conflicts—Tam wouldn't be born for more than decade after the negative images of the early sixties would be published to the world—or the mistaken and decidedly unfair characterization of all Southerners as yahoos and hillbillies. Tam's personalized bias, held since his college days, derived almost exclusively from the cartoon-like tableau generated in his mind upon hearing any reference to either Mississippi or Alabama—apple-cheeked fraternity boys and magnolia-queen debutantes sucking mint juleps even as bullet-headed state police crouched in wait for unsuspecting Yankees. While he felt, at the very worst, indifference toward frat boys and debs, he found the idea of being hassled by cops in mirrored sunglasses disconcerting. Cop-avoidance ranked very high on his roster of priorities. He was aware of the fact that, should he be stopped, full disclosure of his fugitive status would be but a single electronic impulse away. The fact that he was now the legitimate possessor of a Tennessee-plated vehicle helped ease his fear of being a cop magnet. Also—and clearly one of the reasons he found a female travel companion advantageous—Madison's presence, both as a driver and a diversion, would surely insulate him from government scrutiny.

The nearing of the interstate caused another concern to rise like a gaping alligator from the mire of well-preserved resentment. Two months earlier, more out of boredom than genuine interest, he had conducted an Internet search for the current whereabouts of one Roger Malonee. To his surprise, he had discovered that the father he hadn't seen or spoken with for more than twenty years had somehow found his way to a northern Alabama community called Arden. To Tam, this single fact provided all the justification he needed to warrant his detour around the Yellowhammer State. His preferred solution to most of life's difficulties had always been evasion; avoidance, to his mind, an undervalued virtue, generally rendered confrontation unnecessary. Until now, it hadn't been difficult to avoid Roger Malonee. Until now, Tam had always been able to savor bittersweet personal vindication in the sterile bubble of fantasy justice. *Until now.* Now he knew he'd be traveling a path that ran within a few miles of that absconding bastard's home. Once again, he'd been unmistakably steered toward an encounter, unlikely a mere twenty-four hours earlier. He dared not ignore fate now that she had made her imperious will known. Perhaps, he thought, as with the improbable injection of Madison Monroe into his life, it was meant to be.

But Tam's most niggling worry about traveling I-65 had nothing to do with either jail or awkward family reunions. Rather, it concerned complex personal trip logistics and, with the sun sinking in the western sky, the threatened disruption of a treasured daily routine. Sundown to Tam signified time for his daily "Golden Mellow"—his personal code-phrase for the warm relief that came with his evening six-pack of beer. This ritual, one of several he used to help cope with the stresses of daily life, had begun years earlier with the routine consumption of a two-or three-beer nightcap to help him mellow out. The precise quantum of beer required for this purpose had expanded in time to "an even six-pack." He had no loyalty to the brand or brewer of the amber liquid, but, by his own clear, ritualistic preference, it had to be packaged in a can, as opposed to a bottle or keg. There was just something almost sacred about that aluminum vessel—the way it fit his hand, the brushed-metallic finish, the unique and important cracking sound made by the pop-top as it punched through to paradise—that helped enhance the accompanying burnish. What he was after was not slobbering drunkenness, but a full-sensory ritual of conflict avoidance. He had found that three beers usually brought the Mellow; four made it more profound, five helped extend it. The sixth beer was just there, stuck to the others by that obnoxious plastic ring. It seldom helped him deal with the Edge; occasionally it was the precursor of larger problems—the break-in at the Auto Corral office, for example. That event had been facilitated by the unfortunate synergy of disenfranchisement, and the sixth, and possibly a seventh and eighth, tall-boy brew.

That unfortunate type of occurrence hardly ever happened; the sixth beer normally went down without incident. His day typically ended with him languid in his recliner, Edge-free and uninterested in confrontation. That being the usual scenario, he had been completely baffled by Lauren's continuing resistance to this harmless routine. The thing she referred to as a "disgusting addiction," was, in reality, merely a personal therapeutic strategy, something to help make him a more sociable companion. Tam had repeatedly pointed out to her she had her own restorative diversions, including costly weekend-long shopping extravaganzas with her "rich-bitch" friends. Moreover, he had argued, the fact that he limited himself to a fixed daily ration of alcohol and never drank during daylight hours (with the exception of barbecues, picnics, lake outings, softball games, and other social events), established that he was *not* an alcoholic. To the contrary, he argued, his alcohol consumption had proven to be as effective as any pill in quieting the active internal dialogues that made normal married life and sleep impossible.

And now, here was this—this unplanned and disquieting logistical dilemma. His inner organizer always arranged the bulk of his mandatory daily activities around the focal scheduling of his evening routine; this day, as awkwardly disorganized as it had begun, had been no exception. Even as he fled the law, he had managed to mentally arrange his day's travel in discrete activity blocks that concluded with a frosty six-pack in a cheap motel room. His revised itinerary now demanded a new strategy, one that provided both for progress and for countering an ever-expanding Edge.

But scheduling was only a part of his dilemma. Even as he mentally scrolled through the menu of best available travel options, a voice—to be sure, the never heard, yet clearly recognized, voice of Jesse Breedlove—spoke to him. "I know just how you feel," the ghost declared with a purposeful drawl. "You're just like I was—all you want is to be numb. But you're never gonna have a normal life as long as it goes on." And when Tam commenced his ritual of justification, the spectral voice interrupted. "I'm the one person you can't bullshit," it said. "And

I'm telling you, when your liver's aching, and there's nothing left of your life, it'll be too late." When Tam, irritated by this new complication, angrily shook the voice from his head, the face was still there—smiling, almost smirking, at him, just as in the photograph. Of course, Tam reminded himself, he didn't *have* to engage in his routine. He knew he *could* make an exception and drive straight through to Pensacola. It was just that the recent events had triggered an unusually high level of internal dialogue and stress; if he was going to sleep well, he *should* unwind properly. Now, hours behind his original schedule and with Madison in tow, he wasn't sure how it was all going to play out. The fact that Madison had already informed him of her fear of night driving and intolerance for drunk drivers narrowed his options.

He twisted the steering wheel and squirmed in his seat. It was hard enough to fit his six-four frame into the driver's compartment of a subcompact car; the slow creeping of The Edge was making the experience more unpleasant.

"You okay?" Madison asked—the first time she had spoken since they'd left Aileen's house.

"Yeah," Tam replied. "This isn't the most comfortable car for me. Plus, I'm a little tired." He decided not to divulge Uncle Jesse's private scolding.

She nodded.

"So how're *you* doing?" Tam cast a quick glance in Madison's direction. She was folded in half in the passenger seat, upper body inclined forward and hands clasped around tucked legs. She had turned toward the open passenger-side window. She seemed to be staring at a vast field of corn simmering in the late July heat. Tam could see her jaw muscles milling the ever-present pink wad of bubble gum.

"I'm okay," she replied, turning back to Tam. The warm breeze blew her hair across her face. Her jaws worked, grinding and chomping almost without pause.

"What're you thinking about?"

"We used to work that field right there," she replied. She turned back toward the window. "Me and my two brothers, my daddy, and momma. Burley tobacco, they called it. It used to belong to a man name Anderson. I heard some big corporation owns it now." She seemed to be staring past the plants themselves, into the very soul of the land. "They'da been topping it right about now."

Tam slowed the car and looked out at the sea of nearly six-foot stalks. "'Topping it'?"

"Yeah. When the plants started to flower, they'd get these blooms that stuck out the tops. When they got long like that, Daddy and them would go through and lop them off. Sometimes they'd make two runs, depending on what Mister Anderson wanted done."

"I ain't much of a country boy," Tam said, "but that sure looks like corn to me."

She swept the hair off her face and smiled at him. "It *is* corn, silly."

"So what happened to the tobacco?"

"It ain't profitable no more. That's what I hear, anyway. It's all a bunch of mumbo jumbo to me. I hear the guys at Mac's talking—quotas and subsidies. I don't really understand all that mess. All I know is they say they can't get enough for the tobacco at market. The small growers I know have been hurting for years. Now, as you can see, the big growers don't want to fool with it, either."

"From what I heard you say at the funeral, it's probably just as well."

"It's complicated, Tam. I know tobacco ain't no good for you. I mean, look at all the people who use it and get sick. Look at me. I remember stripping leaves in the morning, then feeling dizzy and sick all day at school. That's what the nicotine does to you. But I smoked anyway, just like my brothers. And look at my folks. Both my parents worked around it, both of them smoked, both of them died young. I'm all that's left around here. Momma died when I was about seven. Daddy fell over dead as a doorknob when I was in junior high—bone cancer." She was still chewing her gum, still staring out the window. "I know these growers ain't trying to hurt people, Tam—even the Millers and the Haases. They're farmers—they grow stuff for a living, and it's just another crop to them. And they work hard, they really do. My daddy worked like a dog. He worked part-time at Wal-Mart's, but from April to November, the crop was all he thought about. He grew the plants, set them, applied the herbicides and pesticides. Then there was always a lot of frettin' about the weather, suckers, whatnot. Then the plants have to be topped, then cut, then hung to cure. Then, when the leaves are right, we'd strip them. It's a business, Tam. What I said back at the church, it was true, but probably unfair at the same time. Does that make sense? All these folks, they might grow something bad. To them, they're just growing a crop, same as that corn out yonder. They're still just farmers, all of them, struggling to get by." She took a long breath and sighed. "I guess I was just mad because the preacher didn't have nothing good to say about Jesse."

Tam nodded. He'd heard some of what Madison said, but mostly he'd been thinking that perhaps he could handle two beers and still drive. That, he judged, would probably get them far enough down the road that she'd agree to spend the night somewhere. Then he could crack open another, maybe two, cold ones to put The Edge to sleep for the night. It wasn't his standard Golden Mellow, but then this had been an un-standard day. Or they could stop near this Arden place—Madison, of all people, couldn't argue with the demands of fate—he could knock back a can or two to get his nerves settled, and he could make the dreaded phone call. Either way, there'd be a resolution that everyone, even Uncle Jesse, had to be pleased with. This internal bargain pleased him immensely; immediately a huge weight was lifted from him.

"So what about you?" she asked. She had turned to look at the things, his things, crammed into the sparse backseat and floorboard. The folded easel, the guitar case, the paint-smeared plastic box filled with tubes, jars, brushes. Odd cargo, indeed, for a fleeing felon.

"What about me?" Tam said.

"Well, you had to listen to my sorry story. What's yours?"

Tam smiled and turned back to the road. It lay before him in sweeping bends and cambers, coiling like gunmetal ribbon around steep hillsides where horses and cattle grazed under a merciless Southern sun. He drove for several minutes without speaking, past farm houses, steel grain elevators, and sheds with idle wagons and drills. And then, as they negotiated one last twisting rise, Interstate 65 came into view, and with it, gas stations with their appended convenience stores. And, thought Tam, coolers filled with chilled aluminum cans. Cans filled with golden relief.

"I'll tell you what," he said, at last. "I'm dry as a bone right now. Let's stop up there and get something cold to drink." He turned to her. "Then I'll tell you whatever you want to know."

CHAPTER 4

▼

CHECKING KANDY

At 10:40 PM, Tam closed his fluttering eyelids and began to count to ten. It was his sincere hope that he was in the middle of a bad dream, and that, when he reached "ten" and his eyes popped open, his subconscious—or whatever it was that had generated those disturbing images—would've moved on to the next topic. He suspected he was dreaming because nothing he'd been experiencing made the least bit of sense. Not the smoke-shrouded bar, the one-armed barkeep, or the plus-sized exotic dancer, who didn't so much dance as strut, squat, and rub on the obligatory pole. And certainly not the bizarre dressing room scene, with the mostly naked woman and the angry, biker-looking dude with the chrome-plated pistol.

Nothing had made sense that entire evening.

Beginning back in Tennessee, with Madison's reaction to the purchase of the beer. Tam had rolled giddily back into the car with his sacked treasure under his arm, oblivious to the reproving glare that had been tracking him since he left the mini-mart. He was fifteen miles down the interstate and already getting into the second can before it occurred to him that there might be a problem. This would have come as no surprise to anyone who knew him well: despite his great confidence in his ability to categorize and judge others, his attitude receiver had never been accurately tuned to the precise frequency of human disapproval. Instead, he reacted to this development as he did with any other negativity in his life—processing it, as a terminal cancer patient might, in distinct and identifiable stages.

First came the psychological gymnastics of Denial: Madison's attitude *couldn't* be attributable to his drinking because she was a reasonable person, un-Lauren-like in her relations with others. From what he had seen, she seemed tolerant of the deficiencies of those close to her. Aileen, for example, with her crusty demeanor and little yard of horrors. Or Robert, fighting in church or sprawled, brain-dead and useless, in front of the television set. Or Uncle Jesse who, was an *actual* alcoholic. No, if she could tolerate these glaring and egregious deficiencies, she couldn't find fault with a thirsty man having a few beers at the end of a long and trying day. A few miles further down the road, as he took a closer measure of her now rigid posture and the uncharacteristic icy quiet, he felt a prickle of indignation. How *dare* she react this way when he was doing her a favor? He then conceded they were in her cousin's car, and he *had* planned on asking her to drive. And, true enough, he *was* hopeful of screwing her at some point before they parted company. Still, how could she be so … *so like Lauren?* In the next phases of this process, he Bargained ("I'll hold off on the rest of the six-pack until she's asleep"), then tumbled into the desolate swale of Disappointment ("If this is how she really is, then she *can't be* The One") and finally, as evidenced by his eventual shrug and the strident breaching of the third can's lid, Acceptance.

The phone call to his father had not gone as he had imagined, either. He had placed the call many times in his head; on every occasion, his father had responded to his voice with the stunned silence one might expect from a cornered scoundrel. In those fantasy conversations, Tam had relished his father's discomfort; he refused to do or say anything to relieve the awkwardness of the moment. And why should he? Roger Malonee had done nothing to ease the pain of his fatherless adolescence. He hadn't been around to share his son's triumphs or to help him work through his failures. He was, as it turned out, in *Alabama*, one of the last places Tam would have guessed a brilliant physicist would seek refuge. And, although a part of him now hoped that a life spent in that imagined semi-tropical hell-hole might be, in itself, a satisfactorily cruel punishment, he had long believed that the sudden shock of a cold call such as this would probably be the only penance the man ever paid for his sins. The *actual* call, placed in sweltering heat from a filthy public phone system shelf attached to the side of an access-road convenience store, had played much differently than the fantasy one. In reality, it had been Tam's heart that had pounded, his brow that had gushed sweat. And Roger—quite unlike his fantasy persona—had responded to his son's greeting with an insouciant, "So what brings you around here?" Matter-of-factly, evenly, without the apparent tincture of either guilt or regret. As though it had only been a few weeks since they last spoke. As it turned out, it had been Tam who had stammered incomprehensibly, unsure how to explain either the call or his presence in Arden, Alabama, on a broiling August afternoon. And, when his father had issued a firm invitation for the travelers to come straightaway to his house for a visit, Tam could only mumble an awkward acceptance and, with a shaking right hand, tattoo directions on a sweaty left palm.

Nor had anything about Roger Malonee or his new Southern existence matched any of the images Tam had constructed en route to his father's home. Not the house itself, a handsome split-level with manicured Bermuda grass on an isolated, crape-myrtle-and-magnolia-lined street. Not the long, two-tiered, custom-built ramp that rose gradually from the sidewalk to meet the front porch. Not the city of Arden, a magnificent techno-town sprung from red clay and cotton fields and populated by dozens of self-made millionaires and many thousands of true geniuses—actual rocket scientists, systems analysts, engineers, mathematicians, bio-tech wizards, and generations of their gifted offspring. Not Roger himself, a rail-thin, barely six-foot, professorial figure with thinning gray hair, salt-and-pepper moustache, and wire-rimmed glasses—so unlike the towering, Rasputin-like personage of his visual memory. Not his voice, still as deep and as hardwired to life's ironies as he recalled, but more measured in pace and somber in tone, as it should be. Not the fact that he insisted that Tam refer to him only as "Roger," possibly to block one possible inroad to a dialogue concerning his parental deficiencies. And clearly not Paula, the *new* Mrs. Malonee, a pleasant, forty-something with a husky voice and an aristocratic, deep Southern accent, or Tam's surprise half-brother Roger Jr. ("I go by Rocky"), thirteen years old and, for reasons then unknown to Tam, confined to a wheelchair.

And certainly none of the events that would follow, including the Malonees' spend-the-night invitation to Tam and Madison, Madison's suspiciously quick acceptance of that offer, Roger's declaration that he and Tam were hitting Arden for a "guy's night out," and, most of all, the evening's latest stop—the hideous and threat-filled dressing room of the Exxxstasy Sho-Bar.

None of it could have really happened.

And yet, he was reluctant to open his eyes. If the dressing room scene and all the crazy things that came with it—the half-naked dancer, the mean-looking biker dude, the chrome-plated nine millimeter pointed at his head—were real, then he was a dead man. And he'd have his father to thank for all of it.

As though he needed it, suddenly he had yet another reason to despise Roger Malonee.

*   *   *   *

They had set out to sample the Arden night life in Roger's old Ford F-150 pickup. They drove in silence with the windows open and the sticky night air rushing through the cab. They traveled on one of Arden's more commercial thoroughfares, its range of billboards and business signs rendered marginally less offensive by a legislated uniformity of height and size and, in any event, framed pleasantly by the long ridge of graceful background hills—the Appalachian's verdant lumbar region.

As they rumbled along, the volatile mix of proximity and an almost non-stop flurry of jarring emotional shots blasted open Tam's long-sealed vault of unpleasant memories. His father's present silence caused Tam to recall the way the man had, all those years ago, retreated into what Tam could only assume was a moody, narcissistic universe of one. While he was able to recall a few happy excursions with Roger—to Detroit to see the Tigers play, sledding on a nearby hill, playing hockey with a tin can on a frozen neighborhood pond—he remembered most vividly the man's collapse into an emotional hole, and how he finally—silently—just disappeared. And the age and condition of the truck, another unlikely but potent memory trigger, made Tam recur to his father's extreme frugality. Suddenly, he was seven again, reliving brutal tongue-lashings for the venial sins of waste: letting water run while he brushed his teeth, failure to properly squeeze the toothpaste tube, leaving on lights that weren't being used. The sheer accretion of these unpleasant memories served to reaffirm Tam's long-held belief that Roger Malonee was an insufferable bastard.

*   *   *   *

The Exxxstasy, a low-end strip club housed in an old warehouse near one of Arden's less prosperous neighborhoods, was the third stop on their clubbing circuit. In many respects, it was a standard middle-grade strip club with a ten-stool bar and a dozen tables arranged around the narrow pole-stage. There was a separate area with four love seats arranged at odd angles; Tam assumed—correctly—that this area was reserved for private dances. He had no personal experience with this specific variety of "gentlemen's entertainment," nor did he have any real interest in it. The Exxxstasy had been Roger's idea; Tam was just obeying fate's arbitrary command. It being Saturday night, the club was near capacity. The hostess seated the two men at a small, round table near a door marked "Private."

A surly waitress in a ridiculous short-skirted jumper took their orders and, after some ten minutes, delivered two glasses half-filled with flat beer.

Tam took a sip from the glass and stared at the woman on stage. The club's emcee had introduced her moments before as the "exotic Kotton Kandy." She was a large bleach-blonde with average-sized breasts and wide hips. She had a colorful flower tattoo on the small of her back and other floral-themed illustrations on both ankles. Cellulite dimples creased the pallid flesh of her upper thighs. Tam's eyes began their inventory, as he assumed they must in such a venue, with her breasts and her haunches; they soon moved up to, then settled upon, her face. As was the case with Madison and other interesting-looking people, it was the details of the facescape—especially the defects—that ultimately captured his attention. Her most salient facial feature was her mouth; very full lips, slightly upturned at the corners, were painted a strident shade of red and frozen in a defiant pout. Overdone shadow and mascara hung heavy on her already narrow eyes. Her nose was large and bumpy. High and strong cheekbones gave her face an interesting shape, but she had bad skin; even through an industrial-strength coat of makeup, acne pitting and an ugly chin scar were apparent. As he had with Madison, he worked out her portrait in his mind. Landmark lines to mark the prominent features, mixed dark tones to capture the shadows and shades, the creative combination of reds, yellows, and white to replicate the complex shades of her skin and hair. And, of course, the faithful but compassionate representation of the scars and bumps and pits.

Her routine began with a few minutes of basic stage-strutting, a sequence conducted with the aid of three colored scarves. Tam regarded this phase of the performance as amateurish, unathletic, and decidedly anti-erotic. Even worse, the occasional spasmodic jerking of her head interfered with his study of her face. The strutting soon gave way to a type of swaying two-step. Occasionally she dipped and thrusted, more-or-less in sync with the prurient thump of a mid-eighties hair-band anthem. After a few minutes, she shuffled back to center stage and, wrapping a leg around the pole, began the critical, final phase of her performance.

"That Madison's a fine-looking girl," Roger said, the first words he'd spoken since ordering his beer. His eyes remained on the woman swinging from the pole on the stage ten feet from their table.

Tam nodded. He wasn't sure how to respond other than by tacit agreement.

"So how long you guys been together?"

Tam glanced at his watch. "About seven hours," he said. He watched his father watching the dancer and slowly shook his head. He had initially regarded

Roger's bar-hopping proposal as rational, even if unexpected. "Bonding"—if that indeed was what he was after—would require talking, and any productive discussion touching on their disturbing personal history (how else could they form a new bond without breaking the rusted chains of the past?) would probably be best conducted outside the presence of current wife and son. But the men had bounced from an upscale hotel bar to a noisy bowling-alley pub to the current strip joint without having engaged in any meaningful conversation, and without any effort on Roger's part to broach the subject of abandonment. What Tam had craved was a heartfelt apology; he would have settled for any degree of supplication or reasonable attempt at explanation. He would even have accepted a partially plausible excuse. What he had gotten, instead, was off-the-cuff commentary on the ridiculous cost of bar beer, the serious shortage of local dancing "talent," and the tropical storm gaining strength in the Gulf. And now, a comment on Madison's looks. Tam was beginning to think that his father's true motivation for this night on the town might be to temporarily substitute one domestic disappointment for another.

"No shit," Roger said. His eyes shifted briefly from the dancer to Tam. "Seven hours. And I guess you're already nailing it." He took a sip of beer and snorted in approval. "I shoulda known any son of mine would be a hell of a cocksman."

Tam's jaw dropped, although Roger, who'd already turned back to the half-nude woman on the stage, didn't notice. The remark hit Tam the wrong way, although he couldn't decide what shocked him more—its offensive content, that a father would actually speak that way to a son, or the fact that the words had provoked a reaction at all. Adhering to his usual analytical method, he tried to work out the answer before deciding how, or even if, he should respond. The more he thought about it, the more he became convinced that the problem was something much deeper than any of the suspected possibilities—some obscure but powerful subconscious notion that jabbed at his latent sensibility. It somehow suggested to him that Madison, regardless of who she might be or what she might do, already meant a great deal to him.

"She's just bumming a ride," Tam said, at last. He took another sip of beer, then added the hopeless lie, "I really have no plans to have sex with her."

"Are you serious?" Roger snorted again. "What are you, queer or something?"

"Excuse me?"

"Shoot. I mean, if it was me, and I was your age, I'd be all over that."

Tam did a quick mental calculation and determined that Roger had been *precisely* his age when he had deserted his wife and child. Maybe for another woman, perhaps someone as attractive as Madison. Maybe for no reason at all. A wicked verbal missile assembled itself in his mind; the warhead was sequenced and armed, his shoulder-mounted launcher was ready to blast his adversary off his chair. Then just as quickly—and to Tam's way of thinking, miraculously—an unfamiliar caution light flashed; a guiding voice instructed him to stand down. Somehow, given the briefest moment of reflection, Tam had recognized the lethal nature of his planned assault, the pure pointlessness of executing it. Somewhere between the left side of Tam's brain and the tip of his tongue, the ordnance had been intercepted and disarmed. Through some process he couldn't understand, he'd probably done the right thing. Not a typical result, especially after he'd had a few drinks. No comment by him, no matter how observant, could obliterate his childhood scars. It could only make the current situation even more uncomfortable for all concerned.

"She seems to be a nice person," Tam offered, at last.

Roger grunted and stared at Kotton Kandy. The woman was doing her best, clutching the pole with one hand, her inflexible limbs not quite able to deliver her far beyond the crudest phallic imagery.

Tam took a long drink of now tepid beer and evaluated his state of mellowness. *Nothing.* The beer tasted watered-down and flat and his buzz—if it had ever arrived—had now departed. He tried to calculate how many beers he had in him and arrived at two and a half—one at each of the first two stops, and half of his current drink. Tam didn't count the evening's first four beers since they'd been consumed under less-than-ideal conditions and, in any event, before technical sunset. Now he had no way of knowing how much alcohol he had in him because there was no way of knowing how much the bar was diluting the drinks. Another excellent reason, he told himself, for doing your drinking at home.

There was a scattering of applause as Kandy finished her routine. She waved her scarves and strutted away, stage left. A few moments later, she appeared at the bar in a plunging neckline T-shirt.

"Here we go," Roger said. "Now we're gonna get hit up for drinks or a lap dance."

"No, thanks," Tam said.

"Hey, you wanna have some fun with her?"

Tam watched Kandy roam from patron to patron, unenthusiastically doing management's bidding—slowly working her way toward their table.

"Not really," he said, doing his best to stifle a yawn. "I'm really, I mean really, tired."

"C'mon. This'll be fun." Roger raised his right hand and waved until he had the woman's attention. She squeezed past two other tables and then was right there, next to Tam. Their waitress appeared at almost the exact same time, approaching from the other side. Tam gave both women quick glances and an embarrassed smile then stared down at his empty glass.

"Miss Kandy," Roger announced, "to thank you for your … artistic performance, my son would like to buy you a drink."

Tam's half-open eyes bounced from Roger to Kandy and back, noting in the process that two men seated at the bar's end seemed to have more than a passing interest in this transaction. Even though he did not frequent such places, he understood the essentials of that particular strip-club scam. Suddenly, and for the first time, it occurred to him that less than twenty dollars remained from the hundred he had stolen. He had expensive gas and beer and probably food for two to buy—he didn't have fifteen bucks to throw away on an unskilled dancer's undeserved soft drink.

"I … ah, don't—"

"Thank you," Kandy said. She flashed a slight smile. She nodded to the waitress who, in turn, signaled in the direction of the bar. For the first time, Tam noticed that the bartender, a huge, balding man, had only one arm. His mind was momentarily diverted from the awkwardness of the moment as he watched with the bartender deftly manipulate the mugs, glasses, and bottles with only one hand.

"My son's a doctor," Roger said. He beamed with fake pride, then put his glass to his lips and drained the remaining beer.

Kandy's narrow eyes zeroed in on Tam. "A doctor?"

"Yes, a doctor. He's visiting here from out of state."

"Could you come back to my dressing room and look at something?"

Tam stared at her.

"It won't take but a minute."

"Go on," Roger said, grinning at his son. "Just go give it a quick look-see." Then, turning to the dancer: "He's a little shy."

Tam's large hands locked onto the table's curved edge. "I—"

"C'mon. *Please*." For the first time, an actual smile seemed to cross the woman's face. "I've been worried. I just need to know if it's something serious." She took Tam's right hand in hers and gently tugged on him. "You don't have to buy me a drink. Just do this for me."

Tam shot his father an urgent please-rescue-me look; Roger Malonee did not appear to be interested in either saving his son or terminating the gag. The woman tugged again, harder this time, and managed to pull Tam to his feet.

Drained by exhaustion and the effects of the alcohol, Tam found himself able to offer only nominal resistance. The dancer pulled him through the passageway protected by the "Private" door, down a narrow hallway cluttered with gym bags and small piles of clothing, and into a compact dressing room. Two mirrors hung on one wall just above a scarred folding table cluttered with containers of makeup, plastic drink cups, tissue boxes, a loaded ashtray, and the cardboard tube from a roll of paper towels. There were three metal folding chairs; the one closest to the makeshift dressing table was empty, the other two were piled with clothing. Along the opposite wall was a sturdier, steel-legged table with a half-loaf of moldy bread, two cans of commodity chili, and a hotplate spread out on it. A heavy veil of smoke hung in the air. Another performer, a tall brunette who seemed more concerned with adjusting her costume than Tam's intervening presence, pushed wordlessly past the two intruders as they entered.

"Well, screw you too, bitch," Kandy drawled. She swept the bread and cans off the sturdy table, pulled off her sequined thong bottom, and hoisted herself on the wood-grained laminate surface. She spread her legs apart and stared hopefully at Tam. "It's that thing," she said indicating a purple lump on one of her labia. "Do you see what I'm talkin' about?"

Tam stood in front of her, frozen, his jaw slack, mouth open. He had never before gazed in full light upon a woman's vulva, much less one shaved and exhibited so explicitly.

"Do you see what I'm talking about, Doctor—" She redistributed her weight on her elbows. "What's your name, hon?"

Tam nodded dumbly. He did, in fact, see the pea-sized cyst on the right lower labium. And he did note that it looked inflamed. As unfamiliar as he was with the terrain, he felt fairly sure that it was something that required real medical attention.

"Um—"

"Doctor?"

Tam looked up at her, at the fascinating face that he had once thought he wanted to paint, and said: "I'm not ... ah ..."

"What now?"

"Um ... I'm not really ... I think you need to see a doctor. It looks bad—"

She pulled down her cover-up. "What are you saying? You're *not* a doctor?"

Just then a man pushed the door open and stepped into the room. Tam recognized him as one of the two men who'd been watching him from the bar. He was wearing a Harley-Davidson T-shirt, leather vest, motorcycle boots. But it was the shaved head, Fu-Manchu moustache, and deep frown that informed Tam that he was in serious trouble.

"What's up, hoss?" the man demanded.

"He tricked me, Shane," Kandy whined. She arranged her clothing and jumped from the table. "He told me he was a doctor."

"This true, boy?" The man took several steps into the room and glowered at Tam.

"I never said I was a doctor—"

"So you ain't a doctor?"

"No. I mean, I *am*," Tam protested. "It's just that I'm an, ah, oral surgeon. I don't really ... I'm not really qualified ... ah ... I work on the *other* end." The grin he flashed wilted quickly under the heat of the man's obviously persisting displeasure. "The main thing," he continued awkwardly, "is she needs to see someone—"

"Yeah, just not you."

Tam took a deep breath and exhaled slowly. He knew one thing for sure: he didn't want to have to fight Shane. He was exhausted, and his jaw was still sore from the fracas earlier that afternoon. Besides, they were on this guy's home turf; there was no telling how many similarly disposed friends he had lurking around. He visually measured the distance to the door and decided that running wasn't a viable option, either. Perhaps he could reason with him ...

"So what's your deal?" the man asked. "You just some kind of pervert that tries to trick women?"

Tam sighed and shook his head. "Yeah, you caught me, Shane. That's what I do. I go around to strip clubs and trick the dancers into showing me their twats."

The gun appeared so quickly and unexpectedly that Tam was stunned to see it. But there it was: chrome-plated and proximate and with a barrel that looked to be an inch in diameter.

"You're a real laugh riot, you are," Shane snarled. "You don't often see a pervert with such a smart mouth." The gun's barrel rose until it was pointing right at Tam's chin. "Maybe if I put a hole in your tongue, you'd be even funnier."

That's when Tam shut his eyes and told himself it all had to be a dream. And if it wasn't, it was all Roger's fault.

Just as he began to curse his father's name, he heard his voice, suddenly and improbably, but unmistakably the voice of Roger Malonee.

"It isn't his fault," the voice boomed. "Put the gun away."

Tam opened his eyes to see Roger standing inside the room next to the other large man from the bar.

"He says it was just a misunderstanding, and this guy didn't have nothin' to do with it," the man next to Roger growled.

Shane lowered the gun and stared at Roger.

"Who the hell are *you*?"

"I'm his father," Roger said. "I told the girl he was a doctor, not knowing all this was gonna come down. I was just having some fun with my boy. I didn't know it was gonna turn into all this mess."

Shane's confused look shifted from Tam to Kandy to Roger. "All I know is, he's standing back here starin' at Shirley's private region like he's a dadgum genealogist or somethin'."

"*Shirley?*" Tam mumbled.

"I'll tell you what," Roger said. He pulled his billfold from his back pocket. "Since it was my fault, and since I've upset both of you, let me give you something to make it right." He plucked four bills from the folding money section. "Will forty bucks apiece fix it?"

Shane shrugged and rammed the gun down into his jeans. "I reckon that'd fix it, so far as I'm concerned."

The club bouncer folded his arms across his chest. "The house needs twenty, too."

Blood rushed to Roger's face but he didn't say anything. He pulled another crisp bill from the wallet and handed it to the man.

"And now," the bouncer said, tucking the money in his shirt pocket, "y'all probably want to go ahead on and get your asses out of here." His thick shoulders rolled menacingly forward. "Before everyone changes their minds."

Roger looked like he was prepared to argue the point, but Tam gathered him and shoved him out the door before he could speak.

*   *   *   *

Everyone was in bed by the time the two men arrived back at the Malonee home. Tam asked his father where Madison was and was told that she was probably in the first-floor guest bedroom. Those were the first words spoken between the two since they left the bar. It had occurred to Tam that the ten-minute ride might be a splendid time for his father to apologize—for the inappropriate comments, the practical joke gone bad, in fact, for every rotten thing he'd ever done. But there had only been the faint crackle of country music to fill the void between them.

"You gonna be sleeping with her?" Roger asked now as the two men stood in the darkened living room.

Tam evaluated the question. It didn't seem to be imbued with the carnal tone of Roger's earlier remarks. The question struck Tam as the good faith, factual inquiry of a host into an overnight guest's sleeping preferences.

"I guess not," Tam said. "I'll just sleep on the couch here."

Roger grunted and told Tam he'd go get a blanket and a sheet. He returned in less than a minute with the bedding clutched to his chest.

"Thanks," Tam said. "And thanks for taking me out. It was fun—sort of." His mouth twisted into a slight grin.

"Even after I almost got you killed?"

Tam shrugged. "I figure I better get used to people pointing guns at me."

"I don't follow." Roger took his glasses off and rubbed his eyes.

"It's nothing, really. I'm just thinking that—" He paused, wondering how much more information he should share with this man, this stranger whose blood ran through his veins. He decided that "nothing" was the most appropriate number. Possibly one day—although probably not—but certainly not at that precise seam in their unsettled history. "It's nothing," Tam said. "Just a joke." He tried to meet Roger's bleary-eyed stare, but found himself unable to hold the man's gaze for more than a few seconds. Tam's eyes drifted, finally settling upon a curio cabinet in the corner of the room. The shelves were crammed with objects he assumed had been selected by Paula. Nice things, un-Roger-like, civilized, collectable things. Hummel figurines, mounted blue plates, a crystal angel. And then, on the third shelf, another object that seemed so out of place that it all but smacked him awake.

A baseball. Mounted on a squat, plastic stand. Alone on that third shelf, isolated in odd juxtaposition to the crafted porcelain, above, and the crystal below.

Tam eased toward the cabinet, squinting to see the ball's features in the dim light.

"It's autographed by the '61 Tigers' pitching staff," Roger said proudly. "All the really good starters—Mossi, Bunning, Foytack, Lary." He put his glasses back on and moved closer to the cabinet. He was jolted awake by the fading blue ink on a yellowed horsehide sphere. "Frank Lary," he said, in a tone that reserved for the most significant of humans. "The Yankee-killer, they called him. Did you know he was from Alabama?"

Tam shook his head. He didn't know any of these old Tigers, nor did he really care about them. He remembered now that, at the few Tigers games they attended together, Roger had prattled on, almost non-stop, about the *old* Tigers, the great Tigers of his youth—the Detroit team that had won it all, back when he was a freshman at Michigan. And he probably had mentioned some of these ball-signing old-timers, as well. Tam was sure he would have repressed that specific information. With some effort, he could dredge up the names of some of the 1984 team's luminaries—Jack Morris, Alan Trammell, Kirk Gibson—but they never had mattered to Roger. For some reason, these players only seemed to disappoint him.

For some reason, everything new in his life had seemed to disappoint him.

The two men stood there for another minute, just standing, saying nothing. Even though he found it painful to make eye contact with Roger, Tam noticed for the first time, through stolen, close-up glances at the old man's face that he looked, well, *old*. And tired. Not just it's-real-late-on-a-Saturday-night tired, but life-tired. Like he'd been run through experience's wringer.

"All right, then," Roger said, at last. He thrust the bedding at his son. "I guess I'll see you in the morning."

Tam mumbled thanks again and watched his father walk away. When Roger had disappeared up the stairs, Tam dumped the sheet, pillow, and blanket on the sofa, kicked off his boots, and eased toward the guest bedroom. He gave the mostly closed door a slight push and peeked in. The room was completely dark; by the light of a single lamp in the living room, he could see Madison's T-shirt-clad form curled around a large pillow in the double bed. His guitar case was propped against a chair near the door. Madison's red suitcase was open on the floor not far from the door. Tam noticed that a framed picture of Brandy and an old blue book, green slips of paper protruding from its pages, were resting on top of the neatly folded clothes.

A sensation that was both warm and disquieting sloshed through him. He realized that his attraction to Madison had blossomed well beyond the infatuation he'd felt only twelve hours earlier. Perhaps it'd been Roger's comments at the bar, perhaps his bizarre and sudden brush with death. It wasn't the alcohol talking; the faint buzz he'd achieved had been blasted out of his system by the sight of the gaping gun barrel. Whatever the prompt, he suddenly wanted to be with her—not just for a few days or nights, but for the long haul.

He briefly entertained the notion of crawling in bed with her. Tam knew he wouldn't try anything sexual with her, of course; under all the attendant circumstances, that would be outrageous. Still, he needed the firm embrace of some soft other—someone who was looking more and more like The One. He would've settled for a quick, reassuring hug—any kind of non-confrontational human contact.

It'd been a rough day.

He stood there for a while watching her. Looking at her face—half in shadow, oddly restructured by the fall of the light, still beautiful. Watching her chest rise and fall with every breath.

Completely at peace, by herself, without him.

After a few moments, he carefully pulled the door back to its original position and shuffled back to the sofa. He tucked the sheet between two cushions, lay down, pulled the blanket around his curled-up form.

He was asleep even before the voices could reconstruct the day's events.

CHAPTER 5

▼

THE THEORY OF SOMETHING

August 1, Sunday

Hurricane Gregor
Latest position: 20.4N, 86.8W
Pressure: 970mb
Winds: 75mph
Movement: WNW 8 mph
Location: Approx. 28 mi. SSW Cozumel
Status: Strengthening/Landfall imminent

Kelsoe Babb III:
I first met Tam right after he and Madison got to town. He's certainly someone that you'd remember. He was one of those people that just got your attention. I'm sure you know what I'm talking about. Nice looking boy, with the exception of that scraggly red beard. I've never been a fan of facial hair anyway, but on him it just looked ... well, it made him look ragged. But he was real tall, broad shoulders, big old hands. I think he said he'd been a basketball player in college. He seemed extremely gregarious for a Yankee. You know what I mean—not quite so ... what's the word ... direct? I'm saying he seemed pretty open, laid-back, overall friendly. I don't think it was just

because he wanted me to buy his artwork. Although he clearly was needing the money. The painting he brought to the gallery, a lovely portrait of the girl, he took twenty bucks cash for it. It was one of the four or five paintings that got evacuated with me and the wife. Good thing, too. I ended up selling it for 300 bucks when I was able to open back up. Given all that I was out, I think it was a completely fair settlement for me. I probably could have gotten a lot more for it. Once the story got started about him being washed away in the Surfsider, the value of all his paintings went through the roof.

That's the thing about him that was real surprising. Just looking at him, you'd think he was just another construction worker or landscape guy. Or maybe a painter, but not an artist. I'm talking about the guy who paints walls and trim. Those people are all over the Panhandle. Tam was about as far from that as you can get. He had the two gifts a great portrait artist needs—he could understand the essence of his subjects, and he could make that essence come out the tip of his paintbrush. Quickly, too, without a bunch of touching up or overpainting. Being a gallery owner, I obviously come in contact with a lot of painters. So I think I know what I'm talking about when I say he had more raw potential than anybody. And when I say raw potential, I mean his talent was unrefined yet spectacularly promising. When he told me he painted that picture in twenty minutes, I knew I needed to be in business with him. That's where the idea for the portrait booth came from. I mean, he had the rare ability to pull off that rapid, high-pressure, commercial kind of portrait work. Also, it was clear that he really needed the money.

He did real well with it. For one thing, his fee was, well, dirt cheap. Twenty bucks, that's all. And once that first person sat for him—I think it was a lady on vacation—then everybody walking around that mall got curious and started watching. Next thing you know, he was doing about three an hour. And the portraits were colorful and amazing. He used acrylic paint—you don't see many portraits done in that medium—because it dried much faster.

On Thursday, the day before he took the little girl, I had him and Madison up to my house for lunch. Nothing special, just sandwiches and chips. Things had almost come to a stop on the boardwalk, and they both looked so pitiful. Turns out they were living completely hand to mouth by that time. Anyway, that's when I first suspected something was wrong with their situation. When I asked them about their evacuation plans, they clearly weren't singing from the same page of music. Madison said they would be heading west, but Tam acted like he was headed elsewhere. Kind of odd with the storm clearly heading this way.

Anyway, like I said, he was a great talent. You might even be correct calling him a genius. And his business was good, too, at least for that day and a half.

Tam awoke violently from a nightmare, one that had been recurring with disturbing frequency. In this dream, he is immersed in icy water, having fallen through a weak spot in a frozen pond. No one else is near; nobody hears his frantic cries for help. He fights to pull himself out through the jagged hole in the ice, but he's paralyzed from the scalding cold. Finally he gives up, abandons the fight. His heavy arms fall to his side, and he begins to sink. The faint light recedes as the dark water takes him.

Tam was jolted, as he always was, into heart-pounding wakefulness just as he was inhaling a lethal lungful of ice water. Gasping for air, he propped himself on an elbow, tried to blink away the fog of sleep. His head rotated slightly, his wide eyes doing their best to connect his conscious mind with the unfamiliar surroundings. Gathering information, he struggled to create a clear picture out of the things he knew to be true.

He was on a sofa in the living room in the house of his father and his wife in a place called Arden in the state of Alabama.

It was Sunday.

A traveling companion, whose precise further relationship was exactly that and no more than that when last he saw her, was, to the best of his knowledge, still in a guest bedroom.

Everything he owned was in the guest room next to her bed.

He had come close to being murdered the previous night in a ridiculous turn of events.

He had a paraplegic half-brother about whom he knew nothing.

He was a wanted criminal.

In the sober quiet of a new day, the full weight of this final truth slammed headlong into him. The rebel's euphoria and muted sense of personal empowerment he'd felt only hours before had been replaced overnight by the awareness of his substantial vulnerability. The spotlight of his conscious thought, though dimmed considerably by the fog of drugged sleep, was trained upon images of steel bars and concrete. On what would be, for all practical purposes, the end of his life.

He sat up and put his feet on the floor. This physical readjustment made him aware of all the pain in his body. Radiating from his lower back, in his jaw, in his head, bisecting his abdomen like a surgeon's scalpel. His tongue felt like a slab of sandstone in his arid mouth. He rotated his watch face toward the bay window and saw that the digital block numbers read six o'clock. He knew they needed to be leaving soon, not so much for his benefit, but for Brandy's. And, he supposed, Madison's as well.

Suddenly he didn't want to go.

Suddenly, even though he was an alien presence in Roger's home, he found a reason to want to stay put. Despite the grim history of abandonment and the magma chamber of resentment that boiled just beneath his surface calm, Tam felt sheltered there—from psychos with pistols, from pissed-off ex-fathers-in-law, from cops with warrants, from the lurking threat of imprisonment. He knew this sense of security had little to do with the nurturing chrysalis of family or shared DNA. It was merely the faultless cover of a comfortable home in a leafy neighborhood in a town he'd never be suspected of visiting. Like an unloved animal who'd found a secure lair, he at least now had a place to sleep in peace.

He got to his feet and shuffled toward the kitchen to get a glass of water. As he passed the guest bedroom, he paused and gave the door a gentle push. Peering into the darkness, he could make out Madison's form, still curled around the pillow. He stood and watched her for a full minute, half hoping he'd hear her imagined husky, morning voice invite him in. When it became clear that she was asleep, he pulled the door shut and continued to the kitchen.

There was just enough pre-dawn light leaking in from the windows in adjacent rooms to let Tam see what he was doing. He found glasses in the second cabinet he opened. He removed a plastic tumbler, filled it with water from the tap. He leaned back against the substantial granite counter and drank, his eyes roaming the open kitchen and the rooms beyond. He noticed the warm decorator touches: a set of crystal decanters, embroidered wall-hangings, framed family portraits, knitted afghan folded over the back of a cozy den sofa. An initial leaking of his resentment—this was the idealized home he'd always wanted but never had, not even with Lauren—eventually yielded to a benevolent acceptance of the new Malonee family's good fortune.

His eyes drifted to the adjacent sunroom. He noticed that most of one wall was glass, permitting a spectacular woodland view. His artist's eye was feasting on the diverse shadow-shapes of the surrounding flora when his attention was seized by the sudden, unnerving awareness of another presence.

A shadowy form in the gauzy blue light of the sunroom, something, at once, both alien and familiar.

Rocky in his wheelchair.

Just sitting there, parked in front of the wall of windows. Staring off into the early morning haze. Tam set the tumbler on the granite counter and walked through the open double doors into the sunroom. When the floor creaked, the young man's head snapped around.

"Sorry," Tam said. "I didn't mean to startle you."

Rocky pivoted his chair slightly so that he could see his half-brother. "It's okay," he said. "I'm usually the only one up this early."

Tam moved a few steps closer and, to avoid staring down at the withered legs and steel cambers, he let his gaze drift out the wall of glass. He saw for the first time that the room opened onto a large wooden deck. A green garden hose coiled around two large ferns on the oak decking. Beyond the balusters and rail he could see a small rock garden encircled by season-spent daylilies and withering azaleas. Beyond the landscaped area was a wall of giant oak and hickory trees, their heat-stressed leaves beginning to blanch in anticipation of autumn. A detached garage-apartment near the edge of the woods was connected to the house by another wooden wheelchair ramp-umbilicus.

"It's kind of peaceful out there at this time of day, isn't it?" Tam asked.

"Not always." The boy had turned back to the view. "Sometimes coyotes come out of the woods and grab them a little breakfast."

"No kidding. *Coyotes?*" Tam tried to visualize those ragged little predators—animals he believed to be indigenous to the prairie and other areas of his vaguely conceived western cowboyland—darting among the azaleas and daylilies.

"Yep. I saw two of them chasing some poor critter just yesterday." Rocky turned back to Tam. "We got raccoons, foxes, skunks, possums, groundhogs. Of course, squirrels and chipmunks. And there's red-tail hawks, owls, I think maybe even a bald eagle or two. You name it, it's out there."

For the first time, Tam turned to look directly at his half-brother. He was mildly astonished to behold facial features—eyes, strong jaw, cleft chin—that, at least in the pale wash of morning light, looked eerily like his own. He wondered if Rocky shared his amazement at the common features, all of which, of course, were derivative of the elder Roger. It then occurred to Tam that brothers and sisters growing up together probably never found anything remarkable about their shared common physical features. For complete strangers to suddenly behold almost-mirror images …

He couldn't speak for Rocky, but as far as *he* was concerned, it was a most extraordinary experience.

"That's my dad's office," Rocky said, pointing to the building behind the house. "It's his office and his workshop. He has all kinds of neat tools. He has three big table saws, too."

"Uh-*huh.*"

"He built that ramp for me. He designed it and cut all the boards. He let me help him, too, but I couldn't use the saws. One hundred percent pressure-treated southern yellow pine—my dad said that was the most resistant to decay and insect infestation."

Tam grinned. "Looks nice."

"Do you still play basketball?" Rocky asked.

Tam stared. The sudden shift in the topics was almost as jarring as the subject of the question. "What—?"

"Dad said you played in college. That's so cool."

"Your dad told you that?"

"Yeah. He said you played power forward in college. He said you averaged, like, twenty points a game your sophomore year. I think he read about you on the Internet. I was only about five at the time, but I still remember everything." He reached down into a bag that was hanging from the left armrest and pulled out a folded piece of paper. "Here," he said, handing it out toward Tam. "I found this in my room last night."

Tam took and slowly unfolded the paper. It was a poor quality dot-matrix copy of his posed individual basketball shot. He hadn't seen that photo since college. "No," he said, finally. Ruefully. "I really don't have, ah, time to play anymore."

"So did you ever, like, play in the pros or anything?"

Tam lowered the paper and shook his head.

"What's the matter?" Rocky asked.

"Nothing," Tam replied softly. He was thinking how odd all of this was—odd that his father would be checking up on him after a full decade of not giving a rat's ass whether he lived or died. Also, it seemed strange that he'd been admired by a blood relative he'd never met.

If he had only known that, maybe …

A noise drew Tam's attention to the kitchen. He saw Roger standing by the stove with a coffee pot in his hand.

"I see you and the boy are getting to know one another," Roger said. His voice was both soft and gruff. "That's good."

Rocky asked Tam, "Has Dad showed you his project yet?"

"His *project*? No."

"Dad, why don't you show Tam your project?"

Roger poured water into the top of a coffee brewer. "I don't think Tam's interested in *that* kind of stuff."

"I might be," Tam said. "What kind of stuff?"

Rocky turned his chair so that he was facing his brother. "Dad's working on a theory for time travel and—"

"It's *not* about time travel," Roger corrected him from the kitchen. He was hunched forward with his hands on his knees, staring at the water dripping into the coffee pot. "How many times do I have to tell you?"

"It *could* be," Rocky protested. "You said yourself you didn't know what all it would mean." He turned back to Tam. "It's just so cool. He's gonna win the Nobel Prize some day for this."

Roger, still bent forward, shook his head. "The inexplicable exuberance of youth," he said. He did not seem to be entirely displeased with the boy's spirited promotion of his work.

Tam handed the printed photo back to Rocky. He quickly motioned for him to return it to the bag.

Rocky's grin disappeared. "What's wrong?"

"Nothing," Tam said. He knew there was no way to satisfactorily explain his request without mentioning his issues with Roger. And he knew there was no way to do that without shattering the pedestal upon which Rocky had obviously elevated his dad. Tam didn't want any part of such a destructive endeavor.

The boy shrugged and rotated slightly toward the bag. As he did, Tam's gaze reluctantly fell upon his wheelchair. Cringing, he noted the standard functional features: the grips, pads, levers, rails, cambers. And, of course, the necessary toting equipment—a nylon backpack hanging from the back of the chair and the zippered armrest bag. Metallic, skeletal devices such as the chair had always made him uncomfortable. They represented incapacitation and dependence, two states he feared more than death.

Then, just as he was ready to look elsewhere, he spotted a feature that did *not* appear to be standard: a special chrome rack under the seat, obviously custom-welded to the cambers. The rack held two sliding trays, one with a digital music player, three sets of headphones in a variety of sizes, two cell telephones in holsters, and what appeared to be a walkie-talkie—standard accessories of the New American teenager.

"Pretty sweet, huh?" Rocky asked.

Tam knew the boy had caught him staring at the chair.

"Yeah," he agreed. "Sweet. Got all your tunes right there at your fingertips." Tam felt blood rush to his face as soon as the words left his mouth. The implication was clear: "How very nice for you—being a cripple, you're forced to carry your entertainment around with you!"

"Dad built it for me," Rocky said brightly. If he had been at all insulted, he had suppressed any evidence of it. "Plus, he wired me this special walkie-talkie into the house intercom system." He held it up for Tam to inspect. "I have this toggle where I can call any room in the house." Rocky moved the switch to the setting labeled "5SR" and cued the unit's mike. "See," he said. His parallel voice crackled from an intercom box on a wall just above a light switch. "Pretty neat, huh?"

"Yep. Slick as owl—" Tam stopped himself, reconsidered his choice of similes. "Yes. It's very neat."

"He's also building me a special sport chair, so I can play basketball this winter." Rocky paused a beat. "Of course, there's a chance I'll be walking again by then."

"Good morning, y'all." Paula Malonee's husky drawl preceded her into the kitchen. A second later, she entered the room with Madison following right behind. "Everybody sleep well?"

"Sure did," Tam offered. Paula's sudden appearance was an enormous relief to him. He didn't know the precise nature of Rocky's affliction, but another glance at his legs, all pale and atrophied, told him that the boy was probably deluding himself about walking again.

"That's good," Paula replied. She gave her husband a gentle push in the direction of the great room.

"I was out like a light," Madison said.

Tam felt a knot tie in his abdomen. He interpreted Madison's statement as a slam at him, as evidenced by: (1) the quick repositioning of her body, making it plain that she was directing the comment to Paula, and (2) the fact that she had replied in such an enthusiastic manner made it clear that she *was* speaking again—just not to him.

Paula finished shooing Roger from the kitchen and said, "Why don't you men go look at the TV or something while I fix us some breakfast."

"I'll help," Madison offered.

Tam stood in the sunroom and watched her. Even though her hair was tousled and she wasn't wearing makeup, he thought she still looked beautiful. In fact, he thought she looked even better than she had the previous afternoon. Fresher and a lot less, well, *quirky*. He waited for her to make eye contact with him, but she kept her back turned to the sunroom—punishing him with her savagely purposeful silence, just like Lauren used to do! And for what? For having a few lousy beers? For taking some time with the father he hadn't seen for decades?

Roger sauntered over to the sunroom door. "We got enough time to run out to my office," he said. "That is, if you're interested."

"Sure," Tam replied. His eyes were still fixed on Madison, still awaiting some acknowledgment.

"You're gonna love it," Rocky said to Tam. "It's *very* cool." He pivoted his chair and rolled quickly through the great room toward the double doors and the ramp leading to the garage-office.

Roger intercepted his son near the doorway. "Buddy," he said, "if it's okay with you, let me just show your brother here some stuff real quick—just the two of us. You've heard all this stuff a million times, anyway. We'll be right back in." He pulled open one of the doors and, with the flat of his hand, pushed Tam through the opening.

Tam glanced back at Rocky and noted the distressed look on his face. Then he checked the kitchen and saw Madison—still ignoring him.

He swallowed a lump and followed his host down the long wooden ramp.

*   *   *   *

"So." Roger settled into the worn and uncomfortable-looking seventies chrome-and-fabric office chair and stared at Tam over steepled fingers. "I guess I need to know what you know about quantum cosmology before I start."

Tam's wide eyes roamed the converted workroom in the detached garage as he collected data on the strange creature named Roger Malonee. There was a large desk against one wall, its surface cluttered with two computer monitors, a scanner, a printer, piles of papers, scientific journals, books. The opposite wall was essentially a giant bookcase, its six shelves crowded with folders and more books; more files, additional stacks of paper, and sideways-lying magazines had been squeezed into the narrow space between the bookcase top and the textured ceiling. Much of the scuffed tile floor was covered with storage boxes, bound documents, computer towers, piles of books, and another printer, this one disconnected. Tam noticed that one box near his feet had framed diplomas and numerous plaques crammed into it. The wall behind the desk had three large posters: a spectacular view from the Hubble telescope, a map of the solar system, and a large diagram of a hydrogen atom, with smaller inset illustrations describing and representing smaller subatomic particles. Bolted to the wall to Tam's immediate right was a porcelain whiteboard with an aluminum frame and box tray loaded with marker tubes and dry erasers. Sets of complex equations were scrawled on the board's surface in three different colors.

"What I know about quantum cosmology?" Tam asked. He gave a short, snorting laugh. "I guess that would be pretty much nothing."

Roger's brow furrowed. "*Nothing*? You *did* attend college, didn't you?"

Tam fought the powerful urge to fire back with a sardonic, "Yeah, no thanks to *you*!" For the second time in as many days, he recognized that the injection of a tartly worded verity would do nothing to make their few hours together more meaningful. And, on further reflection, he recalled that Roger had put himself, not just *partly through* undergraduate school (as had he), but *through* enough school to have earned his doctorate. Rare realizations such as this, occurring to Tam with an unprecedented frequency during the past hours, only served to make him slightly less judgmental of the historical objects of his contempt. "Yes," he said, finally. "But I have an excuse. I majored in psychology, with minors in poker and partying." He grinned and paused, waiting for Roger's display of mirthful appreciation. When it didn't come, Tam muttered, "I wish I had it to do over—"

Roger rested his chin on his finger-steeple and nodded solemnly. After a moment of contemplative silence, he said, "We all do things we regret. We've all done dumb shit, things we'd like to redo."

Tam stood in the thunderous silence, wondering if he'd just heard what he thought he'd heard. The thing he'd been waiting most of his life to hear. The fact that his father had excluded Rocky from their conversation, at the very least, suggested the intent to unburden his soul. And the fact that his face clearly confessed his regret …

Then Roger said, "One thing I wish I'da done different was get Rocky to a doctor faster."

Tam immediately recognized that his abandonment was essentially eliminated as the primary object of Roger's regret. *Purposefully, unmistakably, with malice aforethought.* Surely a man that brilliant couldn't be so socially obtuse as to believe that the mere passage of time had healed all the old wounds. Ignoring the ever-tightening stomach knot, Tam swallowed hard and asked, "You mean, with regard to his … legs?"

Roger nodded. "He was almost ten when it happened. Up until then, he was a perfectly normal, happy kid. Played baseball and basketball. *Loved* basketball. Then one day after a game, he complained of a tingling in his feet. We thought it was just some kind of normal post-exercise thing and didn't pay any attention to it. The next day, he said his knees were hurting." Roger twisted in his chair, as though reacting physically to the memory of the experience. "I mean, still, that's not unusual for a kid … I mean, after playing hard—" He paused, his fingers now burrowing under his glasses, rubbing his eyes. "Anyway," he continued, "after another day or two we finally called the doctor. By that time, the poor kid could barely walk. The doctor did a couple of scans, then ordered more tests." He paused again, his now moist eyes meeting Tam's. "It turned out to be TM—transverse myelitis, an inflammation of the spinal cord. They still don't know what caused it. The doctors say it was probably a virus of some type." He snorted. "A virus. Hell, other people get viruses, and all it gives them is a runny nose." He stared at the whiteboard, as though there ought to be an equation there that would solve the mystery. "Anyway," he continued, "*this* virus—if that's what it really was—had the same effect as a traumatic spinal cord injury."

Mindful of Rocky's earlier remark about playing basketball again, Tam asked, "Is there a chance he'll ever—"

"Recover?" Roger picked at the space between his two front teeth with the nail on his right index finger. "I don't know. The doctors don't know. Maybe, maybe not. Damage has been done to the spinal cord. The doctors originally told us that, if he was gonna recover, he'd start showing signs in the first three or four months. It's now been more than three years. Our neurologist tells us there's still a *chance* he could recover, but—" He shrugged. "Hell, I just don't know."

Now Tam felt as bad for Roger as he did for Rocky. At least Rocky didn't feel any guilt over his condition. Tam smoothed his growing beard as a new thought occurred to him. *Maybe it was karma, or fate, or whatever big force was out there just reeling old Rog back in.* After everything he'd done and the crumpled lives he'd left in his wake, maybe this was his destiny. Maybe it's what he had coming to him.

All of a sudden, as though the intervening topics of regret and illness had never come up, Roger jumped to his feet and walked to the whiteboard. "Did you ever take any chemistry? Do you know *anything* about the composition of matter?"

Tam shrugged. "I know what an atom looks like."

"Like a tiny nucleus planet with little orbiting electron-moons?"

Another shrug. "Yeah. I guess."

"Wrong!" Suddenly animated, Roger snatched an eraser and a red marker from the box tray. "That's a cartoon symbol created for schoolchildren and morons." He furiously erased the equations from the board and replaced them with a giant question mark. "We don't know exactly what an atom looks like. Nor do we know what a quark, a lepton, or a boson look like." He walked to Tam, grasped him by the shoulders, steered him to the desk chair. Then, with what Tam thought was an uncharacteristically gentle touch, he pushed him down and into the chair. Returning to the board, he said: "Here's what we *do* know."

For the next fifteen minutes, the teacher dragged his flabbergasted student through a quantum physics crash course. Bits of information flew at Tam like bullets from a rapid-fire knowledge gun. Equations appeared in a manic right-hand scrawl; they were rubbed away into elongated pink smears seconds later by a few left-handed dry-eraser swipes. Numbers that meant nothing by themselves were rendered even more meaningless by the addition of qualifying exponents and imprisoning brackets and braces. Names that Tam recognized (Einstein and Planck) were outnumbered by ones he didn't (de Broglie, Wooters, Kaluza, Zeilinger). But the information was coming at such a frenzied clip that he didn't have time to even be distracted by his empty spaces. Matter, Roger explained, is almost completely air; even the most solid of objects ends up "being" nothing more than frozen energy. "Matter is waves," Roger said, as he scrawled de Broglie's wave-matter equation on the board directly under Einstein's famous energy-mass equivalence formula. "And what are waves?" He paused, whacking the palm of his left hand with the marker.

Tam stared at the board, quietly asked, "Energy?"

"Yes!" Roger beamed at his pupil. "Exactly!" He slashed at the de Broglie equation with the marker. "Right there! The equivalence of waves and mass. What we get from this," he said, the marker alternating between the two equations, "is the equivalence of mass and energy and therefore, the equivalence of what? *Waves and energy.* So matter is energy which is—?"

"Nothing?"

"No! *Not* nothing. *Something.* Energy cannot be nothing, because matter would be nothing. And if the something happens to be vibrating superstrings or some kind of membrane, then we not only *can* have additional dimensions for the theory to work, we *must* have them!" He paused. "Are you with me?"

Tam nodded. He was enough of a scientific blank slate to accept just about any well-presented proposition as truth. "I hate to say it, but, yeah, I think I am."

Apparently buoyed by the willingness of his student, Roger then launched into the particulars of his own theory, which he called dimensional quantum state equalization. As if offering proof to a jury of skeptical math professors, he pulled out two notebooks filled with calculations, hastily scrawled notes, equations. With a face that had grown scarlet with enthusiasm, he showed them to Tam who nodded dumbly. Roger explained that the elementary particles might become like "spindrift" (noting Tam's puzzled look, he defined the term as "tiny, wind-blown units of sand and water") under proper conditions, and that this might facilitate "quantum trans-dimensional streaming." Tam got even more confused when Roger uttered phrases like "latent dimensions," "spin," and "energy equalization."

He *did* manage to get something out of the lesson. Raised on a steady diet of phasers and transporter beams, all Tam could envision as Roger spoke were people breaking into a fine mist like ocean spray, fading into blurry digital bits, then reappearing in some parallel floating dimension. He had paid close enough attention to grasp that Roger's equations seemed to make theoretically possible the reincorporation of matter in other dimensions. All there had to be was *equalization*. Roger had said so.

The fact that the man was talking speculatively—and then only about the smallest units of matter—was lost on his son.

The intercom speaker on the wall crackled. "Breakfast's ready, y'all."

Roger put the cap on the marker. The lesson had concluded. The scarlet receded from his face; his voice reassumed its usual gruff and ironic drag.

He had returned to earth from the heights of his passion.

Tam followed him out the door and onto the ramp. Halfway to the house, Roger stopped and turned back to him.

"I need to tell you something before we get back around everyone," he said. He scratched his head and stared down at the pressure-treated southern pine boards.

Tam grabbed the railing to brace himself. Could *this* be it, at long last—the cathartic moment, the purging of twenty years of guilt?

"You need to take a shower before breakfast," Roger said. "You really stink."

CHAPTER 6

▼

THE ORCHARD

They left the Malonees' house shortly before noon, following handshakes and back-patting hugs and earnest promises to keep in touch. Tam drove to a convenience store a quarter mile down the road and pulled up to the gas pumps. He put ten dollars worth of cheap gas in the tank, holding back just enough cash to buy some roadside fast food along the way. He knew he had an almost-full tank, enough to get Madison to her Florida destination. That was his primary mission now. He'd worry about everything else later. He paid for the gas and a bottle of the most heavily caffeinated soft drink he could find and returned to the car.

It was a brutally hot day. The air was still and saturated with tropical moisture. The shimmer of convection waves distorted the air just above the searing asphalt. Tam slipped into the driver's seat and felt the suffocating heat compress him. He took a long hit off the drink and closed his eyes. He savored the icy burn in his throat.

He turned to Madison. "You sure you don't want some pop or something?"

"I'm fine," she replied, a bead of sweat snaking down the side of her face. She gave him a quick, polite smile before turning back to the window.

Tam shrugged and cranked up the Honda. *Suit yourself.* He adjusted his sunglasses and steered the car onto the interstate spur's westbound entrance lane. It had been that way with her all morning. She had responded—cordially, but without any embellishment—to all direct questions posed to her: What time did you guys get to bed? *Ten-thirty.* Did you sleep well? *Yes, thank you.* What time do you want to head out? *I can be ready in two minutes.* Would you like something to drink? *I'm fine.* The abruptness of her replies convinced him that she was determined to avoid him. She seemed content to chew her gum and stare silently at the passing scenery. After a brief internal debate, Tam decided against demanding an explanation. Sure, he thought, it would've been nice to have had a pleasant travel companion, especially since he was doing her a favor. There could be no doubt, however, that she was angry—*or crazy.* Either way, he decided, he was best rid of her as soon as possible. He'd drop her off in Pensacola and then …

He sighed and gave the steering wheel a squeeze. He wasn't quite sure what was going to come next because he hadn't yet thought the whole thing through. He *had* been planning to let her take the car. He'd just get her to let him out at a pawn shop, someplace where he could raise some money. He could pawn his guitar; a vintage Telecaster like the one in the back ought to bring a few hundred bucks. He'd give her the car and half the cash, then jump on a bus to wherever. That *had* been the plan. Now he wasn't sure what the hell he'd do.

He checked the rear-view mirror for cops, cut another glance at Madison. She was still staring out the open window. Her hair was flying in the rush of hot, tropically humid air. Her hands were wedged between her jean-clad legs. Tam guessed that this was some kind of closed body language, some way of telling him to fuck off, without actually having to speak. He let his eyes trace the curve of the jeans. He thought about what it might be like to touch her, to run his hand from her shapely ass down the length of her firm leg.

Madison shot him a sharp, almost annoyed, glance that quickly terminated his sight-feast. He jettisoned all lustful notions and fixed his eyes on reeled-in roadway. Nothing was going to happen between them, he instructed himself, and it was therefore pointless—perhaps even damaging—to fantasize about it. In about six hours, right after they rolled into Pensacola, she'd be gone from his life, probably forever. He'd later be able to say it'd been an interesting twenty-four hours, but that's about it. She'd go her way, he'd go his. In about ten years, he'd see or hear something that reminded him of her, and he'd think about her, probably in some fabricated and idealized way. It was best just to pretend she wasn't even there.

He slumped back in the seat and let his head fall back against the headrest. A suffocating cloud of depression settled over him. Recent events had punctured what remained of his already-ruptured bubble of self-worth. Passenger-packed vehicles reminded him of vacations he'd never had, family he'd never known. Each mile-marker post clicked off another wasted minute of his life; every destination-distance sign reminded him that he had nowhere to go.

And then, the thing he feared most: the inexorable onset of the dreaded Road Truth. Without the mitigating effect of conversation, the hypnotic road sounds opened up the sluice gates of his brain's deep structures and washed away his willful defenses. Like tiny hammers, discrete chunks of truth thumped his consciousness:

> *You aren't running to something—you're running away from everything.*
> *You aren't a misunderstood artist, you're a selfish asshole. Just like Roger.*
> *Even Roger isn't as selfish as you are now.*
> *Lauren isn't an evil bitch, she only wanted to be happy.*
> *Madison has every reason to be angry with you.*
> *You're a drunk. Just like Jesse Breedlove. A pitiful alcoholic.*
> *You're gonna die miserable and alone.*

An eighteen-wheeler roared by on the Honda's right side, snapping him rudely back to reality. He discovered that he was in the left lane on a bridge over the Tennessee River going ten miles under the speed limit. A car passed him on the right. The driver shot him an angry look.

He eased over to the right lane and glanced at Madison. She was still staring out the window. In the distance, a tug pushed a long barge west on the glittering water.

He decided that he needed a beer.

Correction: *many* beers, the more the better.

*   *   *   *

North Alabama passed by quickly on either side of the cruising Honda. Like many interstate highways, I-65 had been engineered to be primarily an object of pastoral placement; much of its Alabama leg swooped and curved through pine-oak forests, animal-dotted pastures, and kudzu-and-mimosa-shrouded hillsides. To the average traveler, the most significant evidence of human habitation was the periodic clustering of restaurants and service stations at access roads marked with the names of unseen hamlets.

Until Birmingham.

The downtown portion of the city appeared in hazy silhouette over the top of a ridge, momentarily catching Tam off guard. He knew from the road signs that Birmingham was approaching; he never expected such an impressive skyline.

Unlike the rest of the northern state, the interstate didn't bypass Birmingham, but sliced more-or-less through its heart, almost as if to showcase its most inspiring features: the unexpected verticality of the commercial district; the vast urban university campus overlooked by a towering hillside Vulcan; the stunning backdrop vista forged by the Appalachian-ending Shades and Red mountains; the affluent suburban sprawl extending far to the south and east.

Whether it was the unexpected impact of the city, the refreshingly inspirational drive through gorgeous, wooded hills, or some other blessed (but mysterious) reason, Madison suddenly seemed to be in an improved state of mind. Tam first noticed it when she laughed at his half-mumbled remark about a passing truck loaded with port-a-potties; by the time they reached the exit to a verdant Oak Mountain, she was talking again. It took her a few minutes to get warmed up; soon the words came bubbling out in those inimitable non-stop chains, with apparent finishing phrases end-on with new beginnings and peppered with clichés and uniformly trite similes ("that Paula seems like she's as good as gold"; "Rocky is as smart as a whip"). Most of the substance of those word-streams, as it happened, was whooshed away by the blast-furnace flow of unconditioned air through the passenger compartment. That didn't matter to Tam. The only thing that mattered to him now was that she apparently didn't hate him anymore.

Plan A was back on again.

*　　　*　　　*　　　*

"Where you going?" Madison asked.

"There's a cop following me."

They had stopped for burgers at a chain restaurant on the Orchard City interstate exit somewhere north of Montgomery. Tam had pulled through the drive-through lane, placed, and picked up their order. He had first noticed the police cruiser as it rounded the corner of the building. When it began to slowly approach him from the rear, he quickly turned left on the access road—away from the interstate and toward town.

He hadn't gone far when the patrol unit pulled onto the road behind him.

Madison turned in her seat and squinted back into the sunlight glare of the cop's window.

"How do you know he's following you?" she asked.

Tam's sweaty palms twisted the steering wheel. "I watched him turn in from the street," he replied. "He didn't do anything but drive around the building. It's like he spotted me and followed me all the way around."

She spat her gum into a napkin and plucked a french fry from the bag. "It doesn't make sense," she said. "Why would the cops be pulling us over?" She bit off half the fry and laughed. "Wait, I know—you made an illegal turn into the drive-through lane!"

"I'm glad you think it's funny."

"No, it's just … it doesn't make sense. I mean, we weren't doing anything … the car's totally legal—"

"Maybe he recognized me."

She popped the rest of the french fry in her mouth and sat back with an if-you-say-so look on her face.

Tam emitted a mighty sigh of exasperation. "I'm *wanted*, Madison. I thought I explained that to you back in Tennessee."

"So you're saying that this cop recognized you from, like, a hundred yards away?"

He wiped sweat from his forehead. "What if Robert called the cops on me?"

"Robert wouldn't do that."

"How can you be sure?"

"Two reasons. He's very fond of me. He's not that fond of cops."

"All right, what if they came snooping around, found the Olds, and leaned on him. I mean, maybe he didn't have a choice in the matter."

She grabbed another fry. "I think you're just being paranoid."

Tam cut another look in the rear-view mirror. The patrol car was still there. "If you're worried about something, and it turns out you had reason to be worried, that's called justifiable concern, not paranoia."

By now they were in the middle of the block-long Orchard City business district. Tam slowed to a crawl, rolled past a free-standing auto parts store, a row of one-story lawyer and insurance offices, an old-fashioned five-and-dime, and a shoe repair shop. He caught a green light at the next intersection and turned left onto a street marked with county highway signs.

Madison asked, "Do you have any idea where you're going?"

"No. Just south, I think." His eyes were fixed on the rear-view mirror. When he saw that the patrol car had made the same turn, he grimaced. "I'm *so* freakin' busted," he said. "I don't know how or why. All I know is he's locked in on me."

"Just show him your license. I'm sure it's nothing."

"Nothing? It'll be something when he checks the computer. The warrants for me will pop right up."

Madison blinked. "What the hell did you *do*, anyway? I mean, I know it has something to do with that car, that Olestra, or whatever it's called. Did you, like, jack the car from someone?" A long pause. "You didn't *shoot* somebody, did you?"

"No, no, nothing like that. I mean, I committed some felonies, but I didn't hurt anybody." He gave her a look that almost demanded her unconditional trust. "I would never do *anything* like that. I mean, hurt an innocent person."

She bit into another fry. "Could you hurt a *guilty* person if you had to?"

He gave her a puzzled look, didn't reply. They continued down the street, which, despite the assigned county highway number, was a residential area. The houses on the first block were two-story, Victorian-style structures. The second block had smaller homes, mostly older, craftsman bungalows. Thereafter, the number of residences slowly dwindled as Orchard City yielded to the ambient grassy fields and woods of the surrounding county.

Madison turned and glanced back at the patrol car. "Maybe it's just a coincidence," she said. She nervously shifted the warm sack of food and cardboard drink carrier in her lap. The half-smirk on her face had melted into a look of genuine concern.

"He's gone," Tam said. The relieved words rushed out literally in a burst of held breath. "He turned off at that last little road." He sagged visibly behind the wheel.

"Well, I didn't think he could be following us."

Tam began looking for a place to turn around. By this time, they were more than a mile outside town. They were in a rural area now, surrounded by fields and pastures, with only scattered trailers and the occasional farmhouse visible from the road.

"There's a road up yonder," Madison said.

Tam slowed even more and stared at the land surrounding the road. Hundreds of trees no more than twenty feet in height, wide as they were tall, in orderly ranks that rolled up a small hill and into the distance as far as he could see.

"What the hell is *this*?" he muttered.

"Looks like an orchard of some type."

"That makes sense. I mean, wasn't that the name of the town?"

Tam turned onto the road that Madison had indicated. It curved up a grassy hillock before disappearing into the center of the orchard. He followed it for about fifty yards and stopped where it turned into a dirt road—twin grooves worn into the parched loam.

"It's peaches," he said, staring wide-eyed at the ranks of squat trees.

"That's what it looks like."

Tam was looking at the fruit hanging from the tree branches and scattered on the ground. "I didn't know Alabama was a peach-producing state."

Madison ate another french fry and punched a straw through the plastic lid on her drink. "Well, those are peaches and this is Alabama so there you have it," she said.

"Did you know peaches are a member of the rose family?"

She picked out a small bunch of fries and stared at him. "Tam, we need to get back to the interstate."

"Why don't we grab a few for the road?" he asked. The car's idling engine missed, shaking the car. "They are, as they say, ripe for the picking."

"I don't like peaches. Besides, you just got through sweating out this cop back there. You start stealing peaches, you're just askin' for trouble."

Before Tam could respond the Honda's engine sputtered and chugged. He pressed the accelerator and there was one more violent heave.

Then nothing.

"What's going on?" Madison asked.

"Hell if I know. It just quit." Tam put the vehicle in "Park," and turned the ignition key. There was a labored grinding, more sputtering, then the sterile clicking of the starter. He turned to Madison. "It couldn't be the battery. I don't think they just quit like that."

"Is it out of gas?"

Tam peered at the fuel gauge. The indicator needle had fallen to "E," but he knew that "acute fuel starvation" (as Mr. Holdsworthy was fond of calling the condition) was not going to be their problem. "There's gas," he said. "I checked it back on the interstate. There was more than half a tank."

He pulled the hood release and unfolded his considerable frame from the small car's doorway. The sun was almost directly overhead. He pushed up the scorching hood and stared at the engine. Madison appeared on the passenger side near the front of the car. Tam leaned into the engine housing. He tugged on a couple of plug wires and checked the battery cables, then straightened up.

"What do you think?" Madison asked.

He shrugged.

She stared at the engine. "I thought you worked at a car place."

He snorted and wiped away more forehead sweat. "Yeah, I was the loan manager. I only went into the garage one time, and that was to find my father-in-law."

"This is just great," she said. She slumped against the right front fender and crossed her arms.

He ducked under the hood again and tapped on a few parts he couldn't identify. Then he slid back into the driver's seat and tried again to start the car. Once
again, the engine failed to respond. With one foot on the ground, he pulled the
lid from one of the drinks and gulped the watered-down contents. He sat there
for a while, thinking. He knew it was pointless for him to try to make a precise
mechanical diagnosis; the best he would be able to come up with was a general
and uneducated guess about the problem. He knew only four things relative to
the normal operation of an automobile engine: it had to have fuel, it had to be
lubricated, it had to have a spark, it had to be kept cool. He was fairly sure fuel
wasn't an issue (although he knew nothing about fuel pumps or injection systems), there had been no indication of leaking oil, and the car didn't appear to
have overheated. Therefore, he reasoned, the problem must be related to the electrical system. Unfortunately, he only knew two remedial actions for electrical system failure, and he'd already executed both of them.

"You wouldn't happen to have a cell phone, would you?" he asked Madison.
He had gotten out of the car again and was now half-draped over the car's fiery
hot roof.

"No," she said. "Don't you think if I had a cell phone I would've—"

He noticed a slight quiver in her voice. He walked around the car and stood in
front of her.

"I'm sorry," she said. "I know this isn't your fault. It's just … I was just imag-
ining I'd be in Florida last night." Tears began to pool and stream. "I guess I just
had it in my mind that Brandy'd be with me right now, safe."

Tam moved closer to her. He began to reach out, to hold her, but he still
wasn't sure whether he'd been granted the license to do so. Then she leaned
toward him, and he slowly wrapped her in his arms.

"It's gonna be all right," he said.

"What are we gonna do?" she asked. "We're out in the middle of nowhere.
Our car is dead. We don't know anybody around here. There's a cop driving
around a mile away—"

"We don't have any money," he said. "You forgot that."

Her face got even cloudier. "We don't?"

"Do you?"

She shook her head. "Nothin' more than a little tip money I saved up."

"Well, I've only got a few bucks left after getting gas and food."

Madison wilted in his embrace. "I ain't gonna get to Florida," she muttered. "I
should've known better than to think otherwise." She gave him a gentle push. He
pivoted and slumped against the car.

"We do have hamburgers," he said, finally. "And, for what it's worth, each other."

She gave him a disgusted shake of her head and turned away.

He took a deep breath and tried to come up with some kind of plan. He believed that there was an acceptable solution to just about every problem. The difficulty lay in finding it before despair set in—or the problem wiped you out. He searched the barren length of county road they had just driven down. There weren't any houses in the immediate area; not a single vehicle had passed since the car had quit. There was the store down the road, the one the cop had pulled into.

Madison touched him lightly on his left arm. "What's that?" she asked.

"What's *what?*"

"Shh! Listen."

Tam cocked his head and waited, was about to tell her she was hearing things. Then he heard it, too. A rumble—faint as first, then slowly expanding until it took on the proportions of an unmuffled tractor. Then a black pickup truck, belching dark smoke and moving at a decent clip, came into view on the two-lane road.

Madison pushed away from the Honda and began hollering and waving her arms. The truck slowed well before it reached the orchard road. Then it came to a complete stop. It sat there for a full minute idling loudly before turning toward the crippled Honda.

Tam could see two men in the passenger cab. The driver appeared to be older, perhaps in his mid-sixties. The man sitting by the passenger door looked like a teenager. He was wearing a blue ball cap and faded bib overalls without a shirt. He was the first out of the cab. He stepped around to the front of the truck with his thumbs tucked under the overall straps. Tam noticed then that his skin was pallid, almost corpse-like, and that there were many tattoos on his chest, neck, and arms.

"Howdy," Tam said.

The boy nodded. "Y'all having some kinda car trouble?"

"Yes," Madison said, "and are we ever glad to see y'all."

The driver got out of the truck. He was wearing a blue work shirt, cheap tan slacks, plain black lace-up shoes. "Ol' car die on you, did she?" he asked. His voice was gravelly, as if his voice box was mostly scar tissue. He kept walking, past Tam and Madison, finally positioning himself at the left front fender. He began tinkering with the car's distributor cap.

"I think it may be something in the electrical system," Tam offered. He moved next to the older man and rattled on in support of that theory.

The man in the overalls draped himself over the right fender. Tam was trying to see what the driver was doing while still keeping an eye on the tattooed teenager.

"Stupid Jap cars," the older man growled. He continued to tinker with the distributor and plug wires. "You got any tools?"

Tam looked at Madison. She shrugged.

"I don't think so. It's … not our car."

"I wouldn't drive a Jap car myself," said the teenager. He grinned, displaying a set of discolored, chipped, and missing teeth. He walked away from the car, toward the first line of peach trees. When he reached the trees, he stood still, as though pondering his next move. Then he took off his ball cap and began filling the crown with fallen peaches.

"It's kind of all we had," Tam said to the older man, almost apologetically.

"Try to crank it now," the man said.

Madison slid under the wheel and turned the ignition key. There was nothing but a labored whirring.

"It ain't gettin' no far," said the teenager. He had walked back to the car and was eating a ripe peach.

"No, it ain't. Not the least little bit." The older man straightened up and rubbed his grease-blackened fingers together. "Looks like y'all probably got a bad electronic ignition."

"See?" Tam said, savoring a tiny measure of satisfaction. "It *is* electronic."

Madison had gotten out of the car. She handed the older man a couple of napkins and he began wiping the grease from his fingers.

"So what do we do?" she asked.

"Nothin' you can do but replace it," he said. Then, turning to Tam: "Y'all know where there's a good parts store open on a Sunday afternoon?"

Tam shook his head. "We're not from here," he said.

"Us neither. We was just passin' through when we seen y'all."

"I seen a parts place a few miles back," the teenager offered. He spat out a large hunk of rotten peach flesh.

"Me, too," Madison said. "Back just the other side of town."

The older man scratched his stubbly chin and turned to Tam. "Load up with me, partner, and we'll go get us an ignition. Johnny'll stay here and get everything ready while we're gone."

Tam's wide eyes shot from the old man to Madison to the teenager in overalls and back to Madison. "I … maybe you should—"

"If you'd rather not," the man growled, "me and my son, we'll just be on our way."

"No, wait. Just give us one minute, please," Tam said. He grabbed Madison by her elbow and steered her into the taller grass a short distance away.

"What's the problem?" she demanded. "Just go on with him, before they leave us here."

"There's several problems, actually. One, I don't want to leave you here with that—" He shot a glance at the teenager. "—that illustrated banjo boy over there."

Madison put a hand on a hip. "You don't think I can take care of myself?"

"It's not that. It's just … he's a complete stranger. You don't know what kind of mess he's been into."

"*You* were a complete stranger. And I did know what kind of mess you were into." Her eyes burned into his. "It's his *son*, Tam. He ain't gonna do nothing with his daddy comin' right back."

"You don't know that. Don't you remember that crazy mountain man and his son back out in Montana a few years back? They kidnapped a college student together so the son could—" Tam froze in mid-sentence. A large dog had wandered into the area and was playfully darting toward and away from the Honda. The younger man hollered at the dog and then threw one of the ripe peaches at it. The dog scampered a short distance away, barked, and circled. Another peach was launched; it bounced about three feet past the dog and settled in tall grass. The dog barked again and investigated the fallen missile.

"Put more arch on it," said the older man.

Tam shook his head. "I mean, look at that. They're trying to hit that poor animal. What does that tell you?"

"Nothing," she said. "It don't tell me nothing useful about our current situation. Now go on. I'll be fine. If I had to—which I won't—I could just lock myself in the car."

When Tam's frowning face confessed his continuing reluctance, she added: "You're gonna insult the man, then we'll be stranded again."

Tam started to mention his other concern—that he didn't have any money to pay for an electronic ignition. Then he realized it was pointless to even mention it. They had to get out of that orchard, and all he had of value was the old guitar. He didn't want to part with something that valuable just to replace an electronic component in someone else's car, but he really had no choice.

Without saying anything else, he opened one of the car doors and pulled out the guitar case.

He walked over to the older man and sighed. "I'm ready," he muttered, finally.

*   *   *   *

Madison became fearful of the tattooed teenager long before she ever saw the knife.

One minute she was watching him fool with distributor cap and plug wires. Then he was looking at her and making suggestive remarks. She eased away from him, but he slid in her direction.

And then he was pressing against her with his dirty overalls.

"How about a little for a horny ol' country boy who ain't had none in a while," he drawled.

Madison squirmed away from him and moved quickly toward the front passenger door.

"Come on, now," she said, nervously pulling her hair away from her face. "You need to get this engine stuff done before your daddy and Tam gets back."

He emitted a sharp and evil cackle. "Shit. That's funny. He ain't my daddy." He moved toward her again, and was now standing between her and the door.

"What do you mean?"

"Him and me are … how do I put this … on vacation from South Carolina. A place called Darlington. We were at a … camp." The cackle. "You might say we borrowed us a truck and some clothes and left out."

Madison moved quickly around the back of the car; once again the man cut off her attempt to get in the car.

Then she saw the knife. The serrated-edge blade was at least ten inches long.

"I just want a little lovin', that's all," he said. "That's all. You just look so good and I ain't had me none in a long-ass time." He took a step toward her.

Madison turned and ran.

She made it as far as the second line of trees. Then she was slammed, facedown, into the sandy earth. She felt the man's weight crushing into her. She turned her head and begged him not to hurt her.

The man got on a knee and turned her over. "I'm not gonna hurt you," he said. His eyes were wild and large. He straddled her and held the knife to her neck. "As long as you give up that nookie, you'll be fine."

"Tam … my husband … he's gonna be back in a minute or two," she gasped. "He ain't gonna be happy about this."

The evil cackle again. He grabbed her blouse with his free hand and tore the top two buttons off. "I guess I probably shoulda told you," he said. "It don't matter how unhappy he is. You ain't never gonna see him again."

*   *   *   *

"There it is up there on the right," Tam said. He sat on the ripped and mis-shapen front seat with the guitar case turned sideways and wedged snugly between his legs.

The man steered the chugging truck into the parking lot and stopped about twenty feet from the front door.

"Shoot," Tam muttered. "They don't look open."

"There's a sign on the door," the driver said. "Go see what it says."

Still holding the guitar case, Tam got out of the truck and began walking toward the door. When he got close enough to read the sign, he froze. It read:

Gone To the Race
Back Monday
Roll Tide!

He had just begun to turn back toward the truck when he heard its engine rev. He could only watch in disbelief as it roared out of the parking lot. He noticed for the first time that the truck had a South Carolina tag.

He stood with the guitar case twisting in his hand, staring as the truck headed back toward the orchard. His first thought was that they wouldn't be able to fix the car.

His second thought, which exploded into his consciousness within a millisecond of his first, was that Madison was in deep trouble.

He began running after the disappearing truck. His boots clapped at the pavement and the guitar case bounced off his leg as he ran. His breathless curses filled the air.

He'd run nearly half a mile when he had to stop. His feet and knees were aching, a searing pain shot through his shoulder, his lungs screamed for oxygen.

Tam was on the side of the road with his hands on his knees when a chugging roll-back wrecker pulled even with him.

The driver rolled down the passenger-side window and slid over where he could get a good look at the doubled-over man with the guitar case. After a moment, he asked Tam if he was okay.

Tam straightened up and nodded. "But," he added, still gasping for air, "I gotta … get to the peach orchard. This girl … this friend of mine … needs help. I mean, she's in trouble. *Bad.*"

The driver didn't immediately respond. He was slender, almost gaunt, fiftyish, with thinning silver hair that hung down to the collar of a grease-smeared T-shirt. A cigarette dangled from his thin lips. His left eye squinted as the smoke curled up in his face. "What kind of bad trouble?" he asked, at last.

Tam told him what had happened.

The man discharged a stream of smoke, flicked the cigarette out the window. It landed in a smoldering chunk in the scattered gravel at Tam's feet.

"Get in," he said.

*   *   *   *

When the wrecker pulled into the orchard, the older man was walking up a knoll, halfway between the trees and his truck. The black pickup was parked alongside the disabled Honda. The man turned to face the wrecker as it rumbled up the orchard road.

"There's the car, but I don't see Madison," Tam said. And then, pointing: "That's the son of a bitch that left me, right there."

The wrecker driver swung sharply to the left and went off the path to pass the Honda. Then he slammed on the brakes, jammed the truck into reverse, and expertly backed until the bed was aligned with the centerline of the Honda. As soon as he stopped, Tam opened the passenger door and jumped out. Screaming obscenities, he charged toward the pickup truck driver.

"Hold on a minute," the wrecker driver hollered at him. "Here she comes."

Madison ran toward them from the first cut of the orchard. Her blouse was open to her mid-section. She ran with her arms crossed over her chest. Tam met her and wrapped his arms around her.

"Did he hurt you?" Tam asked.

She shook her head, but pointed to a bloody mark on her neck left by the point of the knife.

Tam cursed and glared at the man standing on the hill. The younger man appeared and stood next to the pickup driver. His hands were at his sides at first; after a moment, he lifted the knife in a menacing gesture.

"Did you see that?" the wrecker driver asked. "Hell, I take that as a threat." He jumped from the truck's cab and pulled a pump shotgun from behind his seat.

"Put her in the cab," he said to Tam. His voice was flat and even, as though blowing a hole in another human was just another everyday task.

Tam assisted Madison into the truck and stood by the open passenger-side door.

The wrecker driver took a step away from his truck and racked a shell into the chamber. Leveling the weapon, he fired a shot in the direction of the two men. The reverberation rolled through the grassy depression. The two men on the knoll froze momentarily, then darted into the cover of the trees.

The driver turned to Tam. "You ever shoot one of these?" he asked.

Tam shook his head.

"That's what I thought. There's nothing to it, really. It's sort of like a camera. Just point and shoot. Just get your cheek on the stock. And hold it a little tighter than a camera." He handed the weapon to Tam and said, "I'm gonna hook your car now. If anything comes out of those trees, blow it up."

Tam lifted the weapon, a Mossberg twelve gauge, to his shoulder and pointed it at the trees. The only shooting he'd ever done was a few BB-gun practice pops at tin cans. Nevertheless, he believed that both these men deserved to be shot— the young punk, obviously, for attacking Madison, not to mention for throwing peaches at the dog. And the grizzled old man for leaving him stranded.

He heard the sound of the winch and motor and saw the Honda moving onto the wrecker's rolled-back bed. He shot a quick glance at Madison. Her head was down, her hair hanging in front of her face. He could see that she was closing up her blouse the best she could with the buttons missing.

The driver had locked the car into place and was heading back around to him. He paused at the side of the wrecker and coughed. He bent forward, bracing himself on the boom supporting a rack of amber emergency lights.

Tam shot a concerned look at the orchard and asked the man if he was all right.

He nodded, but didn't say anything. He eventually was able to straighten up and continue toward the front of the vehicle. Tam noticed, for the first time, that he was limping badly. He reached for the gun and Tam handed it to him.

Without hesitation, the man limped to the front of the black truck. "Cover your ears," he said to Tam. Then, indicating Madison: "Tell her to, also."

Then he pumped shot into both front tires and the front grill of the truck. The vehicle lurched forward as if in mechanical submission. Tam could hear the hiss of air and smell the acrid odor of coolant.

"All right, then," the man said, with no visible emotion. "Let's get y'all out of here."

CHAPTER 7

▼

IRISH WHISKEY AND
AMMO DOGS

The northern half of Grayburn County consisted primarily of woodlands, marshy bottom land, undeveloped fields, pastures, and cultivated farmland. Geographically indistinguishable from the surrounding counties, its jagged boundaries had been established by the meandering course of a shallow, rock-strewn stream and by seemingly arbitrary political decisions that remained mysterious to all but the most dedicated of local historians. And, like those neighboring territories, Grayburn County lay completely within the flat coastal plain that stretched from just south of Birmingham all the way to the Gulf of Mexico.

As was generally the case late on Sunday afternoon, traffic was sparse on the county's two-lane roads. The old Chevy wrecker thundered along a series of narrow thoroughfares crowded by steep, wildflower-covered ditches and kudzu-draped banks. A pickup truck passed, then another, and still another. The drivers, following some unwritten rural roadway travel protocol, all acknowledged the oncoming wrecker by half-lifting an index finger from the steering wheel. The driver casually returned the acknowledgments, pushed his truck well in excess of the posted speed limit, and took advantage of the open roads by occasionally allowing the wrecker to straddle the double center lines.

Madison sat between the two men on the bench-style seat, her hands still clutching the top of her blouse. The driver had his left elbow hanging out his open window and his right wrist draped over the steering wheel. Tam said nothing until the driver had put miles between them and the orchard. When he finally spoke, it was to comment on the burned-out shell of a cabin they'd just passed. The driver muttered a terse response that was lost beneath the wrecker's low rumble. After that, Tam decided that he should remain silent the rest of the trip. There wasn't anything else for him to say anyway. Although he had no idea where they might be headed, he had no reason to question the wrecker driver's intentions. He knew they were safer in that truck than on foot in the peach orchard.

"They were escaped prisoners," Madison said at last.

"How do you know that?" Tam asked.

"That ... *pig* told me. He said they'd walked off from this prison camp in South Carolina. Stole this truck from a farm and were on their way to California." She stared straight ahead and shivered as she spoke. "He woulda killed me like a chicken. I'm sure of it."

"There's a pay phone up ahead," the driver said, his first audible words since they'd left the orchard. His voice was hoarse and very low. He seemed to be having some difficulty breathing. "I'll call the sheriff, and they oughta be able to collect them."

They passed a sign that read, "Beddington Town Limits." The road dipped and swung sharply to the right. The wrecker leaned into the curve and chugged into the parking lot of a closed restaurant. A pay telephone hung from the side of the building.

"What are we ... *you* ... gonna do with the car?" Tam asked.

The driver paused with his bad leg dangling out the door. "I reckon I'll fix it, if that's what you want."

"I think it's probably an electrical problem."

The man stared at Tam for a moment, then climbed out of the cab and slammed the door.

"He's not a very talkative person," Tam said as he watched the driver limp toward the building.

"He's a man of action," Madison replied.

Tam stared at her. "What are you saying?"

"I'm not saying anything. I just said he was a man of action. And he is."

"Are you saying I'm *not* a man of action? A man of *inaction*, as it were?"

Madison stared directly ahead and didn't reply.

"Because, I want you to know, I was busting my *ass* trying to get back to you after that ... old goat took off without me. I was running down the road, that damn guitar case banging on my shins." He pulled up the leg of his jeans so that Madison might observe for herself the physical evidence of his suffering.

Madison glanced down and nodded.

"Are you pissed at me for something? I mean, for going off and leaving you? Because, as I distinctly recall, you insisted I go with that old man—"

"I did insist that you go with him. And I'm not pissed at you. All I said was that that guy wasn't a talker. He's a doer." Then she gave him an extended look, a flat, open-eyed stare that carried an implied disclaimer: "The preceding comments were not intended to either hurt your feelings or damage your self-esteem; rather they represent, to the best of my ability to determine such things, my frank impression of all individuals who contributed in some meaningful way to our recent extraction from a difficult situation. Of which you are not one."

Or, at least, that was Tam's interpretation of the look. Whatever Madison had intended by it, it provided a visual exclamation mark to the pointed subtext of her comments. Although she had not consciously selected the exact words, it was clear that what she wanted was a doer—someone who would be able to swiftly, and without complications, deliver her to her desired destination. He tried for a moment to meet this determined stare, to compel her, at the very least, to acknowledge that he had contributed in *some* way to her liberation. He was unable to stare down the Truth that was written there. And so, as was his way, he turned from his accuser and said nothing.

And so, to use Madison's phrase, "there you have it."

He stared out at the restaurant's brick wall and tried to mentally construct a defense to her unread indictment of him. Proceeding point by point, he did his best to frame the argument that would, at once, vindicate him and indict the true situational villains—cruel fate, of course, and (given adequate time) everyone else responsible for his current predicament. Instead, he could only find evidence of his continuing failure: He couldn't provide transportation, he had no money, he couldn't fix a car, and now—the ultimate disappointment—he had to rely on a consumptive, crippled, middle-aged stranger to extract Madison from peril. All he could offer her were explanations and excuses. She made it clear that she found no redemptive value in those things.

Fine, he thought. *Let your man of action deliver your ass to Florida.*

He closed his eyes and focused his thoughts on procuring an icy cold six-pack.

*   *   *   *

The driver yanked open the door and hoisted himself into his seat. "All right," he said, "that's done. Now here are your choices concerning your car. One, I can take you to my garage about five miles from here and see if I can get it fixed. How long it'll take is anybody's guess. It depends on what's wrong and whether it needs parts."

"Did you say *your* garage?" Tam asked.

"Right. I can tow you somewhere else, if you prefer."

"No, no. I was just a little surprised that you ... you're a mechanic, too?"

"Among other things." The driver plucked a cigarette out of the pack in his shirt pocket.

"That will be fine," Madison said. "We just need to get back on the road as soon as possible." After a moment, she added, "I should tell you that we don't have any money."

"No money?"

"Nothing but about ten dollars."

"No credit cards?"

Madison gave Tam a quick look. Tam shook his head.

The driver leaned over the wheel and seemed to turn this information over in his mind. Finally, he said, "I don't mind cutting y'all some slack on the towing and the labor, but the parts aren't gonna be free."

"I've got that guitar," Tam offered. "It's a real sharp old Tele—"

"I ain't a pawn shop," the man interrupted. He twiddled the unlit cigarette between his index and middle fingers. "Neither are the parts stores."

"It's a collector's item. It's probably worth a hell of a lot more than any parts would cost."

The man scratched his chin. "How much?"

"I don't know. A collector might pay a couple of thousand."

Once again, the driver seemed to toss the idea around in his head. "It's not hot, is it?"

"No. *Hell*, no. I bought it from a music store back in high school. I paid five hundred dollars that I had earned cutting yards, washing cars, and scooping ice cream."

"You've had it since high school?"

Tam nodded.

"Then I'm not about to take it from you." He scratched his chin again. "I noticed art supplies on the back floorboard of the Honda. One of y'all a painter?"

"I guess that would be me," Tam answered.

"You any count with a brush?"

Tam's brow furrowed. "Am I any good at it?" He shrugged. "I guess I am. I mean, other people have said so."

"We may be able to work something out. I got some painting that needs doing."

Madison said, "You said there were several options."

The man began laughing, and the laugh soon degenerated into the painful-sounding cough. When he regained his breath, he said, "When I said that, I sort of assumed y'all at least had a credit card. There aren't a whole lot of options for someone with no means of paying. Besides me towing y'all to my garage, the only thing left is for me to just set your car down and let you call someone else."

Madison and Tam again exchanged glances.

"There ain't nobody else *to* call," she said.

"If I have to get parts, it's probably gonna be tomorrow," the driver said.

Madison groaned and buried her face in her hands.

"I don't know where we'd—"

"Y'all are welcome to stay with me until then. I've got a guest room that's not being used." He shrugged. "That's totally up to you."

Tam scratched his head. He found it somewhat curious that someone would open his home to complete strangers—unless he had something underhanded in mind. On the other hand, he *had* just extracted them from a bad situation. And Tam desperately needed a place to crash for the evening. "We hate to impose," he said, offering the driver the standard opportunity to rescind his offer.

Madison looked up at the man with red-rimmed eyes. "You're very kind," she said. "We really don't have anywhere else to go."

"Not a problem at all." The driver extended his hand to his guests, first to Madison, then Tam. "Name's Don Pedro O'Malley," he said. "Everyone just calls me Pete."

*   *   *   *

Pete O'Malley lived in a modest brick rancher in an isolated neighborhood at the western edge of Beddington. The town consisted of a one-block commercial district, three churches (Baptist, Methodist, and AME), a grocery store, the local school complex, a feed and grain store, and Pete's garage, which was appended to his house in a manner that suggested a local reluctance to apply traditional zoning restrictions. Pete's back "yard" was actually an unfenced, two-acre field that ran north until it merged into the central section of the Beddington High football practice field.

The wrecker arrived shortly before five-thirty. A plump, middle-aged basset hound waddled out of the shade of the garage to greet his master and the guests. He sniffed Madison and Tam and, with a thrashing tail and a guttural "woof," indicated his unconditional approval.

"Meet Elvis, y'all," Pete said. He was standing at the right rear of the truck and was operating the deck-tilt controller. "King Elvis, the fifth, to be precise."

"He's absolutely precious," Madison said. She knelt next to the dog and rubbed him behind his floppy ears.

"He's no ordinary dog. He comes down as a direct descendant of some legendary bassets." He unhooked the Honda and instructed Tam to unlatch the hood. When it popped up, he said, "Now try to crank her." He jammed an unlit cigarette in his mouth and chewed on the filter while he listened to the sterile sound of grating ignition brushes.

"It's probably something electrical," Tam said. His left leg sprawled out into the gravel of the parking area.

"How many miles on this thing?"

Tam squinted at the odometer. "One hundred and ten thousand."

"Has the timing belt ever been changed?"

Once again, the two travelers exchanged blank looks.

"Beats me," Tam said.

"Well," Pete said, rolling the cigarette around in his mouth, "my bet is that's gonna be your problem. The good news is it ain't gonna cost that much."

Tam climbed out of the car and shut the driver's door. "And the bad news?"

"The bad news is I don't have that particular belt, and the nearest dealer is sixty miles from here. And he won't even be open until tomorrow morning."

"So we're here for the night," Madison said.

"I guess so. Do y'all like Irish whiskey?"

Madison, still kneeling next to Elvis, frowned. "I don't use alcohol," she said.

"Well, I do," Tam said, brightening visibly. "My personal preference is beer, but—"

Pete lit the cigarette and took a shallow puff. "Don't have beer, ain't gonna have none. This is a dry county and Sunday, on top of that." He discharged a narrow stream of smoke and grinned. "Our bootlegger is a religious man—he charges double on Sunday."

Tam said, "Well, then, I really, *really* like Irish whiskey."

Pete flicked the unlit cigarette into a rusted trash barrel posted next to the garage door. "I'll grill y'all some steaks and we'll try some. The best Irish whiskey in the world."

Tam and Madison collected their things and followed Pete and Elvis into the house's side door.

"So is the timing belt what you would call 'something electrical'?" Tam asked.

Pete paused in the doorway, gave Madison a look that could best be described as sympathetic, then continued into his house.

*   *   *   *

The two men retired to the screened back porch after supper to sample whiskey and watch the sun sink into the roof of the old high school gymnasium. Two heavy cocktail glasses, three bottles, a blue ice bucket, and a glass pitcher of water sat on a wooden tray on a round serving table. Pete poured a modest amount of light-golden liquor from a gold-labeled bottle into both glasses. He handed one glass to his visitor and eased back into an old Adirondack chair with the other. In the violet haze over Pete's shoulder, Tam could see that someone had left the numbers 6-6-6 illuminated under Home, Visitor, and Inning on the deserted baseball field's electric scoreboard. He assumed this to be the handiwork of pranksters set on rankling churchgoing townsfolk. Madison, politely declining an invitation to join them, had retreated to the den with Elvis. Tam turned his head and saw her through the half-drawn den shades—illuminated by the flickering light from a television screen, curled up on the couch, Elvis's contented head in her lap.

Tam was not nearly as comfortable as Madison appeared to be. As relieved as he was to have a safe place to unwind, he still wondered about his host. Who, actually, *was* this Don Pedro O'Malley? What kind of man drove around in a wrecker with a loaded shotgun behind the seat? Was that some kind of standard rural Southern practice, or was he a gun-toting nutcase? Or was he, as Madison envisioned him, a hero—a true man of action? Tam tended toward accepting Madison's view. After all, Pete had already saved them—complete strangers that they were—from two horrible predicaments that very day. And he had provided them with free lodging and food. But that extravagant generosity only raised new questions in Tam's mind. People just didn't behave that way in a world he perceived as completely cruel and self-interested. Did Pete have some twisted ulterior motive? And why, after preparing a delicious steak dinner for his two guests, had he only nibbled on a roll? His initial suspicion was that the man was poisoning them—or at least *him*—but he'd been so ravenous that he'd wolfed down the food anyway. *No, that probably wasn't it—twenty-five minutes had passed, and no symptoms.* Maybe he was just biding his time, hoping to get Tam blind drunk so he could have his way with Madison. Tam would've felt better about the situation if Pete had some kind of family; deranged killers always seemed to be loners. He'd noticed portraits of an attractive woman and a young girl in the living room, but where were they? He studied his host as he splashed another finger of liquor into his glass. For the first time, Tam noticed that Pete's arm was thin and pallid; his hand shook as he returned the bottle to the table. Everything about him—his passive manner, his bad limp, his hacking cough, this conspicuous palsy—made Tam believe that he was too feeble to overpower him. He took a sip of whiskey, closed his eyes, and let the tension sink away from his neck and shoulders. It was probably best, he decided, just to relax and share a drink or two with the man. Despite his mistaken judgments regarding Madison, Tam still retained significant faith in his ability to get the measure of others. And it'd been his experience that nothing melted barricades like the potent solvent of alcohol.

"Could I have possibly trouble you for a few cubes of ice?" Tam asked.

Pete made a face. "Ice? You don't put ice in a glass of Irish whiskey. I don't think they even have ice in Ireland. If you want water, there's the pitcher." When he noticed Tam's puzzled expression, he added, "They have a saying in Ireland: 'You don't screw another man's wife, and you don't pour water in his whiskey.' Or words to that effect."

Tam, choosing not to water his drink, smiled and took another sip. Although unaccustomed to the hard liquor burn, he took progressively longer pulls on the golden liquor in an effort to hasten the anesthetization process.

"How do you like it?" Pete asked.

"Good stuff."

"It's Powers," Pete said. "I brought a couple of bottles of it back from the mother country at great expense."

"So I wouldn't dare think of defiling it with a few cubes of ice. Or *would* I?"

"Fine," Pete groused, as he handed the ice bucket to his guest. "I shoulda known. Someone who's never fired a shotgun sure as hell can't drink his whiskey without ice."

That Pete, the grizzled wrecker driver/mechanic, was also a world traveler was just the first of many revelations concerning the historical Don Pedro O'Malley that would soon be dislodged by the second drink—three fingers of Jameson—and the third, a half-glass of Tullamore Dew.

The second revelation was that Pete had once been a licensed member of the Alabama state bar. He told Tam that it had taken him about three years in private practice to determine that law probably wasn't his best career choice. And, he had added, draining most of the un-iced Jameson's from his glass, three years worth of frustration "sort of exploded in him."

"What happened?"

"I punched out one of my clients," Pete stated matter-of-factly. "He was a huge piece of garbage, to be honest with you. He was a bitter, unprincipled person who'd retained me to take custody of his two children away from their mother. I'd reviewed all the evidence and all the court files, and it was my opinion that the kids were better off with Mom. But he offered me good money, and I had bills to pay—" He paused, swirling the remaining whiskey around in the glass. "Any lawyer will tell you that you gotta take cases you don't want, represent people you don't like. It's part of the canon of ethics. And I'd represented accused druggies, murderers, and so forth. I didn't like those cats either, but I was always ethically able to represent them. With this guy, though, my fee started to feel like dirty money. When we were sitting in the hall outside the courtroom, I could see him huddled up with his kids, working on them, telling them what to say to the judge. The kids were crying, just sobbing." He stopped swirling the whiskey. "And when he tried to get me to put on perjured testimony at another hearing, quite frankly, I had just had it—with him, with everything."

"So you just whipped his ass?"

"Not until he got all in my face. I don't really care for that, anyway. The fact that I knew he was a huge asshole just made it easier."

Tam smiled and nodded. He was just beginning to feel the narcotic warmth of the drink settle into him. To be sure, this wasn't exactly his usual buzz, but it wasn't at all bad. And with every swallow, every esophageal burn, there came an intensifying of the liquor's effect and the fading of his anxiety about Pete. He leaned forward in his chair and picked up the nearly empty bottle. There was something about it—its heft, the antique label, the clear golden liquid inside— that made him think that it might one day replace the cool aluminum can as his preferred vessel of deliverance.

Pete took another sip and continued. After being suspended by the bar association, he said, he voluntarily withdrew from his law partnership and returned to his home county to run the garage his father had opened forty years earlier. The garage he had always assumed he'd run when he completed his tour of duty in Southeast Asia.

"You were in Vietnam?" Tam asked as he placed the bottle back on the table.

"Yes," Pete said at last. "That's where I acquired my delightful limp."

"What was combat like? I mean, the actual fighting."

Pete refreshed his glass with a few fingers of Tullamore Dew and shook his head. "It was like nothing you could imagine," he said, finally. "I don't really think about it all that much anymore."

"I'm sorry. I didn't meant to—"

"Naw, it's fine. Sometimes it's good just to talk about stuff, get it out of you." He paused again for a long while. The only sound besides the chirping of crickets was the metallic chink of ice on Tam's glass. "I was an artillery man, so right off the bat, it was a different ballgame for me. My battery was set up in a bunch of different firebases while I was in country. I was a one-fifty-five gunner, what they called a gun-bunny—a one-fourteen A-one. Best damn gun in the world, at least that's my opinion. Reliable and really accurate. We could pick a fly off Charlie's ass at ten clicks. Anyway, you asked about the fighting." He took a long drink and set his heavy-bottomed glass on the table next to his chair. He lit and took a drag from a cigarette, discharged the thin stream of smoke and stared, glassy-eyed, into the distance. When he continued, he spoke of a place called LZ Betsy where he manned a gun, where the innocence of his youth was finally squashed out of him, and where, on one frighteningly long day, he received a permanent gift of shrapnel courtesy of an NVA artillery round. He took another quick drag off the cigarette, then crushed out its fire in the bottom of the glass. "So, that's about it," he said. "A few weeks later, I'm in Walter Wonderful— that's what they called Walter Reed—having wheelchair races on the big ramp that ran from the Red Cross area past the chapel."

"I was just thinking that you're about my father's age."

"No shit. Was he in 'Nam?"

"No. According to what my mom has told me, he was a student in Ann Arbor, protesting against the war—long-haired, hippie know-it-all."

Pete's laughter quickly became a protracted fit of coughing that left him bent in half with pain.

Tam got to his feet and stood helplessly by his host's side. A moment later, Madison appeared with a glass of water in her hand. Pete took the glass and, wheezing thanks, gulped half of it down. After a moment he sat up straight and, more or less, resumed normal breathing.

"Sorry," he rasped. "I told you I don't need to be smoking."

Elvis came onto the porch with his tail wagging. He took up a position between Madison and Tam and barked at his master. Pete scratched the dog behind the ears.

"You're a good boy, Elvis," Pete said. Then, looking up with red eyes at Madison and Tam, he said, "I think I told y'all before—Elvis is no ordinary dog."

"He seems very smart and sweet," Madison said.

Pete shook his head. "No, no. Not just smart. I'm talking about *legendary* bloodlines. You have no idea." He motioned for his guests to take a seat. Madison settled into the chair Tam had been in; Tam gingerly positioned himself at the edge of a tarp-covered pile of cut wood. Pete poured another shot of Tullamore Dew in the water glass and took a sip. Elvis circled in the middle of the group and finally collapsed with a contented grunt on the cool concrete porch surface. Pete then launched a story that rolled on for nearly fifteen minutes, an account of the unknown "Ammo Dog Brigade," an elite unit of Basset Hounds trained in complete secrecy at Fort Benning in conjunction with the Scout Dog program.

"Now, it's obvious you love dogs, just like I do," Pete said, looking at Madison. "So this may be unpleasant. Some of the dogs—I stress *some* of them, a very select few—were trained for, ah, sacrificial missions."

"What does that mean?" she asked.

"It means they were strapped with explosives and sent into enemy camps to—"

"Uh, *uh*."

"I'm afraid so. Not all of them, just a few. It saved human lives. After a few missions, though, there was so much unease, so much controversy, that particular extreme mission was mostly discontinued."

"What does 'mostly discontinued' mean, exactly?"

"Ah. That's where the story of the legendary Elvis the first begins."

Pete drained his glass then, leaning forward in the slanted seat of his chair, proceeded to take his guests through a narrative that was, by turns, starkly realistic and patently absurd. A platoon of American infantrymen, he said, was pinned down after a jungle ambush. A "Basset Brigade" handler, in the vicinity to root out occupied tunnels, sent his dog, Elvis, into a Viet Cong machine gun nest "strapped with a high-explosive" vest. Elvis, it seemed, had served with distinction as a "scout" dog, and had discovered VC hiding in tunnels, in jungle brush, and underwater, and had sniffed out and foiled a number of ambushes. It broke his handler's heart to have to send him on this mission, Pete said, because this dog was bright and loyal.

"But the remote detonator failed," Pete said, "and Elvis found himself in the midst of an enemy ambush party of at least twelve soldiers."

"I don't want to hear that they shot him," Madison said.

"Oh, they shot him, all right. Once through the back leg and once through the fleshy meat of his neck. But they didn't kill him, and Elvis grabbed one of the gunners by the balls."

Madison and Tam stared at their host.

"It's true. Locked right down on his sweet spot and yanked him away from his gun. When the others saw the dog's ordnance vest, the VC freaked and ended up bugging out. The pinned-downed platoon overran the VC position and found a delirious gunner, the wounded dog, and two abandoned RPD machine guns."

After a long silence, Tam said, "Is this for real?"

"I wouldn't lie."

"How do you know about this? I thought you were in the artillery."

"I met the dog's handler at Walter Wonderful. They'd taken Elvis to the animal hospital at Ton Son Nhat where he was nursed back to health. The Army released Elvis to him and he later bred him." He reached down and scratched Elvis on the head. The dog emitted a soulful woof of appreciation. "And that's where this guy came from. The handler and I kept in touch and, there you are."

"Cool," Tam said.

"Which brings me to something else we need to discuss. I'm gonna need for someone to take Elvis."

"What do you mean *take him*?" Tam asked.

"Take him away with you when you go. Take him and take care of him." He paused and stared down at the empty glass in his hands. "I've noticed how he likes you, and y'all seem to like him. And, honestly, I don't know anyone else I'd trust with him."

His guests' confusion became evident in their frowns and wrinkled brows.

"Don't you have anyone else?" Madison asked. "I mean, family or—?"

"No family," Pete answered abruptly. After an uncomfortable interval of cricket-chirping conversational gap, he added: "I have a friend or two."

"No, I'm sorry. I didn't mean—"

"Oh, it's fine. I actually have a close friend, an attorney in Montgomery. We used to practice together. She actually *still* practices there. Unlike me, she never beat up any of her clients." He flashed a quick grin. "She knows Elvis, and she loves him dearly. Problem is, she and her son are both deathly allergic to him. Every time they're around him, they both can barely breathe." He shrugged. "So—"

Tam shot Madison a look. "We're gonna be traveling around quite a bit—"

"You said you didn't have any money. Take Elvis, take care of him, and I'll get you a car you can drive, first thing in the morning. Won't cost you a dime—"

"And all we gotta do is take Elvis?" Tam asked.

"That and promise to look after him—both of y'all."

Madison said, "We … that is, Tam and I … may not be—" She paused, her face burning crimson as the awkwardness of the moment settled upon her.

"Madison's got some personal, family business to take care of," Tam interposed. "We may not be together much after tomorrow. So I'll take responsibility for Elvis." He gave her another look. "Until, of course, we … get back together."

This seemed to satisfy Pete, and he collapsed back into the Adirondack chair. He smiled, but he looked spent. "There's one more thing you could do for me," he said. His voice was now just a little more than a whisper.

"Name it."

"Paint me a picture of him. You know, just something to have after he's gone."

"Paint you a picture."

"Yeah. You did say you could paint, didn't you?"

Tam stared at Elvis. The dog was sprawled on a throw rug on the porch, his head resting on a wide paw. His rheumy eyes darted from Tam to Pete as though he fully understood the conversation and had a vested interest in the answer.

"I've painted a bunch of portraits and a few landscapes, never an animal." He paused. "I guess I could do it."

Pete laid his head back and closed his eyes. He smiled, and his whole body seemed to melt into the chair.

It was almost as if he'd completed the last task of his final life mission.

CHAPTER 8

▼

SILVER TWINES AND
PURPLE RIDES

"Oh, Lord. I ain't gonna make it. He's gonna kill me before we even get there."
Tam leaned toward the driver, a beautiful woman with skin the color and texture
of caramel, and strained to hear what she was saying. The roar of the Lincoln's
overridden "climate control system," the chop of air rushing through the
half-opened driver's window, and the fact that she seemed to be muttering to herself, combined to drown out all of what she said, with the exception of the omi-
nous phrase "gonna kill me." Because the woman was providing a free shuttle
service to Montgomery, because she was delivering the three of them to their
free-of-charge, "legendary" vehicle, and because she appeared to be in moderate
respiratory distress, he felt some sort of obligation to assist her. Or, at the very
least, to avoid making her current dilemma any worse. When she sneezed—for
the third time in less than a minute—and buried her frowning face in a wad of
tissues snatched from the armrest-console's storage space, he was able to conclude
that Elvis was the source of her anxiety.

Tam repositioned his huge boots around the overstuffed leather briefcase on
the floorboard and turned his gaze to the Towncar's backseat. He made sure not
to engage Madison, with her flat and purposefully distant eyes, for more than a
second. She had made her continuing displeasure with him quite clear the first
thing that morning; upon waking to find his arm draped over her, she had angrily

elbowed and kicked him off the bed. It had taken him a full minute of gasping and thrashing and shaking out the morning-after booze-muddle before he could even place where he was, much less what he might have done to warrant that abuse. At last, after finally struggling to a sitting position on the guestroom floor, he'd held his hangover-ravaged head in his hands and gathered a few random fragments of his last waking experience. He recalled Pete's offer to provide a car in return for a portrait of Elvis, and his ultimate acceptance of that offer by capturing the dog's essence in the acrylic medium. And he also remembered executing the bargained-for project and indulging in a few more celebratory drinks with his host while they admired the drying canvas. And that was about it. He had no memory of crawling in bed with Madison, couldn't recall having groped her or made any sexual advances, unwanted or otherwise. Given this absence of awareness and the fact that they were both fully dressed when he was jostled awake, he was confident that nothing untoward had occurred. Still, he would never have crawled in bed with her completely sober and, inasmuch as she'd made no secret of her displeasure with him when she'd left for bed at around midnight, he could almost understand her current state of mind.

Almost. In truth, Madison seemed to have a problem, not just with him, but in general. Something, he speculated, that was chemical in nature (based on things he'd gleaned from semi-sober afternoons with *Dr. Phil* and *Oprah*) which required the intervention of a trained professional. On the other hand, she'd been nothing but cordial with Roger, Paula, and Pete. So maybe it *was* just him, after all. Whatever the source of her aggravation, he could tell by her current glazed expression that her attitude toward him hadn't improved in the fifteen minutes they'd been in the Towncar. He let his gaze shift to Elvis, who'd drawn himself up on the glove-leather seat like a restive fur comma. The dog seemed to notice Tam looking at him and lifted his head from his twitching paws and emitted a long and pitiful whine.

"Y'all, I'm just gonna have to stop and get some air," the driver said. She yanked the Lincoln over to the side of the road, and it skidded to a stop in the gravel shoulder. Holding the tissue over her face, she climbed from the car while the open door alarm clanged.

Tam watched her prop herself up on the left front fender while she sucked in lungful after lungful of humid but allergen-free air.

"Man," Tam said, "I thought that dog-allergy thing was just a crock, but it looks like she really *does* have it."

The observation hung limply in the hostile air like a week-old party balloon.

Tam exhaled audibly—not quite a sigh, but something more purposefully evocative than would ever be found in the normal expelling of air—and turned away from Madison and her persistent cloud of quiet indignation. *So.* He was right—it *was* just him. Once again, he'd been secretly accused in the Star Chamber of her mind. Once again, he'd been judged guilty on untested and sketchy evidence without having had an opportunity to defend himself. Well, he thought, *this* time he was finished with her, her *and* her foul moods and peeves and her harsh judgments and all the rest of the random, smoldering vexations that continued to darken his journey. Because what had happened in the peach orchard had *not* been his fault (even though it had been his misplaced, albeit justified, fear of police scrutiny that had led them there). And what he had done with Pete was *social* drinking, and social drinking was *not* alcoholism. And, even though she might be offended by any contact, however incidental or innocent, passing out next to her while fully clothed hardly qualified as the indignity of the century.

It was almost enough to explain why her husband had taken their daughter and fled in the first place.

He took a long, calming breath and began structuring his newest plan—one calling for fulfilling his ethical and social obligation to Madison as quickly, as efficiently, and as *impersonally* as possible. He visualized loading their newly acquired vehicle (including a demonstrative trunk-slam, just to remove any ambiguities about how he felt), pointing it down whichever route represented the least time-consuming path to Pensacola, and driving rapidly and *silently* to the residence of her alleged friend. And then, once there, he would disgorge his disagreeable cargo and roar away in a dramatic, tire-spinning, gravel-spitting exit that would provide an evocative visual exclamation point to his unstated commentary on the whole miserable adventure.

He shook Madison from his mind and turned his attention back to the driver. Janelle Burke, the respected Montgomery lawyer Pete had described the previous evening, tall and handsome, meticulously dressed in a beige business suit. She wore sensible gold ear-bobs and expensive aviator sunglasses. That a prominent lawyer would be shuttling them to pick up their loaner car was a development he could not have anticipated.

Then again, he'd already had so many surprises that day.

Beginning with his brutal wake-up call, but followed not long thereafter by his discovery of a "suspicious black dude" lurking near the wrecker and his subsequent frantic charge through the house, dressed only in his shower towel, emitting shrill reports of imminent robberies. His next discoveries—that the "robber" he had so unambiguously identified was, in reality, Sam, a nineteen-year-old scholarship student and the son of Janelle Burke, and that both individuals were present in Pete O'Malley's kitchen—were the most startling of them all.

That's another thing, he reminded himself. He could understand Sam's chagrin over this false report. Nobody wanted to be characterized as suspicious, much less a robber. He could even relate to Janelle's (almost sympathetic) frown of disapproval. Even though he'd had no reason to know who the intruder was, that the young man might have been expected as a guest, or that he was authorized to lurk. In the interest of goodwill, Tam was willing to concede that his report could have offended both mother and son. He could *almost* see how Pete might have been somewhat bothered by it, as well, even though he was the intended beneficiary of the warning. Madison, though—that was a different story. She had slumped against the refrigerator and muttered, "what a stupid and racist thing to say"—her only words to him that morning, other than, "You're drunker than a dadgum bicycle." Madison, of all people, had the nerve to slap the racist label on him. He reminded himself that she probably came from a long line of slave-owning, plantation masters (although the more he allowed this notion to percolate, the more absurd it seemed). The very *nerve* of her! He was *not* a racist. In fact, he was not only not a racist, he should have been certified as racist-tendency-free—by birth and by his sterling midwestern pedigree (marked exclusively by late nineteenth-century immigrants from non-slave-holding European nations and, eventually, at least one Union soldier). And, although he'd never had any friends of color, he still felt inclined toward smug superiority over all people who had (or could have had) an identifiable bigot somewhere in their family trees. In short, somebody should have stepped *immediately forward* to absolve him of any potential wrongdoing.

That's not what had happened. Instead, Janelle Burke and a scowling Madison Monroe, soon joined by the bleary-eyed Pete and slightly perturbed Sam, had stood, statue-like, in the kitchen and glowered at him like he was the Grand Imperial Wizard of the KKK.

Janelle, having recovered from her allergy attack, walked back to the car and slid under the steering wheel.

"I was worried about you there for a second," Tam said, his voice dripping with solicitude—not the kind of comment one might expect from a racist.

"Yes, thank you." Janelle put the Lincoln in gear and pulled out on the highway. "Although I surely hope we get to Theotis's house before it starts up again."

Tam blinked. "Theotis?"

"Theotis Laughinghouse. He's my uncle."

Tam's fingers tightened around the grab strap mounted on the door.

"That's where the car is."

"Oh." Tam shifted in his seat. The whole car-transfer operation had become a little too complicated for his liking, not just as to the number of people involved, but as to potentially complicating issues, as well. For example, who was to say that this Theotis Laughinghouse understood the arrangements he'd made with Pete? What if he refused to release the car? Or what if he demanded payment for it? He reminded himself that all of this was being done for Madison's benefit. As far as Tam was concerned, he would have been happy cooling his heels in Beddington, laying low and sipping Irish whiskey.

"So Pete tells me your family's down in Florida," Janelle said, looking at Madison in the rear-view mirror.

"Oh, no, ma'am," Madison replied. "Just my daughter." After a moment, as if Tam's presence obligated her to provide more accurate information, she added, "Also her father."

"Oh. Well, it's nice you're still on speaking terms with your ex."

Tam twisted slightly in his seat and emitted a tiny snort of appreciation.

"Um, yes, ma'am," Madison said.

Tam recognized the flatness in Madison's voice, the don't-ask-me-anymore-questions tone with which he had acquired more than a passing familiarity.

"Because I do a lot of domestic relations work, and I see a lot of folks who don't get along too well after the decree's issued."

Well, Tam thought. *Not really a question.*

"Yes ma'am," Madison agreed.

Janelle steered the Lincoln onto an interstate on-ramp. Her eyes were starting to water again. "Oh, Lord," she said. "Good thing it's only a few more minutes." She reached into the console storage unit for more tissue and said, "Elvis is a sweet dog, but—"

"He's more than a sweet dog. He's a legendary dog."

Janelle wiped her eyes and turned to Tam. "Lord, Pete's been runnin' that mouth again about the dog." She paused, her teary eyes narrowing. "He hasn't been talking about exploding dogs, has he?"

Tam froze. He didn't want to say anything that was going to cause, extend, or reenergize a problem. One major gaffe was all he could afford that day. "Ah," he hemmed, "he just told me he thought he might've had a famous grandfather."

Janelle gave him a look—a half-smiling, half-nodding, all-knowing look. It was a kinder, less judgmental, version of an expression he'd seen on many other occasions. With Lauren, it had often been accompanied by a chest-heave of exasperation and lip-curl of contempt, and generally signified a deep sense of personal disappointment.

Tam studied Janelle, trying to determine if Pete had just been shining him on, if there had been a barb lurking beneath the snug gloss of whiskey fellowship. He had bought into the whole "ammo dog" saga. Had Pete withheld the critical details of the story from his former law partner, or had he just been jerking his chain? And if the Elvis story was a fabrication, was anything Pete had said true?

At last, Janelle said, "I don't know anything about Elvis's grandfather. I do know Pete had a rough time there in Vietnam—too many explosions, too much death for a young man to—" She let the thought drift away, unfinished; the portentous overtones persisted. After a brief silence, she said, "I have a soft spot in my heart for Vietnam veterans. I like to hear what they have to say, and I tend to not cross-examine them. You see, my brother, Jarrell, was there, too. He went over when he was nineteen, also. Unlike Pete, though, Jarrell will always be nineteen. Unlike Pete, I never got to hear *his* stories."

"I'm so sorry," Tam said.

"Oh, it's fine. He's in a far better place than this world. When I accepted that, my woe turned to joy." She turned to him. "Do you know Blake, the poet?"

Tam shrugged. "Just that he's the dude who wrote the words to that *Chariots of Fire* song."

She laughed again. "Well, I guess that's true. He also wrote, 'Under every grief and pine runs a joy with a silver twine.' I read that poem when I was off at Vanderbilt, a few years after Jarrell passed. At first, I thought it was just silly, naïve. Then, the more I thought about it, the more sense it made. Now I surely do believe it's true. Yes, I do."

Tam began to ask Janelle a question, but instead bit his lip, and engaged in a brief internal dialogue concerning the proposed topic.

"Yes, dear? You have a question?"

"I just wondered if I could ask you something."

"Ask away, honey."

"Why does Pete want us to take Elvis? He made some reference to stuff coming up, but—"

Janelle tipped her sunglasses down. "He didn't tell you about his problem?"

Tam shook his head.

"He's got lung cancer, honey—*bad*. They've already taken one lung. He's, like, stage four."

Tam thought back over the previous evening. *Well, that probably explains the cough, the lack of appetite, the man's general frailty ...*

"He just got through with one bout of radiation last month." Her eyes narrowed again. "You sure he didn't say anything about that?"

"Not to me, he didn't."

"That's strange. He's shuttin' down the garage next week and moving down to Montgomery, you know, so he can be close to the hospital, and to Sam and me, of course. We're about the closest thing to family that he has."

"I was wondering ... I saw a photo of a woman and a child—"

"His wife and little girl were killed in a horrible wreck about ten years ago," she said. "It like to have killed him. They were just about his whole world." She shook her head and made a mournful grunting sound.

"That's terrible," Tam said.

"Yes, it was. Anyway, he's gonna do another round of radiation, see what happens." She pushed her sunglasses back up the bridge of her nose and turned back to the road. "He says he's looking for a miracle, but—" She shook her head and let her thought drift off into silence.

"You say that like he doesn't have a chance."

"Honey, if the medicine and doctors can help him, I suppose he has a chance," she said. "I don't believe in miracles myself."

Tam nodded and allowed his gaze to drift back to the passing scenery. The sun had temporarily disappeared behind a huge cloud. The resulting shadow cast on the sun-dried flora made everything in the world appear dead to him. Or maybe it was just this dreadful news about Pete and his family—in reality, more a confirmation of his own strong suspicion than actual news—that painted itself on his already darkening lens. He struggled to find a "joy with a silver twine" to submarine this particular woe; no comforting thought occurred to him. For a moment, as he stared out at the crosshatch blur of passing milkweed and sedge, he was struck with the oddness of the moment. He felt more of an emotional attachment to a stranger his father's age than he did his father. Then again, his father had never shared his most personal memories with him. Nor had he ever given him a dog. Or a car. Not just a dog and a car, but treasured personal possessions. And not just given, but *entrusted* to him.

"Did Pete tell you anything about this car?" Janelle's voice steered Tam back to the present.

"No," he answered. "Not really. I mean, he said it was, like, a classic or something."

She laughed again. "I see. A legendary car?"

He shrugged. "Yeah. I think that's exactly what he said." He noticed that the wild grass and woodlands had gradually turned into marshy bottomland. In the distance, visible over a clump of oak trees, the haze-enshrouded skyline of down-town Montgomery appeared. "Maybe he was just goofing on me about the car, too."

Janelle smiled, and her face took on a pensive, almost meditative, aspect. Finally she said, "I've heard so many things about that car. Something about being involved in a bank robbery, something else about it belonging to a famous actor. It's kind of like the dog—at some point, I just quit thinking about what's true and what isn't. Pete's like another line from that same Blake poem: 'To see a World in a grain of sand, and a Heaven in a wild flower ...' That's just Pete, dead-out. With him, usual material things mean nothing, and odd, little things mean everything."

Tam began to ask her another question, even more personal than the last. This time he didn't catch himself until the first syllable was hanging awkwardly from his mouth.

"What is it, honey? You can go ahead and ask me anything. As you can see, I don't have a whole lot of secrets."

Tam smiled and nodded in appreciation of Janelle's extravagant openness. Meanwhile, the question had been routed through his appropriateness filter—typically triggered a few seconds after the scanned words had already found their mark—and he determined that it would probably fail the critical "how-could-you-even-ask-me-that?" test. His mind shifted gears as he struggled to quickly structure a less-objectionable form of the same question. But all that issued from his arid mouth was a lame insistence that his inquiry amounted to nothing and should, therefore, be forgotten.

Janelle suddenly burst into laughter. And not *just* laughter, but head-thrown-back, deep-bodied, Geoffrey-Holderesque laughter. Tam found this reaction both confusing and unnerving.

"You want to know about how Pete and I became friends," Janelle said, finally. "You're curious about how and why. A black woman and a white man, close friends in the Deep South." She shot a quick, reaction-gauging glance his way. "Isn't that true?"

Tam felt his face burning. Yes, he thought, that had been his question. And an innocent question, at that, one that he might have posed purely out of benign curiosity. A muffled but persistently anxious voice cautioned him—about what? Would he be revealing the presumptively racist substrate in his clouded chemistry of personal belief?—and he mumbled some obscure response.

"Well, I don't mind talking about it," she said. "It's like the story of the ugly duckling." She turned briefly toward him and smiled. "In a way, it's the story of the Old South and the New South."

Tam nodded.

Without hesitation, she opened *The Book of Pete and Janelle*. She began with a compressed version of her life story, the details of which, she insisted, must be first heard to understand how they came to be friends, then law partners. She told Tam that she'd been born in Montgomery in December 1955, two days after Rosa Parks refused to relinquish her bus seat. More significantly, she asserted, *she had actually ridden* with Mrs. Parks—her pregnant mother often returned from work on the same bus with the legendary seamstress and activist. Her father had died a month before she was born. She grew up in the house of her maternal grandmother with her grandmother, her mother, her brother, and her mother's younger sister, Sadie. Her mother was a maid for two white families, and when the resulting bus boycott went into effect, she had to walk several miles to work. The three most influential people in her life, she said, were Dr. Martin Luther King Jr., Rosa Parks, and her mother.

"I never had to deal with some of the mess that my momma and grand-momma did," she said. "Momma said they were afraid on those buses. She said people got beaten up, and one man got murdered. But I never saw that. It wasn't a perfect world by any means—it still isn't—but I never felt like there was someone out there stopping me from doing things. I never felt hated by anyone. My biggest challenge was overcoming my sense of self-loathing—my ugliness, for lack of a better word."

Tam's brow furrowed. "Ugliness? You're anything but ugly."

"Thank you," she said, "but back then I felt very ugly, indeed. I remember riding on the bus downtown with momma. By then, blacks and whites rode together, and there was never any trouble. But I'd sit there and look at the white girls and think, they're so pretty. They had pretty white skin, pretty blue eyes, straight, blonde hair, pretty little noses, and pretty thin lips. Everything about them was pretty. And everything about me was unlike them. I remember just watching them and thinking, 'Girl, you'll never be pretty. Not like that.' And then when I watched television, I never saw anyone that looked like me. It was only attractive white people." She gave Tam another glance. "Then, one day, I was in my junior high civics class, and my teacher—she was this white lady named Miss Weathers—held up a picture of Rosa Parks. I was very uncomfortable, because more than half the kids in my class were white, and the subject matter—a white man demanding that a black woman surrender her seat—had a lot of shameful history behind it. Then I remember Miss Weathers looking at that picture and saying, 'Isn't she just a beautiful woman?' And I heard some of the boys kind of laughing, but some of the girls nodded and agreed that she was. And you know what? I looked at that picture, and she *was* a beautiful woman! Not based on any subjective, ethnic interpretation of beauty, but objectively and truly. Yes, she was. She was a beautiful woman."

"So is that when you saw your own beauty?"

"Not completely. At least not then," she said. "I still believed that no white man would ever see beauty in me."

Tam nodded. "And that's where Pete comes in."

She laughed. "You got to hear the story, child. A few days after that civics class, I actually met Rosa Parks. Yes, I did. She and her husband were living in Detroit then, but she'd come back home for some kind of event. I walked up and introduced myself, and we talked for a long time. We talked about the fact that I rode the bus with her. I was in my momma, but I was there with her. And we talked about growing up black in the South, what I wanted to do with my life, everything you can imagine." She threw Tam another glance. "And we got around to discussing white folk, too. I was still upset about those boys laughing in civics class." She shook her head. "After all my people had endured, all it took was two dumb boys laughing at Rosa Parks that filled me with anger toward whites."

Tam gave a small, acknowledging shrug.

"But when we talked, everything made sense. She said there was this small percentage of folk—white *and* black—who were mean and hateful, and this small percentage of people who were extraordinarily kind. Everyone else—the biggest chunk of humankind—fit somewhere in-between. They're not good or bad, they're just out there, living their own lives, pretty much unconcerned about other people, other problems. They're not bad people, but, when they choose not to get involved, bad things can happen."

"What about the tool who ordered her out of her seat? Did she say which group he fit into? I mean, I can't even imagine one human being ordering another out of a bus seat for *any* reason."

"She didn't say. And frankly, she seemed so sweet, I can't imagine her *ever* saying. Anyway, our conversation helped me understand the world a little better. I came away believing, as I still do, that there are good people and bad people and neutral people in every group and race."

"And so where, exactly, does Pete fit in?"

"He's one of the really good ones. We met at a Veteran's Day thing in the early eighties. I was a lawyer by that time, and he was in law school. I had gone to the gathering because of my brother. I was wearing his picture and his artillery insignia. Pete hobbled over—he wasn't walking quite as good back then—and we started talking." She smiled. "He became a good friend. We met for coffee a lot, he even told me I was beautiful." She turned and looked at Tam over the frame of her glasses. "That's right. Don't be reading anything crazy into that—just two friends talking about all these self-image issues." She turned back to the road. "He came to my wedding, he was around when Sam was born, when my Marvin passed a few years ago. And I've been there for him."

"When he punched out his client?"

She laughed. "Oh, Lord, yes." There was a long pause before she added, "And when he lost his family, too."

Tam studied her. She was still facing straight ahead, but he was sure she was looking into a space more distant than the buckling interstate. Although it was a long time before she turned back in his direction, he was positive that a tear was inching down her cheek.

✳   ✳   ✳   ✳

The car rolled over the Alabama River and followed the interstate's arc through the middle of the state capital. When they were halfway through the city, Janelle steered onto a busy road lined by small businesses and compact homes.

"I need to stop by my office real quick," she said. "I hope that's okay."

"Fine," Tam replied. "I mean, you're going out of your way for us."

After about a mile, the Lincoln veered onto a diagonally intersecting street; within a matter of minutes, Janelle was pulling into the parking lot of a two-story, brick building. A hinged sign in front of the building read, "Collier & Burke, Attorneys-at-Law." Janelle motioned for Tam to lift his legs, hoisted the stuffed briefcase from the passenger-side floorboard.

"If y'all want to wait out here, I'll only be a few minutes," she said. "Got a few papers to sign."

Tam watched her walk toward the building, then half-turned toward the backseat and said, "That was a really interesting story." When there was no reply from Madison, he turned and saw that she was staring out at the surrounding scenery. After several minutes of sitting in uncomfortable silence, he climbed out of the car and walked back to the street. He was sure they had passed an art gallery not long before they'd turned into the law office. He found the gallery less than a quarter of a mile back up the road. He stood on the sidewalk outside the large display window and looked at the paintings hung there. He noticed that many of them employed the vivid colors offered by the acrylic medium.

An attractive young woman carrying a cardboard drink holder with two large cups wedged into it walked past him and paused at the front door.

"See anything that interests you?" she asked.

"No. I mean, they're all good." He tried to think of a way of explaining his situation without having to admit to being broke. Finally, he grinned and said, "I'm just looking, actually."

"Well," she said, smiling at him, "feel free to come in and browse, if you like."

"You work in there?"

She paused, displaying, for the first time, a guarded attitude toward the tall, scraggly stranger. "I'm the manager," she said, at last.

"Do you buy paintings? From artists, I mean."

The woman stood with the cup holder in her left hand and her right hand on the door knob. Tam interpreted the length of time she spent reflecting on his question an indication that the answer was too complex to be answered in the time they had together on the sidewalk. Finally, she asked, "Are you an artist?"

Tam became flustered. He knew that he was reasonably talented when it came to applying paint to a canvas. But was he an *artist*? To Tam, an artist was someone who had not only produced something of an artistic nature, but also had it judged worthy by the artistic community at large. In his mind, he'd produced nothing that would grant him the right to use such a title of distinction. No, at that moment, he was merely a painter who aspired to be called an artist.

"I'm in the process of … opening a studio now," he stammered, at last.

"Oh. Here in Montgomery?"

"Well, no. Florida, actually."

"Do you have an area of specialization?"

"Portraits, still lifes, pretty much anything." Then he remembered his most recent work, the stunning rendering of Elvis, the legendary basset hound, and he added: "I was recently hired to do a painting of a dog."

The woman nodded and pulled the door open. Tam knew by this prompt that the conversation was, for all practical purposes, over. "We display a lot of local work," she said, as she slipped the coffee and most of her body through the door. "Bring your stuff by. I'll be happy to take a look at it." She gave him another smile, this one more perfunctory than the first, and quickly slipped into the gallery.

He swore under his breath as he walked away. She had shown some spontaneous interest in him; just as quickly, it was gone.

It was the dog painting, he told himself. He should have never mentioned it. In his experience, artists who painted dogs were rarely taken seriously. *Probably the stupid dogs-playing-cards series.* Whatever, the reason, it had obviously been a mistake to bring it up.

He shuffled back down the street, alternately cursing fate and his inability to keep his mouth shut.

CHAPTER 9

▼

PAINTING ROSETTA

Janelle Burke turned into a neighborhood of well-kept, blue-collar houses and a suburban feel. The houses were uniformly compact, similar in design, and wedged end to end, but every plot had plenty of grass and abundant greenery. Wisteria-draped oak and pecan trees shaded backyards bordered by masses of eleagnus, still a good two months away from a fragrantly redemptive autumn blossoming, and wilted clumps of honeysuckle. It was the kind of neighborhood where, in kinder weather, residents strolled the streets or gathered around back-yard grills to make casual conversation about the state of the world. On a fiercely hot day at the back end of an already brutal summer, however, the streets and yards were all but deserted.

Janelle guided her car through a warren of similar-looking streets as if it were her own home neighborhood. She circled around a small park with a swing set, a slide, and a ball-less tetherball pole. The loop spun them into a long street with similarly sized and shaped houses for as far as they could see. A short distance down the street, the Lincoln slowed, easing to a stop by the curb.

"Well," Janelle said. "There it is."

They had stopped in front of a tidy, older brick rancher that, like most of the other houses, had been built on a slab. Window air conditioner units protruded from both windows on the east end of the house. A rectangular planter made of the same brick as the house ran the length of the front walkway and separated the walk from the front yard. A huge oak tree sat more-or-less in the geometric center of the grass-starved front yard. A group of people, mostly adult men and small children, were clustered in the vicinity of a car parked just off the driveway in the browning grass.

But all Tam saw was the car.

A 1973 Plymouth Fury III, a classic American land-barge. Long and wide and boxy. And purple. Not just purple—radiant metallic purple. A color that could be fairly described as lurid when, as now, it seemed to burn with electric intensity under a barely filtered mid-morning sun. The words "Purple People Eater" had been painted on the trunk lid in white Algerian script. Tam stared at the Fury and tried to imagine how it would *not* attract the attention of every cop he passed.

Then he noticed the people, particularly the young, T-shirt-and-baseball-cap-wearing male leaning into the vehicle through the open passenger door and the denim-clad lower torso protruding indecently from the driver's side.

"Are they gonna be, um, okay with us taking it?" Tam asked. A sudden stab of pain behind his right eye caused a shallow wave of nausea to burble through his empty stomach.

Janelle's brow furrowed. "They who? Ain't no *they* to it, honey. This car belongs to Pete. Bought, paid for, and rebuilt by him." She paused and cast a reproachful stare at the young men in and on the car. "He loaned it to my nephew, and now he's calling it back. Don't worry about those boys."

She opened the door and marched quickly around the vehicle. A beautiful young pigtailed girl dressed in a red-striped shirt and overalls met her halfway to the Plymouth and wrapped her in an exuberant embrace. Tam watched as Janelle hoisted the girl into her arms and continued toward the purple car. An older man with a splay of white hair ranging from beneath a ball cap and wearing a red foot-ball jersey with the name *Vick* on the back—Tam assumed that this must be Uncle Theotis—hobbled toward Janelle as she addressed the young man in the T-shirt. Tam couldn't hear what was being said, but, a moment later, when Janelle directed her stern attention to the individual stretched across the car's front seat, the T-shirted youth dealt Tam his fiercest scowl.

"Are you sure we can't just wait for the Honda to be fixed?" Tam said, retracting from the young man's harsh stare. Although this question was intended for Madison, he appeared to have directed it to the vacant driver's seat.

"I was supposed to be in Florida Saturday night," Madison replied. Her voice was high-pitched and quivering, as if her stress was reaching critical mass. "Nobody cares what happens to Brandy—"

Reacting angrily to her initial comment, Tam had wheeled toward the back-seat, fully prepared to unload on Madison for what he felt was her selfishness, her ungratefulness, her coldly critical grousing. But the reference to Brandy stopped him with his mouth open and the indignation spring-loaded on the tip of his tongue. And when Madison's voice broke, he bit his lip and shrank from the attack. He sagged and dropped his head.

"That's not true," he finally said. He began massaging his throbbing temples with his fingertips. "I *do* care what happens to Brandy. She's the whole reason—" He paused to again recalibrate the next string of words already locked and loaded. Even though he'd already posted Madison's dismissal notice on the bulletin board of his consciousness, there seemed to be some powerful and relentless part of his unconscious self—his *soul*—that wanted for her to need him. While he was bothered by the thought of Brandy being abused, she remained a theoretical entity to him. What truly had motivated him was Madison herself and, for what-ever time they might spend together, the continuing possibility that he could possess her. "Brandy was one of the reasons I agreed to do this," he offered, satis-fied with that self-arbitrated semantic amendment. He turned back to Madison with his most earnest look. "I'll have you in Pensacola before midnight. I promise."

Madison nodded and wiped away tears with the back of her hand. She turned to look out the window.

*   *   *   *

Her gaze settled on the old man in the football jersey, at the beautiful child in the overalls and pigtails, and the huge, purple car. She tried to process the recent events, the detours, disappointments, and distress. She instructed herself to believe in Tam, to trust that, despite his apparent commitment to a destructive and disordered life, he would somehow do as he'd promised. And she promised herself to forgive the Fury's clunky inelegance if it could only reunite her with her own beautiful child.

*   *   *   *

The Laughinghouse living room was open on the foyer side and rectangular in shape with two doorways—one that led to a side hallway and another that allowed access to the kitchen. Two framed portraits, a heavenward-gazing Jesus and a pensive Martin Luther King Jr., had been hung on a lavender wall above a floral-print love seat. A squat console television crouched directly under the room's large picture window. The huge and variegated swirl that was Hurricane Gregor's enhanced radar image glared from the screen. The bright, early-afternoon sunlight streamed through the window's open louvered blinds and painted blinding stripes on the worn, tan carpet.

Tam sat rigidly on the love seat and gazed at Sadie Laughinghouse, that royal salon's plus-sized matriarch. Sadie, regally arrayed in a silky silver caftan-and-pant set and comfortably established on her overstuffed, recliner-throne, had something that Tam needed, but she would have commanded his attention under any other circumstances. Her hair was solid white and cropped close to her skull. She wore large beige-framed glasses and had an engraved silver choker, dangly silver earrings, and silver Taureg bracelets on both wrists. Her fingernails were painted bright red and curled a full two inches past the tips of her fleshy fingers. Her left arm was draped around her granddaughter, Rosetta. The girl leaned into Sadie and eyed, alternately, the audacious stranger on the love seat and Theotis, who stood in the doorway to the kitchen. Tam judged Sadie to be in her late fifties to early sixties, although he couldn't be sure. All he knew for a fact was that she seemed to be the house's benevolent but iron-willed dictator, and that Theotis, for whatever authority he might wield in the outside world, was only a dutiful courtier in this salon.

"What exactly do you mean, you want to paint Rosetta?" Sadie asked. She spoke in a slow cadence, enunciating each syllable of every word. Her manner was polite, even genial, but businesslike; she seemed intent on making clear to this Tam Malonee that he would do nothing with any member of her family without first obtaining her royal imprimatur. She had been previously briefed by Tam and Janelle on Madison's quest and exigencies. Now, in her niece's absence, she was receiving testimony on the merits of the traveling couple's urgent petition for financial assistance.

Tam quickly tried to organize the thoughts that had been flitting like electrons through his aching head. He knew he had a major crisis on his hands—he had less than seven dollars in his pocket, the four-barreled, fuel-guzzling Fury had an empty gas tank, and Madison, currently pacing outside with the increasingly anxious Elvis, was getting close to a complete meltdown—and his attempt to make a coherent and dignified sales pitch to Sadie under less-than-ideal conditions was not going well. He wished that Janelle, who'd been called back to her office, was still there to negotiate for him.

"I'd like to paint a picture of her," he said. He found himself failing in his attempt to maintain a deep and well-modulated voice. Instead, it was taking all his effort just to stave off hyperventilation. "Kind of a portrait. With the dog, in a swing. I found a gallery here that, I think—" He paused as he gulped involuntarily, his Adam's apple convulsing unexpectedly around the innocent next word in the queue. "—they will buy it from me." Another pause, this time to suck down precious oxygen, even as the plan's exploitive purpose and essential improbability swirled through his mind. "With the money I earn from this, I can buy gas to get us to Pensacola."

The queen's lush nails undulated almost silently on the chair's wooden arm cap.

"Thus," continued Tam, interpreting Sadie's silence to mean that more information was required, "allowing us to proceed to reunite this mother and her abused child without further delay or expense to anyone else."

"You wanna paint her with the dog in the swing?" Theotis asked, his pleated brow glistening under the frayed brim of his ball cap. This was the first time Theotis had really said anything. It became obvious by his pronunciation and lisp that he was in need of the dentures that, Tam assumed, were soaking in some jar at that moment.

Tam paused, mentally backtracking through the last minute of the conversation. Before he could identify the precise point of confusion, Sadie said: "You're saying you can paint this child's picture, sell it, and get on the road to Pensacola? All in one day?"

"Yeah. I mean, yes, ma'am."

The fingernails clicked off tiny, rhythmic beats. "Well, that would be something to see."

"Yes, ma'am, it would. But, if you guys give me the chance, I think I can—"

"Young man, let me see if I understand. You and your—" She paused to give Tam the opportunity to characterize Madison. When Tam only sat, gape-mouthed, she continued: "You and your *friend* are going to Pensacola. And you have no money." Another pause, this one more dramatic. Tam took this to represent the prickly obstacle of a substantial, but in his view ill-informed, intervening judgment.

"Like I said, I have seven dollars."

"And the lady friend?"

"She's got about twenty bucks. Twenty-two fifty, to be exact. It's her tip money from her job. But she's gotta hold that for her and her kid. *So*—" He let the explanation trail off, satisfied that he'd provided all the essential information necessary to nudge the conversation in the direction of its excruciatingly distant finish line.

"And you have no credit cards." Her eyes drifted toward the television screen where some poor reporter was getting blown sideways by wind and rain.

"No. No, ma'am."

"Mm … hmmm." Her eyes shot back to Tam and locked on him like a weapon targeting system. "Then let me ask you this: Have the authorities been contacted regarding the abuse to this child in Pensacola?"

Tam sagged deeper into the love seat. He wondered why nobody would ask him a question he could answer. He stammered a reply that contained a few "I'm sures" and one "couldn't really say." He closed with an optimistic, "Hey, I figure a mom and a child together is a good thing."

Sadie gave him a polite smile. "That's not necessarily true, Mister Mal-oh-nay. You see, I worked for the Department of Human Resources for twenty years, and I saw many cases of abuse by mothers." The fingernails drummed, more audibly now.

"All I know is, Madison seems like a decent person to me, and I promised her I'd get her down there by tonight." He shrugged. "So—"

The questions persisted for nearly fifteen minutes. More accurately, questions, intermingled with a fractured mini-lecture on parental neglect and the epidemic of child abuse. Included in Sadie's polemic was a harsh, statistics-based commentary that noted that most pedophiles were single, white males in Tam's general age category. During this interstice, Tam nodded politely, but nevertheless permitted himself to drift away to his "freeze zone," a conjured *tabula rasa* upon which any bizarre present experience could morph into a surreal dreamscape. He traced this reality-conversion "skill" directly to a childhood playground incident in which an older boy persuaded him to hold his breath while a combination Heimlich maneuver-bear-hug-lift was performed on him. At some point in the course of this stunt, Tam had lost consciousness; he recalled waking to distant voices and a murky quasi-reality. *Just like now.* Now, as he drifted away, Sadie was sitting there in a fuzzy lump with a voice enunciating words that floated above him, but didn't register. All the while, *it*—the whole thing—was transforming into the bizarre coda of a monstrous bad dream-symphony.

"Is that a possibility, Mister Mal-oh-nay?"

The question snatched Tam back to reality. "Um … sorry … I …"

"I say, if you're truly a professional artist, why can't you just paint Rosetta right here? Right here in her own house?"

Tam glanced quickly at the girl. "Well, my vision was her on a swing—her on a swing, maybe with the dog sitting nearby, in bold, acrylic colors. We passed a park—I'm just saying that this was my creative vision. It seems like that would be something this gallery would go for." He paused, allowing himself another, longer and more critical, view of Rosetta's sweet face. "Then there's the whole question of light," he said. "Outside light's different—"

"Then you can paint her in the kitchen." She gestured toward the bright room just beyond the slumping Theotis. "As you can see, there's a nice, big window that lets in the morning sun just fine."

"I guess I could, but—"

"And what about us? We donate to you this child and our time so you can make some fast money—"

"I'll paint one for you guys, too."

"Two paintings. This afternoon." Sadie had let go of Rosetta and was sitting back in the chair with her arms folded across her massive chest. Having beaten Tam down as a negotiator, she was assuming the role of play-by-play commentator. "Painted right here in this child's own house."

"Sure. I mean, yes, ma'am. If you'd like, that's what I'll do."

Sadie smiled. "We'll see how it goes," she said. She then gestured for Tam to begin.

He sighed. With his head pounding and Madison pacing impatiently with Elvis outside the window, there was no choice but to make the best of what had been offered.

He got to his feet and headed for the car, where his paints and tools had already been stashed.

*   *   *   *

Tam embarked upon a seemingly impossible mission under circumstances that would've caused any normal portrait artist to melt down. He was surrounded by an audience—Theotis, Martay, another grandchild, and a neighbor (who had dropped in to see who the white visitors were) were arrayed in a semi-circle around one end of the kitchen table; Sadie was parked in a chair close enough to Tam to repeatedly bump his foot with her own. Madison was standing in one corner of the room with Elvis, who was greedily slurping water from a plastic whipped cream container. Rosetta sat on a stool in the opposite corner. More accurately, she sat on the stool for no more than two minutes before darting away to play with Martay. And Tam was wedged between the refrigerator and stove with his palette and paint tubes balanced atop a stack of mail and old magazines on the kitchen table's edge. The lighting, although indeed quite bright, was all wrong for an outdoor scene. If all this wasn't enough of a burden, his head was throbbing and his hand trembled as he tried to sketch his basic scene from visual memory. On any other day, Tam Malonee would have folded his tent and walked away. He would have found himself a comfortable chair and knocked down brews until the problem went away. This day was different. He knew he was in the crucible and that much was at stake—not just his promise to Madison, but also the answer to his biggest question: *Was he an artist, or was he something else?* Which, in essence, meant that he was nothing.

The sketch went well, and that was critical. Tam was delighted with the face—its shape, the critical landmarks, the essential features. He had a bit more difficulty capturing the girl's basic form on the constructed swing, but he managed to finish the whole rough-out in less than five minutes. As the essence of Rosetta began to emerge on the canvas, the persistent chatter among the grown-ups at the table began to slow. At last, as it became clear to them that they were in the presence of something approaching artistic genius, the room fell into hushed silence.

He next turned his attention to the tricky problem of his palette. Not only had he never painted a darker-skinned person before, he'd never tried to capture skin tones using acrylic colors, *period.* As a rule, acrylics were brighter and bolder than oils; Tam, therefore, had always been reluctant to use them in portrait work. If this gallery liked to hang acrylic paintings, though, that's what he would use. This had plainly become an urgent and mercenary—as opposed to leisurely cre-ative—endeavor. He squeezed out his eight available colors and stood there frowning.

"What's the problem?" Sadie asked.

"Nothing. I'm just not sure yet how this is gonna work." Indeed, Rosetta wasn't black. She wasn't even brown. She was generally a lighter caramel shade— the same as Janelle—but, in the bright kitchen light, her face reflected every shade from warm honey to dazzling pure white. Tam swallowed hard, feeling the added stress of having four pairs of judgmental adult eyes watching every twitch of his palette knife, every dab of his brush. He took a deep breath, shut his eyes, and tried to visualize how he wanted the painting to look. To his surprise, a men-tal image took shape, an interesting montage of tone, color, and texture. Without hesitation, he exhaled slowly and picked up his brush. He'd been trained (if a few sessions of drinking wine and being playfully critiqued by his art professor "friend" could qualify as training) to forgo any initial underpainting of the whole canvas in favor of "attacking" the subject to be painted. *Alla prima,* she had called it: literally "according to the first." He dabbed the brush tip in a mixed blob of paint and made his first strokes.

"Make sure you get that skin color right," Theotis said in his mushy toothless lisp. "Rosetta, she light. She ain't like me." He gave a coarse cackle. "'Course, I been out in the sun all summer." When he saw Tam's puzzled expression, he said, "What, you not think the sun make black people skin darker?"

Tam stood with his mouth open, his narrow-tip filbert brush suspended in mid-air.

"'Cause we do, ain't that right, Sadie? I been out all summer and look at me— I'm *smoky* dark."

Sadie gently touched him on the arm. "Theotis, dear, Mister Mal-oh-nay is trying to concentrate." She smiled at Tam. "Please accept my apology and continue."

Tam continued. He worked the quick-drying acrylics on his palette, mixing blobs of cadmium yellow and red, buff titanium, burnt sienna, and white, until he was generally satisfied with the resulting tones. Then for the next half hour, he worked his magic with the brushes, slashing, dabbing, feathering, until Rosetta appeared on Tam's imagined swing, complete with a stunning diversity of tonality.

When, at last, the artist laid down his brush, Theotis grinned and clapped him on the back. Sadie clutched him tightly to her ample bosom. And, as his chin disappeared into the caftan silk, Tam glanced over at Madison. She looked weary, but pleased.

He slumped into a vacant chair, overcome by the immenseness of the moment.

He'd finally done something right.

CHAPTER 10

▼

BLUE BOOKS & RAINBOWS

The Montgomery to Mobile run of Interstate 65 is as tedious and uninteresting a thoroughfare as any in the southeastern United States. Slicing in a gently curved northeast-to-southwest diagonal across south Alabama, it tracks through one-hundred-sixty-odd miles of dense evergreen and oak forest on a generally flat coastal plain. With the exception of the late-summer blooming crape myrtles in the median and the occasional eyebrow-raising roadside sign, there is nothing to look at beyond the tree-lined corridor and the endless unwinding of asphalt ribbon.

As it happened, looking at scenery wasn't Tam's highest priority as he nudged the chugging Plymouth southward. When he wasn't checking the rear-view mirror for state troopers, scanning the instrument panel for the fully anticipated verifications of mechanical malfunctions, or playfully glaring back at the gawking occupants of passing cars, he was either monitoring his speed, checking his watch, or ticking off the trip's remaining distance against the roadside mile markers.

By the time they reached the journey's halfway point (according to Tam's best calculation), it was already late afternoon. The sun that had scorched the land for the best part of the day had mostly disappeared behind by a menacing cloud-billow that had seemed to boil up from the evergreen horizon. Confident that he was at least substantially on schedule, Tam eased off the accelerator and tried to let his rigid muscles melt into the two-toned, vinyl-covered seat. He eventually let his left arm hang out the open driver's-side window where he caught the heavy air in his fluttering open hand.

But cars, trucks, and motor homes continued to pass them and the apparently intrigued occupants continued to stare. The seventy miles worth of persistent public attention was doing nothing to make him more comfortable behind the Purple People Eater's wheel. Even with his identity obscured by the dark glasses, Tam could not help but feel that, sooner or later, he'd be recognized. For all he knew, his scowling visage—courtesy of the ever-helpful Lauren, photographic chronicler of his every miserable married moment—had already appeared on one of the "most wanted" television shows. He had feared that the car's garish paint job might attract attention; he could never have imagined that the stares would have been as bold or as unrelenting as they had been. He muttered to himself that he might as well have been driving a giant wiener-mobile or a freak-show trailer.

"What is it?" Madison shouted. The intervention of her voice, especially at the volume required to be heard over the wind rush, surprised Tam.

"What is what?"

"You seem a little nervous."

"Um, I don't know. I guess it's all these people ... have you noticed everyone staring at us?"

She grinned and worked her gum. "Actually, I think they're all just looking at Elvis."

Tam looked over his left shoulder and saw that the dog's gape-mouthed head was extruded from the notch in the rear window. Glancing in the side mirror, he could see that Elvis's soulful eyes were almost forced shut, and his long ears and tongue were fluttering in the breeze. The look on his face could only be described as ecstatic.

Tam laughed and shook his head. "I guess you're right," he said. "I was probably just being paranoid again."

"You've had a pretty good day," Madison replied. She tucked her left leg under her and smoothed back her wind-blown hair.

He checked the rear-view mirror and shrugged. The rough morning and the persistent attention of passing strangers notwithstanding, it had been, all in all, a decent day. Madison's serial dark mood had once again given way to her sunnier side. And the exhilaration he had felt on the completion of Rosetta's portrait had been extended and intensified by the painting's sale *and* by the reaction of the Montgomery gallery manager. Despite his pride in the finished work, despite the praise heaped on him by the Laughinghouse observers, he had not known whether the portrait would be accepted by a discerning member of the cognoscenti. But Alicia Farber, the gallery manager from his earlier sidewalk encounter, had seemed enthusiastic about Rosetta's portrait. And not just about the color and composition, but about the *truth* it represented. This praise, this essential validation of him as an artist, had been as significant to Tam as the fifty-dollar, "cash-on-the-barrelhead" payment, which, Ms. Farber had assured him, represented a significant departure from the gallery's usual policy of accepting new artists' work on a consignment-only basis. While the money had filled the gas tank, the enthusiastic acceptance of him and his work had been ambrosia for his soul.

"So where did you learn to paint like that?"

"The same way I learned just about everything I know," he said. "From an older woman."

Madison gave him a long, analytical look. "The way you said that makes me believe there's more to that story."

"An older woman, that's all I said." He flashed a coy smile.

The old Plymouth now rumbled past a green sign announcing the mileage to Pensacola. Tam shot another quick glance at his watch and the sky and, realizing that he'd previously plugged a wrong number into his mental calculator, began to question whether they would, indeed, make Madison's destination before dark. His foot fell heavier on the accelerator pedal. He reminded himself that he had made a promise to Madison, and he wasn't going to break it.

"So who was this older woman?" Madison persisted.

This question directed Tam's memory to one of his most important promises and the woman to whom it was made. Lindsay Kitchens, the voluptuous thirty-something Lakeland art professor who had taught him the *alla prima* "flashpainting" technique, even as she had done her best to restructure his entire belief system. And, yes, she had taught him other worldly things as well, for he was but a sexually naive nineteen-year-old when she had taken him in. Tam permitted himself now to lapse further, into the visual and tactile memory of her mounted on him, the feel of her breasts and soft and ample hips, her hand gently guiding his to her specific pleasure zones, the taste of her body. Others might say that she had seduced him, and that, for a recently tenured professor to have had a sexual relationship with a student—and one nearly half her age, at that—would have been regarded as positively scandalous. "Others" never did know of their liaison, because Tam had promised never to tell anyone. After he suddenly and unilaterally withdrew from the relationship, Lindsay had tearfully confessed to him her one most paralyzing fear—not that he wouldn't return to her, not that she would stagger miserable and alone into middle age, but that he'd breach his promise to her. That he would be indiscreet. He had lived up to his word and never told a soul, not even his goatish peers on the basketball team. Now, as details of his later indiscretions displaced the memory of her in the viewing window of his mind, he asked himself: Why that singular act of integrity? This precise question had never before occurred to him. Now that it had, the answer absolutely intrigued him. It certainly wasn't because the teenaged version of Tam Malonee was strictly bound by codes, covenants, and conventions; by the time he was fifteen, he'd already broken a dozen ordinances and most of the commandments. Nor could it have owed to his great fondness for Lindsay Kitchens, the talented artist, the human being beneath the remarkable physical attributes—he found the urgent demands of her feminist agenda intimidating, her periodic displays of smug superiority irritating, and her frequent, occasionally dramatic, mood swings symptomatic of some diagnosable mental disorder. He certainly hadn't gained anything by keeping their relationship to himself. *Or had he?* Perhaps his reward was simply the knowledge that he'd done a decent and honorable thing. Perhaps this new, and largely unfamiliar, sense of personal rectitude was a major dividend that could only be bestowed by time.

"Tam?"

Madison's voice brought Tam back to the present just as an eighteen-wheeler roared by on the left. A brief, mirthful-sounding blast from the truck's air horn—the driver's way of chuckling at the lolling Elvis and the rumbling, purple monstrosity—established audibly to Tam what he was unable to confirm visually.

"It was just a woman who taught art there at Lakeland," he said, finally. He had decided against sharing any more information about Lindsay Kitchens, even though he had possibly already suggested too much. "I'm not even sure I can remember her name," he lied. His brows arched above his dark sunglass lenses as he turned toward her. "Why are you so interested in it?"

She shrugged. "Don't know. Just was."

He twisted the steering wheel and his thoughts retreated to the issue of his companion's moods. While he was happy to have the upbeat Madison back by his side, he wondered what, if anything, he'd done—or not done, as the case might be—to facilitate that change. Could it have been that he had impressed her (at last!) with his artistic talent? Was her attitude improving only because she was closer to being shed of him? Or did her moods just naturally shift with the metered regularity of a pendulum from chirpily talkative to morose? It was quite possible that, in just a few hours, she'd be gone and he'd never know. At last, he made the decision to simply throw the topic out for discussion.

"Can you, maybe … answer something for me?" he sputtered. "It's just that … I don't know … earlier today you wouldn't even talk to me, and now you want details about my past—"

She stared at him and twisted her hair. Finally she said, "I like you, Tam. A lot. You seem basically like … I don't know. A basically decent person."

"Well, thanks. I like you, too. Also a lot." He did his rolling check of mirrors, watch, and instrument panel, then shot a quick glance in her direction. "Why do I get the feeling that there's a huge but still coming?"

"It's the drinking, Tam. The drinking's the but."

He shook his head and groaned. "I can't believe it. You, too?"

"It's destructive, Tam. You can't have a normal relationship with someone who's an alcoholic."

Tam gave her an irritated look. "First of all, I'm *not* an alcoholic—"

"Yes, you are!"

"How do you know what an alcoholic is? You don't even drink. You were probably brought up in this super-religious home where alcohol was forbidden. You probably think that anyone who drinks a beer—"

"My daddy was an alcoholic," she interrupted, her eyes passionate and moist. "Do *not* tell me I don't know what it is. I watched him get drunk every single night for years. I saw what it did to my momma. I saw what it did to my family." She turned away from him. "I saw what it did to *him*."

"But I only—"

"Don't tell me you're not an alcoholic because you only drink at night."

He felt his face reddening. His planned rebuttal was checked by the sudden memory of having lost that same hopeless fight too many times before; instead, he retreated into a brooding silence. He checked his watch. One more hour, he told himself. Then she could just take her misconceptions and wrong conclusions and go her own way. He'd find himself a bar and—

His last thought screeched to a halt just before slamming into the ugly wall of grim possibility. *Could she be right?* He entertained this notion briefly before summarily rejecting it. She—like Lauren, like so many others—was just lumping him into a tub with lesser people, the pathetic schmucks and boobs who drank, but who couldn't handle their alcohol. He wasn't *anything* like them. He was smarter, more disciplined. He understood his limitations. He knew when to say when.

"Tam," Madison said, as softly as she could speak and still be heard, "there's a place up ahead where we can get something to eat."

"I'm really not that hungry."

"Well, then we'll get Elvis some water and let him relieve himself." She pulled her hair back and smiled. "You do have new responsibilities, you know."

Another glance at his watch. "We'll get behind schedule."

"I don't care about the schedule."

"Well, I do. I promised you—"

"Tam, I don't care about that. I don't care if we're fifteen minutes later getting into Pensacola. I've waited for three days to get there." She paused, then said, "There's something you need to see."

He gave her a brow-furrowed look. "What?"

"It's a book," she said. "I want you to look at this book."

He didn't speak for almost a minute. At last, nodding toward a passing billboard, he said, "I guess I could go for some boiled peanuts."

She shrugged. "Okay. That'll work."

"I wasn't serious! What in the hell even *are* boiled peanuts?"

She shook her head and gently punched him on the arm. "You're such a … a … *Yankee!*"

*   *   *   *

The Fury left the interstate at the next exit and rumbled into the parking lot of an old roadside snack stand. The building was small and dilapidated—it looked like it had been more than twenty years since the last time the siding had been painted. A weather-beaten wooden picnic table with two wobbly looking benches sat in the loamy soil between the parking lot and the access road. A tin "Drink Coke" thermometer hung on the front wall near the door. There was a rusted Coca-Cola sign nailed to the building's front overhang; another sign reading, "Best Boiled Peanuts" hung from one side of the building. Not seeing any other cars in the area, Tam parked the Plymouth under the wide overhang. He and Madison left Elvis in the car and pushed open the creaking wooden door.

The inside of the business was as austere as the exterior. The paint on the walls was chipped and peeling. The structure's only window, located on the side of the building with the sign, was so dirty that neither Tam nor Madison could see through it. There was a cracked serving counter sitting atop a glass case where a dozen or so packets of peanuts glowed like reactor fuel under a red warming light. A tiny black-and-white television sat on a shelf protruding from the back wall. There was an old-style soft drink cooler along the wall under the window. Next to the cooler was a framed cartoon of a gray-clad Rebel officer declaring, "Fergit HELL!" A vast man with a shaggy white beard was parked on a wooden stool behind the counter. He wore a Florida Marlins T-shirt that appeared to be three sizes too small for his thick neck and ponderous torso. The visor of a sun-bleached ball cap had been tugged down so low on his forehead that his hooded eyes looked like finger holes in a flesh bowling ball. A sign secured to the wall above his head indicated the prices for peanuts and soft drinks—apparently the only two items in the establishment for sale.

"Afternoon," the man said. He granted his visitors a cursory nod, then rolled his huge head back in the direction of television.

Tam muttered a marginally incoherent return greeting.

"Y'all comin' or goin'?" the man asked, his eyes still fixed on the TV screen.

Tam stared blankly for a moment, then looked to Madison as though she were a certified translator of arcane alien tongues. When she appeared to be as confused as he, he said, "We're on our way to Pensacola."

The man grunted. "Comin', then. Well, won't be long, you'll be headin' back this way." He emitted a hoarse, throaty cackle. "At least, if you can believe 'em weather people." His cap bobbed in the direction of the television. "I'm startin' to think they's all dumber'n cow chips."

Tam looked up at the screen and saw displayed, in a variety of shades of gray, the same swirl patterns that he had seen on the Laughinghouses' television almost six hours earlier.

"Hits a hurricane, they sayin' now. Gregory, whatever they callin' it. First they said it was gonna hit Mexico. Then it was Texas. Then, yesterday, they sayin' somewheres in Louisiana. Now they sayin' Biloxi. If they keep on that-a way, she's gonna turn all the way around and go back the way she come in!" Another cackle, long and dreadful.

"He," Tam corrected, smiling cordially.

"Excuse me?"

"I actually think it's a he, not a she." He shrugged and shook his head as if to say it really didn't matter. He honestly didn't care about the hurricane, or about listening to this man's jabber. He didn't even want the stupid boiled peanuts; he was there only because Madison had insisted on it.

"You ain't from Brewton, are you?" the man asked, the dark eye holes suddenly narrowing into almost accusatory slits.

Tam froze. "Uh, *no*—"

"'Cause you the spittin' image of an ol' boy from there I used to know. Got killed a few years ago by a deer."

Tam threw Madison another bewildered look then turned back to the man on the stool. "Well, then, it wouldn't be me anyway, would it?"

"No, no. I wasn't sayin' you was *him*. Just kin, or somethin'."

Tam shook his head. "Nope. Never been to anywhere called Brewton in my life." He paused. "How in the hell do you get killed by a deer?"

"Shoot. Folks get killed by deers all the dadgum time. They run out in the road in front of your car—next thing, you're sucking on an antler."

"Nope. Haven't heard about any of my relatives sucking any antlers."

"Any-*way*," the man continued. "What can I do y'all for?"

"Two packs of peanuts," Madison said. "And a couple of Cokes. Diet, if you got it."

"Ain't got Coke. Got Royal Crown. And ain't got no diet neither." He made a face and shuddered, as if he were repulsed by the very thought of an artificially sweetened beverage.

"You have a Coke sign hanging out front," Tam protested. "You got a freaking Coke *thermometer*."

"Shoot. Them things been hangin' there since this was a barbecue place twenty year ago. What I got now is regular Royal Crown." He crossed his arms across his wide chest.

"Fine," Madison said. She ordered two regular Royal Crowns. She pulled a wad of bills from her handbag and told Tam it was her treat.

Tam shrugged and glanced again at the television screen. A man holding a microphone was standing in abundant sunshine, delivering a report on the threatening storm. Behind him, obvious vacationers leisurely strolled on sand dunes among gently swaying sea oats.

See there, Tam said to himself as he collected his peanuts and drink. So much damn fuss over absolutely nothing.

*   *   *   *

Tam and Madison sat at the rotting picnic table while the sky darkened above them. They drank their canned RCs and ate from the soggy packets while Elvis lapped water from his dish.

"Well, what do you think?" Madison asked, after Tam had popped a few peanuts into his mouth.

Tam chewed politely but unenthusiastically and did his best to suppress the look of disgust that was spreading from squinting eyes to retracted chin.

"Oh, come on," she protested, "they aren't that bad."

"They're just *gross*," he said. He turned and spat his only sampling of the Southern snack specialty out on the ground. "It's like eating mashed-up bugs, or something."

She sighed. "I guess I'll never make a Southerner out of you."

He shrugged. "Oh, well. If being a Southerner means having to eat grits and bug larvae, I'll gladly pass."

"You know, Confederate soldiers used to live off boiled peanuts. Toward the end of the war, that's about all they had."

"Confederate soldiers?"

"Yeah, you know—the guys who fought on my side in the Civil War. The War of Northern Aggression, as Daddy used to call it."

"Maybe the boiled peanuts will explain why you guys lost."

Madison's face collapsed into a mask of mock fury. "Careful about that kind of talk in these parts, Yankee."

"I apologize," he said, finally. "I didn't mean to be disrespectful."

Madison studied him, apparently searching for some sign of insincerity. When she didn't find it, she reached into her handbag and pulled out a blue, cloth-bound book. It was old and worn and had several slips of colored paper and yellowed newspaper stock protruding from the discolored pages. She placed the volume reverently on the table in front of Tam.

He took a sip of RC and frowned at her. "What's this?"

"I want you to read something in here."

He picked up the book and examined it more closely. He'd seen it before—in her open suitcase at his father's house. There was nothing printed on the cover. Tam had to turn the book several directions before he found the title printed in gold ink on the spine—simply, *Alcoholics Anonymous*. He rolled his eyes, frowned, and laid the book back on the table.

"Now, hold on just a sec before you get all negative," Madison said. "There's one story in here I want you to read. And I want you to read the clipping that's in there, too."

"And then, what? What is that gonna change?"

"What do you mean exactly?" she asked.

"I mean, what if I *did* read this? What if read it and was to say, okay, I have a problem—even though I clearly don't—and agree to go along with whatever this schmuck has to say? I mean, how does that change anything for me?"

She dropped several peanuts into her can and swished them around in the fizzy liquid. "That's what this program, this book, is about," she said. "Most of the people with this problem think it's only about them. It's not, Tam. It hurts everyone. It especially hurts the people close to you."

Tam shook his head slowly. "That's just the thing, Mad. I don't have anyone close to me. It has to be about me, because all I got is me."

She stopped sloshing the contents of the can and stared at him. "What about me?"

"What *about* you? I'm gonna drop you off in an hour or so and, for all I know, that's the last time I ever see you." He rocked the soft drink can on the table's rugged surface. "After that, it's back to just me again. And, as I've already said several times, *I* don't have any problem with me having a few beers at night."

"It doesn't have to be that way, Tam. That you never see me again, I mean. Maybe we could be together some day. True enough, I don't want you involved in getting Brandy. That's my thing, my problem. If Mark tries to get the law after me, I don't want nobody else getting in trouble." She took a sip of her drink. "But after that, who's to say? I mean, like I said, I like you a lot. I wouldn't mind seeing you again after I get this all straightened out. The only problem to me is your drinking." She picked up the book and began to return it to her handbag. "But, as anyone can plainly see, you aren't—"

Tam grabbed her arm. "Hold on a second. You're saying that, if I read this book and cut back on my drinking—"

"Not cut back, Tam. *Quit.* The first thing you gotta do is admit you're an alcoholic. Once that's done, you gotta walk away from it."

Tam sagged in obvious exasperation, his hand still on Madison's arm. He really didn't want to have to give up his evening six-pack. It had been his best friend, providing him with the warmth, comfort, and succor he couldn't find elsewhere. It was the only thing he could look forward to in his miserable life. *At least it had been until that moment.* Now he looked into her eyes and told himself that he could actually have something better than the temporary warmth of alcohol. *Something real, something that lasted all day, every day.* All he had to do was quit drinking.

But *could* he?

"Let me see the book," he said at last.

She smiled and handed it to him.

He took it from her and regarded its worn exterior with a puzzled expression.

"What is it?" she asked.

"I was just wondering why a healthy, chemical-free young woman such as yourself would travel around the country with an Alcoholics Anonymous book in your suitcase."

"Open it up," she said. She popped two pieces of bubble gum in her mouth.

He opened it to the place marked by a green slip of paper and a folded newspaper clipping. He saw that the chapter was entitled, "Me, An Alcoholic?"

"Read the newspaper article first," she said.

He unfolded the clipping. It was from *The Nashville Banner* and was dated April 22, 1994. There was a black-and-white photograph of a man sitting on a farm tractor. The caption read, "New lease on life." The accompanying article told of Henry M.'s life-long struggle with alcohol. How AA helped hoist him from his well of despair.

"That's my daddy," she said. "He only drank at night, too. He worked two jobs, worked like a dog, never touched a drop during the day. At night, though, after dinner, he drank like a sponge." She paused, seemed to briefly revisit memories too painful to sustain. "This was his book. He got it from the program and it changed his life. Changed all of our lives. After he passed away, I took it for my own. It's the only thing he had to leave me."

Elvis let out a small woof of concurrence.

He read the first paragraph of the chapter and felt himself start to shiver. He wasn't sure why. He absolutely ached for her: the feel of her body against his, the imagined bliss of being inside her. At the same time, the thought of being alcohol-free absolutely terrified him. Would he able to sleep at night? What if his personality changed and all his pent-up demons came charging out?

He knew this much: He wanted to be with her and she was saying that it was all possible. *It was all possible.* All he had to do was walk away from the beer.

Thunder swelled and rumbled in the distance.

He placed the book on the table. His left hand remained on it for a full minute before he spoke.

"What are *you* gonna give up?" he asked.

"What am *I* gonna give up?"

"Yeah. It's only fair."

Without further hesitation, she spat out her gum. "That," she said. "I love my gum, but, if you'll do this, I'll give it up."

He exhaled slowly. "Okay," he finally said. "I'll do it."

She darted around the table and fell on both knees in the loamy soil in front of him. "You'll quit, not just cut back?"

"Will you catch back up with me when all this is over with?"

"I told you I would."

He shrugged. "Then I guess I'll do what I need to."

"Tam, promise me that you'll quit. Say the words."

Tam frowned. *Another promise.*

She took his hands in hers and pulled them close to her chest. "Say the words, Tam."

All he could think about was her chest and the heart racing inside it.

"I'll stop drinking," he said. "I ... promise."

$$*\qquad*\qquad*\qquad*$$

With Madison at the wheel, they descended quickly from the interstate on a state highway that, with the exception of a slight westward bow, seemed to be the best available pathway to Pensacola. The road passed through several sleepy towns—Madison impatiently endured the seemingly standard jogs that routed traffic at posted snail speeds around one-block "business districts"—but was otherwise a fast track through flat and open countryside. From Tam's perspective, having Madison behind the wheel gave them the opportunity to let the Fury make up some lost time.

Tam couldn't stop thinking about the new bargain he'd made. Until the peanut stand stop, he hadn't done a lot of thinking about his evening's drinking activities. He had just assumed that, at some point, Madison would go and he'd be free to have a six-pack at his leisure. Now, of course, things were less clear. If it happened that they were separated and Madison stayed with her friend, he'd be faced with either honoring his promise—the burdens of which were now beginning to outweigh the potential benefits in his anxious mind—or sneaking a few drinks behind her back. As far as he was concerned, having a couple of harmless beers to celebrate his first art sale would be totally appropriate. Furthermore, he could now see that the *intelligent* way to stop drinking would *not* be to stop cold-turkey, but to slowly wean himself off the peace-bringing amber liquid. Even the shadowy authors (assuming they were, in fact, real people) of the blue book propaganda pieces would have to agree that such a forward-thinking, slow-withdrawal approach to detoxification would serve him better in the long run.

On the other hand, what if he and Madison, for whatever reason, stayed together that night, and the next? He'd have no choice but to keep his promise to her. There could be no situational exceptions, no gradual and humane withdrawal.

That thought sent another ripple of anxiety through him. It'd been years since he'd fallen into night without the warm, comforting cushion of alcohol.

Of course, he told himself, he'd have Madison. *There was that.* If she turned out to be even half the treasure he'd imagined her to be, he'd never have to worry about alcohol again. Madison could become his drug of choice.

Then again, what if they didn't get along? What if they just weren't good together, or if, as he'd suspected for days, the problem with her wasn't his drinking, after all, but some unfortunate chemical imbalance? Some malignant, hidden pathology that compelled her to despise him at least part of the time. Then it would be just like it had been with Lauren. Except now he would have no money, no job, no comfortable den chair, *and* the stress of living on the run. And, by the terms of his oppressive and duress-ridden contract, he'd have no beer. He would have made the biggest sacrifice for—

He angrily shook these thorny doubts from his mind. Madison was right, he now admitted—he obviously had a problem. The drinking *had* taken him over. So powerful was its hold on him that he couldn't even permit himself to imagine how much better his life would be if he were soberly in love with Madison.

There, he thought—you've taken the first step.

And the second step, he instructed himself, was just as easy—don't drink any more. Should Madison turn out to be The One, alcohol wasn't going to be the thing that destroyed them. He wasn't sure of the precise AA methodology—nor did he really care—he just knew that he'd have to find his comfort in something besides a cool aluminum can. Madison would be his joy with a silver twine.

"Look at that!" she exclaimed. She pointed to the wall of black clouds that divided the stormy eastern sky from the sunny west. Rain was falling in a discernable curtain that covered miles of the wide, flat plain. At the end of the cloud wall, the gorgeous bow of a primary rainbow arced across the highway.

"That's beautiful," he said. "I wonder if there's a pot of gold at the end." He shot a quick glance at the sagging fuel gauge needle and grinned at her. "Because we're gonna need the money."

"Why don't we find out?"

He frowned. "I don't feel like dealing with a bunch of leprechauns right now."

"I'm serious. I never had the chance to do that before."

Tam said, "I'm pretty sure it's a myth, Madison. A rainbow is just the colored light we see refracted—"

"Have you ever tried to find the end of a rainbow?"

A short, derisive snort. "Ah, *no*. Never really saw the point in it."

"How will we know what's there if we don't try?"

Tam gave a shrug of submission. Madison was driving; she was the one with the urgent timetable.

They had entered the police jurisdiction of another Panhandle town. It looked basically the same as the other small towns they had passed through—flat, sun-burned, unhurried. Unlike the other towns, though, this one had a paper mill, and a powerful, almost sickening, chemical reek hung in the oppressive air. Madison steered the Fury off the state highway onto a road that, after bypassing a compact golf course, seemed to run right into the mill itself.

"Look," she said. "I think that's it."

Tam couldn't believe what he was seeing: gorgeous bands of color shimmering in the mist at the entrance to the paper mill. Madison pulled off the road and she, Tam, and Elvis got out of the car. They walked into the mist impregnated with both spectral light and paper mill stink.

"This is *so* cool," she said. She danced around in the mist as the dog scampered around her feet.

"But no pot of gold," Tam said.

"We don't need a pot of gold. We got an ammo dog and a big-ass purple car." She held out her hand to Tam. "Dance with me."

Tam made a face. "I'm not really a dancer."

"C'mon. It'll be gone in a second."

He took her hand and she twirled around him. And Tam held onto her as color exploded from prism-raindrops and they fell, wet and laughing, into each other's arms.

*   *   *   *

"She's not here," Madison called to Tam from the apartment's front door. The apartment of her friend, her mysterious and unnamed coconspirator. The southern terminus of their journey together, the gateway to the restoration of her motherhood. Given Madison's numerous references to The Plan, her friend, her friend's surplus vehicles, and, most importantly, her friend's "you-go-girl" encouragement and strategic contributions, the detached observer (a role Tam had resignedly come to accept) might have anticipated a more enthusiastic recep-tion. Far from coming to life with an open-flung door and warm and welcoming lights, the unit, located at one end of a strip of one-story garden-home-style apartments, remained shut tight and completely dark. The only vehicle in the parking lot was a crumpled foreign car stationed in front of an apartment three doors down. Madison threw up her hands in frustration and stared at the closed and presumably locked door. "I am *not* believing this."

Tam squirmed in the Plymouth's driver's seat. This latest glitch—why would he ever have imagined that *this* phase of the journey would have gone smoothly?—only fortified his already substantial level of anxiety. His heart was pounding, his clammy skin was beginning to crawl. He assumed that this was his nervous system's response to the absence of his long-established evening ritual of sedation. He held his watch up to the meager street lamp light and saw that it was nearly nine o'clock. Normally, he would have had two or three calming beers in his system by that time. And now this. Thinking back on it, he should have been suspicious of the Pensacola hookup. Madison had been intentionally vague as to the critical particulars—the when, where, and with whom—of the plan. As she had put it, she didn't want him "involved." His responsibility had been clearly defined: get her to her friend's apartment, then disappear. As a result, now, even after all they'd shared on their adventure, he felt more like a manipulated driver-for-hire than any kind of trusted accomplice.

The process of disengagement from Madison, however, had a new complication. Not only had they acquired some level of personal involvement, now her "plan," such as it was, was at last revealed to be a blueprint for disaster. Tam cursed himself for not having pressed the issue earlier. After all, planning was his forte. The fact that the burglary of the Auto Corral office was rash, impetuous, and highly imprudent did not mean he was incapable of generating great master plans. But Madison had not sought his counsel, and this plan was, well, *obviously* deficient. For starters, there was no indication that she'd ever given her "friend" any advance warning that she was about to arrive. Furthermore, one didn't just breeze into a strange and hostile town and simply walk away with a child in someone else's lawful custody. Not even if she was your own flesh and blood.

He watched Madison walk to the apartment with the car parked in front, the only unit in the building with any sign of habitation. After a minute, the door opened and she had a brief conversation with an occupant unseen by Tam. When the door closed, she started back toward the car. She moved slowly, perhaps even fearfully, as though each step represented a discrete element in a procession of personal failure.

She shuffled to the driver's window and stared at her feet.

"What's the story?" Tam asked.

"She's not here. She—" Madison pawed at loose gravel and shook her head.

"She *what*?"

"Her neighbor says she's having a baby."

Tam's jaw dropped. "Having a baby."

"Like, right now."

"You gotta be kidding me."

Madison shot him a fierce look.

"I mean, I just assumed that you guys—"

"Well, she's having a baby, Tam. There's no point fussing about who didn't do what, because it's happening. It's like, two weeks early, the guy said. I mean, you know, what I am I supposed to—" Her voice, initially defensive and shrill, receded into a low mutter, tinged with exasperation. *Defeat.*

Tam stared at her. He felt fairly defeated himself. He'd stopped for directions no less than four times and had used a quarter-tank of gas finding the apartment complex. And now he was in the middle of a strange town with little money, no tangible idea of what to do next, and a powerful craving for a calming drink. He briefly envisioned himself as he *could have been* just then: reclining on a cheap motel love seat with a cool can of beer in his hand. Completely mellow without a single worry on his mind. Then he noticed that Madison's eyes were flat and unfocused—emotional black holes that seemed no longer able to either absorb or reflect disappointment.

He squeezed the steering wheel and sighed. "Well, what do we do now?"

She stared at the wet pavement and didn't reply.

"Madison?"

"All right, look," she said, at last. "Just pop open the trunk and let me get my stuff. You can go on, I'll be fine."

Tam frowned at her. "C'mon, now. Just—"

"No, I'm serious. This is the thing I originally asked you to do, and you did it. I appreciate it more than you know." She moved toward the rear of the car and slumped against the back fender.

"Madison. Quit being like that. I won't leave you here in the middle of … wherever this is."

She crossed her arms and stared at the ground.

"Madison. C'mon and get in. Please?"

"I don't want to hold you back. You have places to go."

Tam got out of the car and leaned back on a massive purple fender. Elvis popped his head out the back window and whined.

"Look," Tam said, moving closer to her. "I know you didn't ask me to participate in this thing, but I will. I'm sure not gonna leave you here. If you won't get in the car, I'll just follow you until you do."

"I've got to get Brandy," she said. Her voice broke.

"I know you do," he said. "And I'll help you." He wrapped his arms around her.

She remained quietly in his embrace for a long while. In the background, the non-stop drone of crickets and other night creatures, the incidental music to their exhausting Southern drama, filled the heavy, pine-scented air. Finally, she said, "I really don't want you to get in trouble."

He laughed. "I'm *already* in trouble. One more thing probably won't make any difference."

She glanced up at him and smiled.

"Besides, if her father's abusing her … if we can get to a court with a fair and honest judge—" He rocked her slowly as he struggled to organize his thoughts. He was too wired from his need for a drink to think clearly. Still, it seemed that somewhere there should be justice for an abused child and an aggrieved mother. *She just needed a new plan, something with a little more thought behind it.* And he was willing to help her. If it was important to Madison—and it certainly seemed to be—then it'd be important to him, as well. "We'll figure it out," he said, at last. "The first thing we need to do is get us a room for the night."

"Tam, we don't have any money."

He squeezed her tighter. The closeness of her, the feel of her body pressed against his, helped relieve his shrill internal demand for a drink.

"I'll think of something," he said.

CHAPTER 11

▼

A COOKIE FORTUNE

August 3, Tuesday, 12:00 AM CDT
Hurricane Gregor
Latest position: 25.1N, 92.3W
Pressure: 966mb
Winds: 105mph
Movement: N 13 mph
Location: Approx. 300 mi. E of Brownsville, TX
Status: Strengthening

Kelsoe Babb III:

Where was I when Gregor came ashore? With my wife at a friend's house on the other side of Mobile. I know from experience that the worst part of the storm is always from the eyewall east. In this case, that would have been pretty much from Pensacola over almost to Panama City. At least, that's where the most damage was. Needless to say, St. Bart's took a huge hit. Winds of more than 100 miles per hour, twenty foot storm surge. Most of the beach houses and smaller condos were just ... well, to tell you the truth, there wasn't anything left of them. I guess the winds tore them apart and the wall of water washed away what remained. My wife and I were pretty lucky, all things considered. The gallery had a good bit of water damage—we ended up having to replace the flooring and some of the drywall—but we eventually got it opened up again. Our house—we live just off the main highway, about seventeen miles north-west of Mangrove Key—had a big old tree come through the roof, so that was pretty unpleasant. We had anticipated a pretty good bit of damage, given the storm's intensity. What we hadn't expected, though, was the missing property.

"This was probably a huge mistake," the woman said. She reached up with her left hand and attempted to hold her blowing hair in place. "The wind's so strong, and that." She emitted an odd, half-shriek, half-nervous laugh and shot a glance at her traveling companion, another middle-aged woman who seemed to have a death grip on the boardwalk railing. "Don't really need a picture of me with my hair going every which way. Also, we're kind of in a hurry." She flashed Tam a quick and nervous smile. "I mean with the hurricane and that."

Tam took a deep breath and tried to put the woman's latest concern out of his mind. He was having a difficult enough time keeping the canvas tethered to his easel, talking himself through his billowing anxiety, and fighting his obstinate, almost desperate, need for a drink. The woman, who had previously identified herself as Eleanor Morelli from Akron, was a pleasant, silver blue-haired tourist and Tam's first customer at his boardwalk booth outside the Mangrove Point Gallery. And, for her patronage, he was most grateful. He and Madison were once again down to her tip money and desperately in need of cash. Despite the tacit resistance of her companion, Eleanor had allowed Tam to persuade her to sit for a "flash" portrait. Tam already had it in his mind that acrylics would be the appropriate medium for such a project, not only because of its rapid drying time, but also because he saw it as a way of carving out a distinctive niche for himself in the congested domain of boardwalk-mall artists. "You're doing great," he reassured her now, as he made three long, smooth strokes on the canvas. "And don't worry about your hair. I've already got it sketched in just like when you sat down."

"Oh, I'm not sure that's a good thing," she laughed. "I don't think I even washed it yesterday." She turned to her friend for apparent verification of her claim. By now the other woman had released the railing and moved to the entrance to the boardwalk pier. Like the others gathered nearby, she was staring out at the gulf. After noticing the small group a few seconds earlier, Tam assumed that they were all looking for the big storm. Or, as he derisively characterized it to Madison earlier that day, "the stupid swirl of clouds" that was "still, like, a half-million miles away."

"Don't worry—it's gonna look great," Tam told his model. He executed a few short strokes, then leaned back, frowned, and added: "Could you try to hold just a little stiller for me?"

"I'm sorry," she said. "I've never done anything like this before."

Tam flashed a polite smile and wiped his brush. He wanted to admit that he'd never done anything like that before, either. Even the hastily produced, highly supervised portrait of Rosetta hadn't been as stressful to produce. When he had agreed with the boardwalk gallery owner earlier that morning to give the "flash portrait" booth a shot, he'd been flush with confidence. After all, he'd managed to produce and sell Rosetta's portrait in just a few hours' time. And his motivation level was still quite high. He wanted the money, of course, but he also had other, non-material, needs: artistic validation and impressing Madison. Now that he was actually in the middle of a portrait, however, he feared his reach might have exceeded his grasp. He couldn't imagine a more difficult subject (aging skin, unfashionable eyeglasses, perm-fried, bluish hair, etc.) or working conditions (rapidly changing lighting, brisk wind, cynical stares from passersby). Furthermore, the knowledge that Ms. Morelli was paying thirty dollars for a product that, he assumed, she wanted to feel good about only intensified his stress. Although he had certainly *hoped* to execute and sell the painting of Rosetta, it had clearly been a speculative artistic venture from the get-go. This was plainly different. Mrs. Morelli was an actual paying customer vested with every reasonable hope and expectation of satisfaction. As such, she not only had the incontestable rights to judge and critique his work, she also had (at least in theory) the prerogative to withhold payment. He just *couldn't* get it wrong. Especially not with all the observers lurking about. His reputation, maybe his entire future as a portrait artist, hung in the balance. He ducked behind the canvas, took a deep breath, exhaled slowly.

"You from Ohio, too?" the woman asked. "Because you sound midwestern. Definitely not from around here."

"Michigan," Tam replied. He loaded a number six filbert brush with a reddish blend of paint mixed on his makeshift waxed paper palette. He filled in an area in the center of her face, blotted it, then backed away and grimaced. He was still experimenting with skin tones, still unsure how—or even *whether*—to represent wrinkles, blotches, dark circles. To be sure, he'd gotten a crash course in tone and value in the makeshift art institute that was the Laughinghouse kitchen. But the composition of Ms. Morelli's face was far more complex than that of the blemish-free, caramel-skinned Rosetta. He swabbed the brush in a pre-mixed blob of crimson, white, and yellow and tried again. This time, as he retreated to evaluate the overall tonal composition of her face, he was marginally more satisfied. He paused and tried to clear his head so that he could decide what to do next.

Clearing his head was not an easy task for him that day.

In addition to the immediate stressors bearing down on him, Tam couldn't stop thinking about the remarkable changes—two huge blessings, one material loss—he'd experienced in the preceding hours. He regarded the mere fact that he was *there*, with no professional training, no venture capital, no assets other than his minimal painting tools and his natural artistic gift, as an absolute godsend. He had wandered to the boardwalk soon after arriving in St. Bartholomew, hopeful of selling a few "flash"-produced portraits or seascapes; he could never have imagined that the first person he would meet would be local arts patron and gallery owner, Kelsoe Babb. After Tam had described (with both creative embellishments and appropriate omissions) his essential plight, Babb, sixty-something, with a wry smile, drooping moustache, and a full head of flowing white hair, agreed to give the young artist's work a look. Tam had then produced from his canvas bag a stunningly rendered acrylic portrait of an attractive young woman. Babb commented on the "remarkable" way the painting portrayed a subject in conflict; he specifically mentioned the way a few vagrant strands of hair fell carelessly across her forehead, the sad, tired eyes, the mysterious, Mona Lisa-like smile. He offered to buy the painting outright for fifty dollars; Tam, assuming that this sum represented, more or less, the standard discounted value of his work, accepted without hesitation. The gallery owner had then suggested that the artist set up his proposed boardwalk booth under the auspices and control of the gallery, thus relieving Tam of the additional burdens of licensure, bookkeeping, "and other enemies of creativity." The only stipulations insisted upon by Babb: (1) all fees earned from his boardwalk painting would be paid directly to the gallery (Tam in turn would receive a 50 percent "contract employee" share, payable at the end of each day); and (2) Tam was completely responsible for purchasing his own supplies and canvases. Those terms having been quickly accepted, Babb provided Tam with a small table, a sitting chair, a stool, a pitcher of water, used rolls of waxed paper and paper towels, and a hand-lettered sign. He had then retreated to the air-conditioned comfort of his office to tend to official gallery business and to observe how the joint artistic venture "played out."

The blessing that was the boardwalk booth came on the heels of a painful valediction. In order to raise money the previous night, Tam had parted with his beloved guitar—the only item of personal property he had retained from his teenage years. He was unsure of the Telecaster's exact worth, although he'd heard that the vintage instrument might've been worth thousands. Faced with gouging hunger and the prospect of spending the night with a flatulent basset hound in a Plymouth, he sold the guitar to a scraggly haired night clerk at a lower-echelon motel. The sales price: a free night's lodging along with enough boot cash to re-fill the Fury's tank and buy a late-night, fast-food dinner for three. Tam had found solace in the thought that he'd one day (when he became a famous artist) be able to buy a dozen vintage Telecasters, and by the fact that he'd very soon, and at last, be sleeping with Madison.

He did, in fact, sleep with her, although their interlude of intimacy had not begun quite as he had hoped. After devouring a meal of tacos and nachos, they had watched television before retiring to separate beds. This hadn't been discussed or demanded; Madison had simply brushed her teeth and slipped, fully dressed, under the covers of one of the twin beds. After Elvis draped himself protectively over Madison's legs, Tam had sighed, turned out the lights, and, lying atop the other bed, resigned himself to a long, sleepless night of craving and discomfort. He lay on his back for a full hour, watching the dance of light on the textured ceiling and listening to Elvis making an unlimited variety of licking and smacking sounds. Shortly after midnight, he was seized with a powerful urge to slip out for a quick beer or two. An internal debate on the ethics of succumbing to that temptation then played out in his mind, during which time his eloquent inner pragmatist made a very persuasive case in favor of getting shit-faced wasted. Before he brought himself to act on that inclination, however, Madison intervened.

At first, he'd only been vaguely aware that she was awake and standing in the space between the two beds. What he could make out, in the dim light leaking from the space above the curtains, was the object of his periodic lust, wordlessly removing her clothing. Unable to avert his gaze, he watched each item fall away: her shirt, followed by her bra, jeans, and panties. Aroused, yet still, under all the attendant circumstances, uncertain of Madison's intentions, he remained motionless—paralyzed by both doubt and the perfectly thrilling possibilities.

She climbed onto his bed, and, straddling him, bent forward and gently kissed his neck. Tam literally gasped; Madison unbuttoned his shirt and continued kissing his now-bared chest. Tam wrapped his arms around her and they rolled over, almost falling off the narrow mattress. Now he recalled the taste of her skin as he devoured her, the feel of her body, the shuddering orgasms: first his—far too quick for objectively decent lovemaking—then hers, and finally, theirs.

And then, he remembered with an audible laugh, the unexpected and slobbering intervention of Elvis—clamping Madison's calf in a furry vise, tongue-wagging, happily humping away—

"Excuse me," Eleanor Morelli said now, her encroaching voice yanking Tam away—and not a second too soon—from the memory of the lovemaking session's comedic conclusion. "Are you about done?"

Tam blinked. "Um, yeah," he said, finally. "Just about got it."

"Because I think my friend is ready to go back to the condo."

"Got it. Almost done."

Now fully returned to the task at hand, Tam reached for his fan brush and turned his attention to the only remaining problem area: his model's hair. He dabbed the brush into the hardening blob of white paint, then danced the fan over the blurs of dark and light to give some flattering feather texture to her hairdo. He leaned back again and nodded. The essential physical features—the face shape, the eyes, the nose, the mouth—had been rendered as perfectly as he was able. The hair was very close; not perfect, but better than the woman's actual hair. Her skin tones weren't just right, either; then again, this was a twenty-minute, sidewalk rendering, not a full-scale studio portrait. He was most proud, however, of having nailed what he perceived to be Ms. Morelli's personality and character—sweet, simple, decent.

"Done!" he exclaimed, collapsing as far back as he dared on his backless stool. Both artist and model froze momentarily, neither quite sure of the next step in the process. Finally, as Tam got to his feet, the woman followed his lead.

"I'm a little nervous about seeing it," she said, even as she slowly angled around the easel to take a peek at the canvas. "It's for my son and daughter-in-law."

Tam felt an impulse to admit his own anxiety over the finished product. As he had been putting the finishing touches on her hair, the previously scattered boardwalkers had begun to quietly gather behind him. Now, at the moment of truth, he dreaded their reactions as, he imagined, an exhausted gladiator might dread the judgment of a stone-faced mass of coliseum spectators.

Tam turned the easel in her direction. She took a step forward, paused, stared at the canvas. He watched her face, breathlessly awaiting a reaction. He saw that she was smiling, but it was essentially the same tense smile she'd worn throughout the sitting. He could recall Lauren having borne a similar countenance when she'd professed to be "at wit's end" over him. He couldn't tell now whether it indicated pleasure or pain. Or, for that matter, suppressed dissatisfaction.

"My goodness," she said, at last.

Tam felt a sudden sinking sensation. *My goodness?* What the hell did *that* mean? "Ah," he sputtered, "if there's something you don't care for, I can—"

"No," she said. Her right hand went to her chest and then to the edge of the canvas stretcher. "No. My goodness."

The boardwalk observers began to shift positions to give themselves a view of the finished painting.

"That's her, dead-out," one of spectators suddenly offered.

Another observer agreed.

Tam acknowledged the comments, then turned back to Eleanor Morelli from Akron. "So," he asked, quietly. Hopefully. "Is it … okay?"

"I love it," she replied. Her hand went back to her chest. "You made me look so … *beautiful.*"

The crowd burst into applause. The sound brought Kelsoe Babb out of his office. He beamed with approval as the woman took possession of her canvas, hugged Tam, and headed toward the gallery door to pay the portrait fee.

Tam rested an arm on the easel and watched her. He felt both relief and the rare ecstasy afforded by creative success.

He didn't have time to savor the feeling.

While he was looking away, two more people had gotten in line to have their portraits done.

✳   ✳   ✳   ✳

"This is *so* good," Madison said, as she took a huge bite out of an oily egg roll. She chewed, her eyes closed in ecstatic concentration, then added: "I am *so* freaking hungry."

Tam reached across the table and wiped a bit of shredded cabbage from her chin. His thumb and index finger were still speckled with multi-colored dots of acrylic paint. "Better be careful, Mad. It looks like it's starting to unravel on you."

With spending money in their collective pocket for the first time since they'd been together, the two travelers decided to splurge that night and dine at a real restaurant. Tam suggested the nearby Mandarin Palace; Madison, who'd never before eaten at a Chinese restaurant, hesitatingly agreed. After some discussion, they'd made the decision to leave Elvis in the car while they ate. The condo they had just checked into had a no-pets policy and they feared Elvis would bark the whole time they were gone. They felt fortunate to have found a cheap unit with a day-to-day rental option; given the exigencies of their situation, they really didn't want to have to search for new accommodations. True, it was hardly a luxurious unit—the shag carpet was old and ugly and there was a mysterious and disgusting stain on a sofa cushion that penetrated from one surface to the other—but it was an effective staging center for their rescue mission.

At Tam's suggestion, Madison had ordered the moo goo gai pan, an egg roll, hot tea. After staring with a look of dread at her steaming plate, she had taken a tentative, exploratory bite. Soon she was eating ravenously, alternating heaping forkfuls of her entrée with small slurps from her porcelain tea cup.

"So you like it?" Tam asked. The words spilled out in a murky jumble around his own mouthful of food. He had ordered both hot-and-sour pork and Mongolian beef and, after blending them into an unattractive, MSG-laden mishmash, was eating at the same furious pace as Madison.

She held up the half-eaten roll and, for the first time, closely examined its contents. "What the heck's in this thing, anyway?" she asked.

"I'm not really sure."

"It looks like fried leftovers."

Tam laughed. "I never really thought about it, but you may be exactly right."

She shrugged and took another bite. When she finished chewing, she said, "You have, like, a nightmare last night?"

Tam gave Madison a puzzled look. He had, in fact, had the falling-through-the-ice dream again, although he was genuinely surprised that Madison would know that. "Yeah," he said. "I guess I did. How did—"

"You were all clawing around and gasping and everything. Liked to have knocked me off the bed. I thought you were having a heart attack, or something."

"Oh. Sorry. It's just—" He considered sharing the details of the true-life experience he had had as a nine-year-old—the near-fatal plunge into the icy pond water that served as the childhood memory spur for that still-frightening dream. On the other hand, he had absolutely no desire to divulge the fact of the dream's recurrence, or his two-decade-old belief that he was destined to die by drowning. He *especially* wanted to avoid any horoscope/astrology-based analysis of other unresolved issues that might be percolating in the unconscious froth of his mind. He determined that it would be best not to reveal any content-specific information about the dream. "Sorry," he repeated. "It's not a big thing. Just the result of all the stress, I guess."

Madison considered his answer and gave a small shrug of acceptance. She continued to inspect the egg roll with the kind of clinical curiosity a botanist might display toward an unfamiliar root or seed pod. Finally she winced and popped the remaining half into her mouth.

"You guys not have Chinese restaurants around Middleboro?" Tam asked.

She shook her head. "Other than burger joints and the diner, we don't have *any* places to eat in Middleboro." She took a sip of tea. "We never went out to eat when I was growing up, anyhow. Daddy didn't believe in that—thought it was extravagant and wasteful. Shoot, we used to grow our own food. We had some chickens to eat on Sunday. Daddy taught me how to wring their necks, momma taught me how to clean and cook them. And we put up vegetables to eat during the winter."

"Geez," Tam said. "Sounds like you had a tough time of it."

"Shoot. Not getting to eat out wasn't the bad part. Working the tobacco, before and after school—now *that* was harsh." She proceeded to recount her specific duties in the field: setting the young plants in the early spring, helping to spread the chemicals, topping and cutting the mature plants, stripping off the leaves. She grew pensive as she described the hours, the working conditions, the gnawing perception of being trapped in a dead-end life. She took another sip of tea, settled back into the plush booth, and added: "Of course, daddy's drinking made it all even worse."

"All I had to do was take out the garbage and do my homework," Tam said. "Most of the time I didn't do either one."

"Did y'all eat out a lot?"

"We didn't go to restaurants a lot. Hardly ever, actually. I think it had something to do with Mom's sense of shame over having been abandoned. I guess she thought that if she was seen in public without Dad, everyone would know he'd walked out on us. On the plus side, we did go through the McDonald's drive-through a lot. And we had pizza delivered every Friday night."

"Wow. Pizza every week. Sounds like you had a pretty nice mom."

Tam shrugged. "I don't know. I guess she was. I used to hate her, though."

"Was she an ... ah, did she have an alcohol problem, too?"

"No. I mean, she'd have a little wine every now and then, but—"

Madison took a bite of her moo goo gai pan but never took her eyes off Tam. "Did she, like, beat you or something like that?"

Tam made a face. "*No.* I mean, no, she never even touched me."

Madison's brow knitted as she chewed. "Well, if she didn't make you do a lot of chores, never beat you, wasn't an alcoholic, and got you pizza every week, why did you hate her?"

He poked at a lump of fried pork with his fork. A sudden, appalling glimpse into the stained cross section of his soul flashed through his mind. "I don't really know," he mumbled.

"I'm sorry. I don't mean to pry into your personal life. It's just ... I'm trying to understand what makes a kid hate a parent." She paused and swirled the tea around in her squat ceramic cup. "Specifically, a mother."

Tam stared at her.

"The thing is, I'm sure Mark's turned Brandy against me. Just one of the many abusive things he's done. He's made her hate me."

"Why do you say that?"

"Just her attitude the last few times we've talked. You can tell."

"What could he possibly say to make her hate you?"

She didn't reply.

"I mean, it's not like you're some kind of drug-addled prostitute running around town and raising hell."

She held the cup up to her mouth for a long time. When she set it back down, Tam could see a tear running down her cheek. "I'm not a perfect person," she said, her lip quivering. More tears fell. "I think you've already seen that."

Tam watched her swab away the streams with a broad swipe of her napkin and felt a surge of emotion race through him. *There*, he thought. That swipe, that simple, inelegant, profoundly *human* gesture, was the reason he was so fond of her. By comparison, Lauren was a corner dabber—she used the neatly folded point of a tissue or napkin to gently dab her lash margins like television talk show subjects afraid of smearing their makeup. Not that there were ever any real tears to be blotted. With Lauren, the dabbing had always seemed like a grand theatrical gesture, intended primarily to convey her profound sense of personal suffering.

Obviously, he thought, it wasn't *just* the tear-removal technique that endeared Madison to him. More than anything, it was simply emblematic of that which *was* important—her personality, her history, her character. She was beautiful, but her austere upbringing had kept her from being spoiled by it. He looked at her hands and imagined them, as she had described, stripping tobacco leaf—blue from the cold, brown-stained from the nicotine. Lauren had never done work like that, or for that matter, of any kind. While Madison had been working in the searing fields and chilly curing sheds, Lauren had been strolling in air-conditioned comfort with her friends—all of them with perfect hair, perfect makeup, perfectly done nails—through the local mall. He couldn't even imagine Madison in a mall. There were other things, as well. He loved the fact that she had broken nails, that her makeup was slightly overdone, that her worldview was a little shallow and uncomplicated. Her defects just made her human—*the un-Lauren.*

The more he thought about her, the more convinced he became that she was probably The One.

He reached across the table and took her left hand in his. "You're close enough to perfect for me," he said.

She shook her head and pulled her hand away. "Tam, what if she does hate me now? I mean, really and truly *hate* me?"

"I don't know, Madison. I mean, I've never been around kids that much, but I can't imagine a six-year-old hating anyone, much less her own mother." The waiter, a slim Asian man, placed a tray with the check and two fortune cookies on the table. Tam nodded and smiled at him and he slipped quietly away. "I think kids have a tremendous capacity for forgiveness and love," Tam continued. "I know I had every reason to hate my father when I was young, but I didn't."

"Did your father nearly kill you in a car wreck?" she blurted out. Tears were streaming freely now.

Confused by the question, Tam could do little more than wait for an explanation.

"When Brand was about four, right after we separated, I had picked her up at her day care." Another swipe of the napkin. "I ran a red light. I ran a light and a car T-boned us on the passenger side, right where she was sitting. I mean, there's no other way to explain it. I've played back that moment ten thousand times in my mind, trying to figure out what happened. I just … I don't know. I just didn't see it." She twisted the napkin into a soggy paper rope.

"You didn't … I mean, she wasn't—"

"It broke her right arm and a couple of ribs. That was bad, but it could've been much worse. I guess she was just lucky. I mean, *I* was lucky. I don't think I could have lived if—" She shook her head and her voice trailed away to a hoarse whisper.

"Well, hell, Madison. I mean, that's bad, all right, but it was a freaking accident. Shit like that happens to people. My mom wrecked with me in the car two or three times. Once she dropped a lit cigarette on the floor and we ran into the back of a car. Once we skidded on ice and hit a telephone pole. I had to have thirty stitches in my head with that one."

She snorted. "Yeah, and you hated your mom, too. She raised you by herself, took you to McDonalds, got you pizza every week, and you still hated her."

He picked a fortune cookie off the tray and pulled on the ends of the cellophane wrapper. "I don't hate her now." He stared at the cookie for a long time, then said, "I guess I didn't hate her then, either. I think I just resented the fact that we lived like we did. She was such a religious freak, always going off to see this relic or that shrine or some so-called miracle sighting. Our house looked like a freaking religious grotto, all dark and sealed up, statues and pictures and candles everywhere. I guess I resented the way we lived because I felt that's what drove my dad away. It didn't have *anything* to do with the accidents. If anything, they brought a little bit of excitement to my otherwise boring-ass life." He looked up at her and grinned. "I got to ride in ambulances with the lights and siren on."

She sighed. "Well, whatever. Mark used my wreck as an excuse to take Brandy away. That and other stuff he and his lawyer made up. He took her, ran to Florida, and that was that. The judge agreed that I was a horrible mother."

Tam took her hand again. "We'll get her back, Mad. We'll get her back for you and then she can get to know you. Once she does, you'll see everything will be fine."

She smiled and nodded.

"Now," he said, "we have to come up with a plan."

"I already done that. There ain't no plan to it. I called Mark's office over in Sperry today and found out that he carried Brandy up to his mom and dad's house—"

"Wait, a minute. You *called* his office?"

"Don't worry. I called long-distance collect, like I always do. Talked to Millie, his assistant. She's sweet as she can be, but dumb as a brick. As far as she's concerned, I'm still up in Middleboro. As far as she knows, everything's business-as-usual. Anyway, she says Mark carried Brandy up to Azalea Spring because the weather was gonna get bad and all. *Huh.* More like he wanted to clear her out so he could screw some nineteen-year-old cheerleader at his beach house." She yanked on the napkin and it tore in half. "Brandy spent most of the summer up at Azalea Spring, and not on account of the weather, either. Anyway, that's where she's at. So I'll just drive up there and wait. When she comes out to play, I'll call her over to the car, and *bam*. Away we go." She slumped back in the booth and swiped at her red eyes one more time.

Tam rubbed his beard. "Wait a second. That's your whole plan?"

"Well, yeah. I mean, it couldn't get any dadgum easier. Mark's folks are getting older, probably in their late sixties. Brandy's told me about this big playground they built for her back behind the house. I imagine that's where she spends most of her time. Brandy was always big on the outdoors. I'm sure she'll come with me if I ask her to. And Mark will be on the coast looking after his business." She shrugged. "Like I said, it couldn't be any easier."

Tam stared silently down at the fortune cookie.

"What's wrong?"

"I don't know. It doesn't sound like you've put much thought in this part of the plan, either."

"*Huh.* In what way?"

"I don't know, Mad. Something like this … you gotta think the whole thing through. I mean, *all the way* through. Stuff can go wrong—"

She swept her hair out of her face. "Such as..?"

"Well, the car, for one. I mean, you don't go do something like this with a giant purple car from the middle of the last century. That's just like saying to the cops, 'Hey, it's me, everybody. I'm right here and easy to find and I dare you guys to get me'."

"Good point," she said. "I didn't really think of that." She paused a beat, then added: "And now that you bring it up, you should probably go instead of me."

Tam's eyes narrowed as he studied her. He had fully expected a sarcastic rejoinder—if she'd been the least bit Lauren-like, she would've said something like, "Then we'll just take one of the many less-noticeable cars in our garage," or words to that effect. Or she might've brought up any one of his many schemes that had ended in chaotic unraveling. Additionally, he decided, she would have demanded that he immediately reveal *his* plan, whereupon she would have begun shredding it with her piercing eyes and razor tongue. Instead, what he had gotten from Madison wasn't sarcastic, defensive, or even ironic. If anything, it was cooperative and helpful. Something you might expect from a true partner.

Either that, or—

"I'm lucky to have a really smart person around," she continued. "So tell me everything we need to do."

"I don't know exactly yet," he answered. "I'll come up with something." He glanced at the check and pulled a wad of bills out of the right front pocket of his blue jeans. He slid the bills onto the tray.

"I hope we can get this done tomorrow," she said.

"No way," he answered as he cracked open the fortune cookie. "Not if we have any hope of making it out of here with Brandy. There's way too many details to take care of."

Her face clouded momentarily. Then she flashed a tight smile, cleared her throat, and nodded.

Tam plucked the narrow strip of white paper wedged into half of the brittle pastry. He unfolded it and held it up to the light. He read it aloud to Madison: "When the time comes, you will know what to do."

She shrugged dismissively. "So..?"

"So nothing. Aren't you gonna look at your fortune?"

She snorted, almost derisively. "I don't believe in that mess," she said. "I think people make their own fortunes."

Tam nodded. He refolded, then crumpled, the fortune strip.

They slid out of the booth and headed for the door. Along the way Tam spotted a man with a dewy pilsner glass filled with foam-topped golden liquid. The intense craving, briefly suppressed in the day's bustle, was suddenly rekindled within him. Temptation thoughts, easy pathways to relief from his desire, boiled in his mind. It would be so easy, he thought—and not entirely wrong—for him to have one or two cold beers. He could almost feel the initial frigid burn, the eventual softening of his edge, and, finally, the narcotic relief of sleep.

Then his eyes fell on Madison, striding confidently a few steps in front of him. He reminded himself that, if he didn't want to lose her, he'd have to deny himself that beer. More than just *that* beer—he could never again submit to his old desires. *Never.* She'd have to become his drug, his source of comfort. The mere thought of her warm touch would have to buoy his spirits on cold and difficult afternoons. Whatever became of *them*, he knew he had to fulfill his promises. If, after he'd fulfilled those obligations, it all fell apart … well, he thought, he'd ford that stream when he was knee-deep in it.

He followed her out into the eerily warm and humid night.

*   *   *   *

He lay wide awake at 1:00 AM, his brain, absent its accustomed anesthetic fetter, revved to maximum capacity. A dozen different thoughts, shaped and colored by overdriven cognitive processes, flew from his mind's dark staging areas into his consciousness. He tried to synchronize his respiration with Madison's measured breathing, but it was no use. His heart was pounding and sleep seemed to be an elusive, almost unattainable, indulgence.

He made a decision not to fight the wakefulness; rather, he'd use the energy and the long-muffled inner voices to instruct him.

The plan for Brandy's rescue was his first and least complicated thought. He had already isolated the scheme's most salient issues. Who should be the person to take Brandy? How could she best be lured away? Where could they obtain another, more suitable, vehicle for that task?

Answering those questions was a little trickier. One solution was clear to him: plainly *he*, not Madison, should be the one executing the plan. True, being a stranger, he'd have a more difficult time luring the child into the car; on the other hand, once she was with her mother, he could melt away into the fuzzy margins of society, while Madison could travel unimpeded by suspicion. At first, anyway. In time, maybe within hours, she'd become a suspect; eventually she'd become *the* suspect. By then, however, assuming all had gone as planned, she would've installed Brandy in a secret and neutral location where she'd be safe, and where proper custody proceedings—unbiased and free from the influences of money and power—could be instituted.

The vehicle issue was slightly more complicated. He somehow had to obtain an automobile that was so unremarkable it would fail to register in the mind of the casual observer. Obviously, they didn't have the resources to rent a car, and he certainly didn't want to manufacture an additional obstacle by stealing one. Nor were they in a beneficial position to borrow one, unless—

One shining possibility darted into his awareness. While he had only a passing familiarity with Kelsoe Babb, the gallery owner, he'd generated more than eighty dollars in pure profit for him in that one day. More importantly, Babb seemed to clearly recognize Tam's artistic genius *and* his potential as a cash cowboy. *And* he drove a brown Chevy Cavalier, the ideal car for his purposes. All that remained was a means, some simple, yet foolproof contrivance that would put him in the car for a few hours. If he executed his overall plan flawlessly, nobody would notice his car; if people were to notice something unusual, the car probably wouldn't register with them; and, in the very unlikely event that somebody noticed something *and* identified a vehicle, it could never—or, at least, not easily—be easily traced back to him.

Satisfied with the progress he'd made with his master plan, Tam decided to leave the remaining items—coming up with a premise that would entice Babb to loan him the Cavalier, and the precise ploy that would lure Brandy into it—for the next day.

As his cookie fortune had said: *He'd know what to do when the time came.*

The cookie fortune. He thought about Madison's comment about people making their own fortunes. Not so long ago, he thought, that's exactly what he would have said, as well. Now, however, he wasn't so confident in that belief. What had begun for him as brute drunken rebellion followed by random and disorganized flight had become a chain of events clearly anchored in this mission of mercy. Call it fate, providence, kismet, whatever. Virtually every meeting and experience he'd had since that Middleboro intersection seemed to unerringly refer him to the task of Brandy's liberation. Nor could he discount the significance of the dream—that vivid and recurring death-by-drowning scenario. That nightmare, he now knew, was only fate's reminder of how his own grim personal history connected him cosmically to Brandy Monroe. Although he'd chosen not to share with Madison the details of his own near-death experience, he had no difficulty remembering everything about that February afternoon: the mottled and tired ice of the park's skating pond, his scuffed black hockey skates, his mother's Ford receding into the distance as she headed out to run her errands. There had been nobody else at the pond that day, and, as it turned out, for good reason—the ice was perilously thin in several places. Tam had found one of those weak spots within minutes after his mother had gone. He fell into the icy water, and, but for the fact that the tips of his skate blades touched the pond bottom, he would have drowned in minutes. But he was able to break enough ice to work his way to shallower water and thicker ice. He had been able to prop himself on his elbows, but couldn't pull himself out of the water. So he held on and waited while the flame in his lower extremities burned sensation completely out of his nerve endings. Then, just when he was about to give up, the stranger—a man in an overcoat and shiny black shoes—appeared and pulled him to safety. The more Tam thought about those details, the more striking the parallel with Brandy's plight: a young child in peril waits for an absent mother and is, at last, rescued by a stranger. There was no doubt in his mind now that he was meant to be the stranger in the shiny black shoes. Not literally in shiny black shoes, obviously; all he had were his scuffed boots. He was a stranger to Brandy, however, and he'd be there—also out of nowhere—just when she needed him.

Handed these clear mandates by fate, it wasn't totally absurd to assume that a seemingly generic fortune stuck in a cookie might actually have been meant to guide him.

He turned to look at Madison. She was on the far side of their queen-sized bed, curled around a pillow. Elvis lay on the bed between them, his chin resting on crossed front paws. He was twitching and emitting tiny yelps. Tam assumed he was having his own disturbing dream. He glanced at his watch and turned back to the ceiling.

He listened to the distant crash of the heavy surf until, at last, his eyes closed and sleep enveloped him.

CHAPTER 12

▼

PINKIE PROMISES

August 5, Thursday, 11:00 AM CDT
Hurricane Gregor
Latest position: 27.2N, 90.4W
Pressure: 935mb
Winds: 130 mph
Movement: NW 11 mph
Location: Approx. 170 mi. SSE of New Orleans
Status: Continuing to Strengthen

Kelsoe Babb:

Did I know what Tam and Madison were up to when he borrowed my car? The simple answer is, obviously, no—I never suspected anything. And I really can't say now that there was anything that might have tipped me off. Perhaps I could've figured it out later if I'd checked the call itemization on my monthly cell phone bill. But who does that, right? Not that I'd have automatically suspected something had I noticed an unfamiliar number. I mean, I rely on that phone an awful lot in my business anyway, but that August, what with our "evacuation" to Mobile and all, it became our absolute lifeline. I think the "Call Detail" on that month's bill ended up with more than two hundred calls itemized. And it clearly wouldn't have mattered, anyhow—by the time my bill was mailed out, the whole episode was long since over. And there was absolutely nothing about the car to arouse my suspicion. Not even the dog hair on the back seat, because Tam had told me that he needed to run that hound by the veterinarian's office. As for the kidnapping—if it actually was a kidnapping in the eyes of the law—they couldn't have picked a better time to pull it off. You might even say that, timing-wise, the plan was a stroke of absolute genius. I mean, with the hurricane about to hit, everyone in the community who might have picked up on something— myself included—was busy trying to tie stuff down, get supplies, head out of town. Law enforcement had its hands full, too. Every available cop was running around notifying folks of the evacuation orders, directing traffic, and so on. And, as I think everyone now knows, the girl's father was down in Sperry when all this mess was going on. So, no—I was completely oblivious to what was going on. I think it's safe to say that everyone in Mangrove County was oblivious to what was going on. In fact, to this day, there're only two non-participants who know the whole story, from beginning to end—you and me. Since Tam and Madison used my property to execute their plan, you can understand why I'd want to know the story behind the ... I hate to label it a crime, but my guess is that it might be.

What initially aroused my curiosity about everything, though, was the painting. Just to look at it, it's one of the most remarkable works of art I've ever seen. I guess you already know that or you wouldn't be interested in seeing it. It's not perfect, that's for sure. It is very basic, almost primitive in its style. But not abstract—highly figurative. I know now that the whole thing was painted in a few hours. And that just makes it all the more remarkable. Also, it wasn't finished—the last frame was boxed in and labeled, but never painted. And, of course, it suffered some damage from the elements during the storm. When the workmen found it, it was buried under about a ton of debris from those beachside condos. If it hadn't been sealed in that plastic blanket protector, there wouldn't be anything left of it. But it somehow managed to survive, and it's a treasure. I'm not even sure what the proper name for it is. One art dealer I know called it a panel painting. And that may be what it is, although I tend to think of it as a tableau or a montage. I'm just not sure—and here I am in the art business! The only works I can think of that it can be compared to are a few of Basquiat's paintings and that Stella montage of New York scenes. Maybe, in a way, it's like a compressed, canvas version of a Benton wall painting. However you characterize it, I knew who had painted it the first minute I laid eyes on it. Of course, knowing that made me all the more interested in investigating the stories behind those twelve frames.

As you of all people know, when you're an actual part of those stories, it becomes very special, indeed.

Tam sunk behind the steering wheel and surveyed the space between the road
and the immense playground spread out along the rear perimeter of the provincial estate. The first thing that occurred to him as he gave his working environment a strategic once-over was that the expansive play area had been placed with
little or no regard for young Brandy's welfare. A kidnapper, he thought, could
park *exactly where he was*, wait until the isolated child was completely out of the
view and reach of any friendly observers, and easily lure her away. This security
lapse was sufficient to fortify Tam's otherwise unsubstantiated new belief that
Brandy's grandparents were, at best, negligent guardians—an affirmation of
Madison's earlier characterization of the Monroes. What failed to occur to him
was that he might be regarded as one of the individuals whose bad intentions
made the playground placement so dangerous. In his mind, of course, he was
anything but a lurking predator. To the contrary, he saw himself as a noble liber-
ator, a completely well-intentioned agent of the child's sole loving parent. He
ended that particular thought sequence by concluding that the security lapses
were necessary elements in the fate-based algorithm he had constructed.

He was next struck by the pure opulence of the layout. The estate's dwelling
house (as distinguished from the many other house-like structures scattered
across the vast property) was massive and overwhelming: observed from the rear,
he saw what appeared to be a three-story central structure with two single-story
wings protruding from either side to flank a patio and Olympic-sized swimming
pool. The second floor of the main section had a distinctive balcony with an ivory
parapet and balustrade overlooking the pool. Almost as impressive was the play
compound, which featured a full, playground-style swing set connecting, at
either end, a gazebo (with a protruding spiral tube-style slide) and a two-story
play tower with even more slides sprouting off in the direction of a walk-in play
house. Tam tried to (but could not) imagine what it might have been like to have
had that kind of indulged childhood. That thought was immediately followed by
the anxiety-charged realization that Brandy might actually harbor resentment for
having been removed from those extravagant accommodations. That jarring
thought was followed almost as quickly by his internal pledge to begin acquiring
such things for her the minute his plan had been executed.

His plan. The plan had, at least up to that point, worked out pretty well,
although it was clearly not *his* plan. His vehicle procurement strategy, in its final,
complex rendering, had burgeoned to clearly unworkable proportions. It required
that he present Kelsoe Babb with an elaborately fraudulent scenario in which the
gallery owner took the Fury as "collateral" for a loan of two hundred dollars (for
painting supplies and spending money), thus providing the circumstance in

which Tam would have a need to borrow the Cavalier—ostensibly to "run a few errands." After this preliminary subterfuge, as Tam had noted in explaining to Madison his sub-strategy for reacquiring the Fury, the plan got "just a little complicated." After passively absorbing these convolutions, Madison (as she sat on the stained sofa, putting on her makeup) had matter-of-factly inquired why he couldn't just *ask* Babb to borrow the car for an hour or so. Tam had sputtered a number of arguments in support of his strategies; in the end, realizing that he was persuading no one—not even himself—he had shrugged and agreed to give her suggestion a shot.

As it happened, Madison had also been the one to come up with the most plausible scheme for quickly luring Brandy into the car. According to her plan, Tam, armed with details about her personal life that no stranger could possibly know, would approach the child with the news that he, a trusted employee of her father, had been sent to deliver her new pet basset hound and to return them both immediately to her home in Sperry.

But adroit planning notwithstanding, things were on the verge of falling completely apart. What might have been, at some other time, a leisurely operation, had been rendered extraordinarily time-sensitive. For one thing, the longer he remained there, parked behind a small clump of mangrove trees on a washed-out dirt road, the greater the chance he'd be discovered. He did have the dog there with him and a prepared cover story (involving Elvis and a fictitious digestive disorder with plague-like symptoms), but that wouldn't necessarily stop an inquisitive police officer from checking his identity. Also, he had told Mr. Babb that he'd have his car back in an hour—an "hour and a half, tops"—and he'd already been camped there for almost an hour. But his greatest urgency came courtesy of the approaching storm. It didn't concern him that the communal alert level had shot up, in the matter of a single day, from cautious passivity to outright panic mode. Mass confusion and clotted evacuation routes could only work to their advantage as they fled the Panhandle. The wind and the threatening skies did present a huge threat to the plan's critical element: once it began raining, it was unlikely that the girl would leave the big house for the playground. If the television weather "threat mongers" knew what they were talking about, the rain, once it began, wouldn't let up for days.

He knew that Brandy had to show up soon, or he was going back to the Surfsider alone.

The breeze sent an empty soda bottle scuttling along in front of the car. He shot a nervous look at his watch and again scanned the sun-bleached acreage for some sign of the girl.

"It ain't looking good," he said in a loud, stress-freighted voice. He cursed and began to pound the steering wheel with his fists.

Elvis whimpered sympathetically in the backseat.

Tam took a deep breath and let the air and his frustration out in a slow, heavy stream. For the first time, he allowed himself to consider that failure of the mission was not only possible, it was becoming more likely with each passing minute. He felt his spirits sink, his sense of self-worth dropping to the subterranean levels he had known well before Madison had come along and before his portrait painting successes. He told himself he had done everything he had promised to do. *More*, actually, for his initial covenant was simply to deliver Madison to her friend's house. He began to ask himself whether he could have done anything differently, but quickly pulled the plug on that futile redemptory exercise. Madison would be eternally enabled, if she chose to be so petty, to assert that his delays, especially the overnight stop in Arden and the paranoid Orchard City detour, had collapsed their window of opportunity. He tried to imagine how Madison might react if—more likely, *when*—he returned without Brandy. Disappointment, obviously, but would it go further than that? Would she seethe, as Lauren might have, and dismiss him as a complete loser? Or would she acknowledge the effort he'd made and calmly begin work on a new plan?

It wasn't necessary for him to immediately answer those questions for, just at that moment, Brandy appeared.

When he first saw her, she was moving quickly from the house toward him, alternately skipping and running. She paused to examine a piece of metal that had been deposited by the gusting wind in an azalea bush. He sank a little lower in the driver's seat and studied her. She was dressed in a red T-shirt, green shorts, and florid, oversized plastic shoes that slapped at her bare soles as she bounced along. She was a little taller and more slightly built than he'd imagined. Her brown hair had been pulled back into a ponytail. She had a round, pretty face; as she neared, he could see the strong resemblance to Madison. A cloth doll flopped from her closed right fist. As she reached the playhouse, he felt a sudden sinking, the same feeling he used to get before an important basketball game. Except, as he was well aware, there was far more at stake here than any athletic contest. Throughout days of planning and strategizing, Brandy had remained a theoretical entity to him. Suddenly, she was a very real little person, surrounded by other real people, all of whom would profess to have an interest in her.

Suddenly it became easy for him to question what he was doing.

He quickly redirected his thoughts to the reasons for the mission. First and foremost, of course, was that the father was an abusive man, and the grandparents—assuming, as Madison had asserted, they'd used their influence to cut Madison out of the girl's life—had to be complicit in the abuse. Beyond that, Brandy's custody had been unfairly stolen from Madison; justice demanded a determination by a neutral and impartial tribunal. And, of course, it was clear to him that Madison desperately needed Brandy as much as her daughter needed her.

His mind now purged of creeping doubt, he reminded himself that he *had* to be successful. Not just for Madison, but for the girl.

He took a few deep breaths and opened the door. "Here goes nothing," he said.

Elvis stirred on the backseat and gave a hearty woof of support.

Tam moved quickly around the mangroves and a row of low bordering hedges and crossed onto the Monroe property. Keeping close to the bulky towers to avoid being spotted, he threaded his way through the half-dozen swings until he reached the playhouse.

"Who are you?" The unexpected voice of the girl, surprisingly mature for her age, stopped him cold. He saw that she was peeking at him from around a shuttered side window of the miniature building.

"Hi, Brandy. I'm, ah … Fred … um … Swingley." Tam had been mulling over a variety of identities and opening lines as he walked. Brandy's interposition now demanded that he select and run with one. He rammed his hands into his pockets and grinned at her. "I work with your dad. He sent me to—"

"I've never seen you before," she said. She thrust out her chin and fixed him squarely in her narrowed eyes.

"That's because I work in … Pensacola most of the time."

"Doing what?"

"Procurement," he improvised. "Plumbing and sheet metal procurement." He struggled to maintain his awkward grin.

She pushed open the shutter and frowned at him. "I'll have to call on my cell phone and check this out," she said. She disappeared from the window and seemed to be talking to someone else.

Fear shot like electric current through him, melted his grin. That the girl might have a cell phone at her disposal was a contingency he hadn't even considered. To be sure, it had never occurred to him that a six-year-old might even know what the term "cell phone" meant. Then, too, he hadn't been around many six-year-olds in recent years. He quickly scanned the yard, cut a glance back at the Cavalier, calculated his escape lead time. As much as he wanted to succeed in this mission, he wished to avoid prison even more.

The girl reappeared at the window, still talking into the black oblong pressed against her face. Tam took an oblique step in the direction of the car before realizing that the object in Brandy's hand was just a toy phone, a playhouse accessory. He exhaled and let his rigid shoulders slump forward.

"I have my daddy's secretary on the line," she said, cradling the toy against her shoulder. "She wants to know your name again."

"Fred Swing—" He paused, now unsure of his fabricated surname. "Just tell her it's Freddy." He smiled at her. "From Pensacola."

The girl repeated the information into the plastic object and began pacing around the inside of her house. After a full minute of generating actual conversation-like chatter, she returned to the window.

"She says she knows you."

"Good. I—"

"But she wants to know why we're going back to the beach when granddaddy said a hurricane's coming."

Tam clawed at his beard with fingernails that had grown a few millimeters longer than he was accustomed. "We're just gonna stop by there for a minute. Just long enough to get the dog's stuff. Then we're coming back here."

Brandy's eyes got very wide. She set the toy phone down and came out the house's four-foot front door. "Dog? What dog?"

"Your new dog. He's waiting in the car." Tam nodded in the direction of the Cavalier.

"But Daddy said I couldn't get a dog."

"Well, he's, ah, changed his mind."

Her face lit up and, for a moment, a wide smile spread across her face. Tam noticed for the first time that her two top front teeth were missing. Then her brow furrowed and the look of happiness melted into a serious mien. "You're not a kidnapper, are you?"

Tam swallowed hard and stared in amazement at her. "A kidnapper? No, of course not. I told you why I'm here."

"Because my dad said that a kidnapper might try to give me a dog."

"Well, um, he's exactly right. But I'm not a kidnapper."

"You pinkie promise?" she asked. She raised her right hand, balled-up except for an extended little finger.

He continued to stare at her. "I'm not sure what—"

"A pinkie promise means you promise with all your heart that it's true and it can't be a lie." She thrust the extended digit closer to his face. "Not ever."

Tam could feel a weakness in his knees. "Well, yeah, sure. I mean—"

"Then do it. Wrap pinkies and say it."

He put out his hand and she wrapped her little finger around his.

"Now say it."

"I promise I'm not a kidnapper."

"Say you pinkie promise."

Tam sighed. "I, ah, pinkie promise."

The smile returned to her face. "Do Mee-Maw and Paw-Paw know we're going?" she asked.

Tam felt his face reddening. "Of course, they know, silly. Your daddy talked to them about fifteen minutes ago."

"Will you be my robot? Say yes."

Tam stared at her. "I—"

"I tell you what to do and you say 'yes, master' in a robot voice."

Tam cast a nervous glance around the property. "I guess so—"

"Say it like a robot."

A heavy sigh. "Yes, master."

She smiled and gave her head a regal toss. "Good," she said. Then she held up a finger and said, "One minute. I have to get Estella."

He frowned and watched the girl duck back into the playhouse. She emerged in a moment with the doll. He could see that its blonde yarn hair was drawn into huge clumps; its green, midriff-baring top was emblazoned with a pink guitar and the words, "Chicks Rock."

"Okay," the girl said. She allowed her open free hand to be enveloped in his.

They walked off together—Brandy with her carefree, shoe-slapping bounce, Tam with a stiff-legged robot walk. He had imagined that he would feel elation at this particular moment, yet he didn't. What he felt was slightly foolish, and slightly guilty for fudging on his pinkie promise.

Mostly, though, he felt a swelling sense of sadness over the relative ease with which the precious child had been stolen.

*   *   *   *

"*Uh*-oh," Tam murmured. Yet another jolt of anxiety raced through him as he spotted the two police officers directing traffic at an intersection a quarter mile ahead of him. With Brandy belted into the backseat and gleefully stroking a grateful Elvis, Tam had sped west on the two-lane Panhandle road, putting as much distance as possible between the Cavalier and the Monroe estate. A quick check of the odometer told him he only had ten miles more to St. Bart's, a

hoped-for joyous reunion, and, more importantly, the critical exchange of vehicles that would be their safe-passage ticket out of town. But he hadn't planned on
the highway they were about to cross, a major north-south hurricane evacuation
route, being paralyzed with bumper-to-bumper traffic. A quick check of the
rear-view mirror confirmed the growing line of cars behind him; with only
knee-high grass and narrow, loamy shoulders on either side of the road, he was
committed to proceeding through the intersection.

"Why did you say uh-oh?" Brandy asked.

"Um, heavy traffic up ahead," Tam replied. The cops were holding up all
east-west movement and his lane of traffic had come to a complete stop. He again
considered bailing out, executing a quick "U"-turn and heading back east, but he
quickly abandoned that idea. He knew that, as bold as it might be to drive right
under the cop's noses with Brandy, heading back toward the scene of the abduction—just as the cops were responding to the grandmother's panicked call—
would be even riskier. He took a long calming breath and reorganized his available options in descending order of viability. At last he determined that his best
chance was to proceed through the intersection as though there was nothing
wrong. And, of course, hope that the officers didn't detain him.

"This is taking a long time," Brandy said.

"I know. It won't be much longer." Tam's eyes shot from his watch, to the
rear-view mirror, back to the traffic mess in front of him. Then he spotted Kelsoe
Babb's cell phone wedged into the space between the gearshift stick and the air
conditioner controls. He picked up the phone, considered it for a moment, then
punched in the number of the Surfsider unit. When Madison answered, he stated
curtly that Brandy was with him.

"Where the hell are you?" she asked.

"On the road. Almost back. The traffic's a mess."

"Was everything..?"

"It went fine. Everything's good."

"Who is that?" Brandy called out from the backseat.

Tam muffled the phone against his chest. "Um ... it's a man that works with
your dad."

"Can you call Mee-Maw and tell her it's taking a long time?"

Tam shot an alarmed look at the girl in the mirror. "Brandy, I really don't—"

"Please? Pretty, *pretty* please? I really want to talk to her."

Tam lifted the cell phone and said, "I'm gonna have to go. I'll be there ...
soon."

"What's going on?" Madison demanded.

"She wants to call her grandma. She—"

"Tam, don't you dare! Just tell her the phone's battery is dead. Whatever. You just can't. It's absolutely out of the question."

Tam whispered into the phone, "She's a little bit worried, Mad. What if I just called and said—"

"No! Are you insane? Do you want to go to prison? Do you realize that, if they have caller ID, they'll be able to trace the number?"

"It's not our phone—"

"Tam! Use your head! Is it Mister Babb's phone?"

"Yes."

"Then don't you think the cops will go to him? And don't you think he'll figure out who had used it?"

Blood rushed to Tam's face. Suddenly everything was wrong. Suddenly he was the well-meaning but obtuse one, Madison shrewd and coldly calculating. "Yes, I guess so," he muttered at last.

"You *guess* so?"

The traffic had begun to move again. Tam nudged the Cavalier closer to the intersection and the police. "I gotta go," he said. "I'm coming up to a checkpoint. I'll be there in a little while." He closed the phone and disconnected the call.

"I want to call Mee-Maw," Brandy called out. "I never got to tell her goodbye."

"The cell phone's dead," Tam said. "The battery just went out." He frowned as a few fat raindrops splattered against the windshield.

Brandy leaned forward, peering at the console as if to verify his claim. After a few moments, she said, "Well, you can call from one of those phones you put money in."

Tam's fingers tightened on the steering wheel. The girl's voice had grown louder, more insistent. He agreed with Madison that calling the Monroes would be a risky—perhaps even, as Madison characterized it, *insane*—act. On the other hand, it was something that seemed to matter a lot to Brandy, and the last thing he needed, as he was rolling slowly between two police officers, was for Brandy to be vocally dissatisfied. "Okay," he said, as the Chevy reached the intersection, "as soon as we get through this traffic mess I'll stop and call her."

"You pinkie promise?"

"Yeah, sure," Tam said, "if you pinkie promise not to say anything to these co … police officers up here."

Brandy leaned toward the center of the car to get a look at the officers at issue. "Why?" she asked. "Aren't the police supposed to be our friends?"

"Yes, of course. And they're very busy now directing traffic, so … we just don't want to do or say anything that distracts them."

The girl's face assumed a serious mien as she appeared to be, at once, evaluating the logic of Tam's statement and the general worthiness of the proposed bargain. Finally she shrugged in tacit acceptance, rubbed Elvis's wrinkled head, and turned to look out the side window.

"Well, okay, then," Tam said. He clenched his jaw and accelerated into the intersection. One of the police officers, a huge man with a whistle dangling from his lips, finished pulling a rain poncho over his head and turned in Tam's direction. Tam held his breath and tried to focus on the bumper of the car directly in front of him. A few more feet, he repeated to himself, and he was home free.

And then he heard the whistle—clearly a shrill command blast, as opposed to a polite heads-up tweet—and saw another officer stepping obliquely in the direction of his left front fender. His heart began pounding and his mouth went completely dry. He hit the brake pedal and the car lurched to a stop. The second cop tapped the driver's window with his flashlight; Tam responded by forcing a smile and rolling the window halfway down.

"Howdy," he said, trying, despite his anxious, reedy voice, to sound both casual and local.

The officer leaned forward and peered into the backseat. Tam glanced in the rear-view mirror and was relieved to see that Brandy was still placidly staring out at the swaying trees.

"Where y'all headed to?" the cop asked.

"Just running a few errands. Trying to get some things done before the rain starts."

"You know evacuation's mandatory now?"

A plump, wind-driven raindrop splashed into Tam's left eye. He grimaced and blinked. "Ah, no, sir. I did not know that."

"They say the hurricane's turned again. S'posed to be heading right for us now." He nodded skyward. "As you can see, the outer rain band's already here."

"Yes, sir. Well, like I said, we're just doing—"

"It's fixin' to get bad here after a while. A child don't need to be out in it, that's what I'm saying."

Tam nodded. "Yes, sir. I totally agree. We're in the process of taking care of that."

"This is my new dog," Brandy offered. She gave the cop a broad, gap-toothed grin.

Tam shot the girl an alarmed look in the rear-view mirror.

"She's a fine looking dog," the officer answered. Then he grinned, straightened up, and gave a forward sweeping motion with the flashlight. "Y'all be careful, now."

Tam thanked him and rolled up the window. A feeling of immense relief washed over him as he eased the car forward.

And, as the traffic in front of him thinned and the clogged intersection receded in the rear-view mirror, he dared to allow himself to believe that he had pulled it off.

✳   ✳   ✳   ✳

"Why ... aren't ... we ... going?" Brandy asked in a flat, monotone voice. Her head was tilted back and slightly to the side in a listless, almost defeated, posture. Elvis's head and a single paw were resting on her lap. The rain was starting to come down harder now. Driven by rolling gusts, individual drops struck the stationary car with disturbing little smacks.

"Just a second," Tam replied. "I'm thinking."

He was slouched in the driver's seat, eyes shut, his thumb and index finger pinching the bridge of his nose. Sweat poured down the sides of his face. The Cavalier was parked at the oblique rear of a closed convenience store a short distance from the freestanding shelf pay-phone where, just minutes before, he had abruptly ended his conversation with Brandy's grandmother. The woman's last words, an anguished plea for the girl's return, were burning like acid in his mind. He had made the call, not just to placate Brandy, but to assure Mrs. Monroe that no harm would come to the girl. When the woman had hysterically accused Madison of being behind the abduction, he had denied it—convincingly so, in his estimation. He had insisted that he was an "independent contractor for an established New England family," and further assured her that he had never known a woman of that name. But he had also asked who "this Madison person" was (so that he could "keep the child out of her hands"), and what it was about her that Mrs. Monroe found so objectionable. The things the woman then said had left him in a state of shock. He had fully anticipated some of the general accusations. The bad blood between Madison and her ex-in-laws was hardly a secret. But the specific charges, the jarring revelations, had torn into his gut. If they were true—and he suddenly had no reason to believe otherwise—he had been used. Played like the pitiful chump he apparently was.

"Can we go now, robot?" Brandy whined. "*Please.*"

He twisted in the seat so that he could see the girl. "I need to ask you something," he said. "This is real important, so I need you to tell me the absolute truth."

Brandy nodded.

"Is your daddy ever mean to you? I mean, does he ever hit you or do anything bad to you?"

A puzzled expression crossed her face. "No," she said.

"Never hits you?"

"He spanked me once with the remote control." She grinned. "I stuck a jelly toast in the VCR."

"He just spanked you that one time?"

"Yeah. But it didn't hurt."

"Besides that."

"Uh, uh."

"Does he ever—" Tam paused, unsure of how—or whether—to broach the topic of possible sexual abuse. To be sure, while Madison had insinuated that something like that was going on, she'd never come right out and made specific allegations. Finally, Tam swallowed and said, "Brandy, has anyone ever touched you in a way that made you feel uncomfortable?"

She made a face. "No. Why are you asking me all these things?"

"I'm-just-acquiring-family-related-data," he said in a clipped, robotic voice. "So-that-I-might-better-serve-your-fam-i-ly."

Her perplexed look softened into a grin. Her right foot rhythmically kicked at the back of the front passenger seat.

"So," Tam continued, reverting to his normal voice, "your dad is a good dad. Right?"

"Yes. He's sad a lot, though."

Tam blinked. "What do you mean, 'sad'?"

She shrugged. "He just seems sad all the time. He reads me funny stories at night and doesn't laugh. He never laughs and never smiles. He just sits in his chair and watches the television."

"What about your mom?"

"She's sick. That's why she doesn't live with us."

"Who told you that?"

"Daddy and Gran-Gran. But Daddy said she's trying to get better."

"That's what he told you about her?"

"Yep."

"What else has he told you?"

"He said I could go stay with her when she comes on the bus. She was supposed to come at Christmas, but didn't." Her head lolled back toward the window. "Now can we *please* go?"

Tam turned on the windshield wipers and watched the blades flick the spreading veins of water from the glass. He imagined all the things he believed being swept away with each stroke. Gone were his imagined roles as the silver twine that bore joy, the man in black shoes. Gone was every delusional metaphor that had driven and sustained him. And suddenly erased was the moral integrity of his mission. If her father's only sin was depression, if Madison's past behavior had truly endangered the girl, and if her grandparents treasured her, then this wasn't a mission of mercy. And he clearly wasn't the rescuer he'd imagined himself to be.

He knew then that only two things he'd experienced seemed at all relevant at that moment. The first, the fortune cookie, predicted that he would know what to do when the time came. The second was his most recent covenant: the promise to Brandy that he wasn't a kidnapper.

The time had come, and he knew precisely what to do.

"Okay," he said, finally. "We're going now."

He drove to the edge of the road, paused briefly, steered the car into the eastbound lane. He pushed his foot into the accelerator pedal and the Cavalier gathered speed.

"Where are we going, robot?" Brandy asked.

"Back to your Gran-Gran's," he said. Then, glancing back at her through the thinnest film of mist, he added: "Back to where you belong."

*   *   *   *

"I don't even know what to say," Madison sputtered. "I'm just ... not *believing* you could do this." She was pacing back and forth in the restricted space between the tiny kitchenette's sink and stubby counter. For ten minutes, she'd cycled from incredulity to rage to despondency; now all of those states seemed to have merged into a tearfully angry sense of disbelief. "It certainly explains how you've managed to be such a—" She stopped herself in mid-sentence, tore off a section of paper towel from a roll lying on the countertop, blotted her bloodshot eyes.

Tam sat on the edge of the sofa, his hands wrapped around Estelle, the "Chicks Rock" doll, and a plastic blanket cover. Brandy had given Tam the cover, one of two stacked in the corner of her playhouse, so that he could keep the rain off his head when he was returning to his car. The doll had been left on the Cavalier's backseat. By the time they'd returned to the Monroe estate, uninterrupted, gale-force sheets of rain were sweeping through the area; they'd both gotten soaked during their sprint from the Cavalier to the playhouse. He recalled the girl's face the moment he had turned to leave. She'd seemed contented and oblivious to the turmoil and threat churning just beyond her field of vision. Her only concern had been that he'd return the dog to her, as once again pinkie promised, when the storm had passed. This soon-to-be-broken promise, he now realized, wasn't nearly his most egregious misrepresentation of the day. It was, however, the final step in the whole choreographed dance of deceit and therefore deserved to burn his conscience with particular intensity. Logging his performance bottom line in his personal Ledger of Failure, he recorded: one bewildered and disappointed young girl; one heartbroken grandmother; one manipulated gallery owner. And, of course, one angry and betrayed traveling companion. *Not a bad day's work.* Anticipating Madison's shock and anger, he had almost not cared that the cavalcade of approaching police vehicles were en route to the Monroe home. He had almost been tempted to flag them down, to turn himself in. He almost didn't care anymore what happened to him. "How I've managed to be such a complete *loser*?" he said at last, completing Madison's unfinished comment for her. "Isn't that what you were going to say?"

She sniffed and folded the towel into a small square. "I'm leaving," she declared, finally. She shuffled, zombie-like, past the curled ball of Elvis and into the bedroom.

"That's it?" Tam called out. "Just, 'I'm leaving'?"

She laid her open suitcase on the bed and began gathering clothing from the dresser.

"And just how are you planning to leave?"

"I'll find a ride. Anybody with any sense is evacuating this place." She threw a wad of blouses and bras into the suitcase. "I'll walk if I have to."

Still clutching the bag and the doll, Tam got to his feet and walked to the bedroom doorway. "It was the right thing to do, Madison," he said.

"That's your opinion, Tam Malonee. Of course, it's not your child, either."

"You withheld important information from me," he said. "Worse than that, you lied to me." Sensing the contention in the air, Elvis raised his head and emitted a whimper of concern.

She wheeled angrily in his direction. "She's my child, Tam. I was the one who carried her for nine months. I'm the one who gave birth to her after spending ten hours in labor. I'm the one who got up four times a night to change her and feed her. I'm the one that carried her to the doctor and bought her clothes and taught her how to read. I did all that, and then they just took her away from me like I was a complete stranger." Tears of anger once again rolled down burning cheeks. "So please don't sit there and judge the tactics I used to get her back."

"You're also the one who abandoned her to support your drug addiction by dancing topless in a stinking Nashville strip club." He paused and studied her face, half-hoping to see a reaction that would call into question his decision to abort Brandy's rescue, but also would establish that Madison wasn't the clucking and reproving dissembler he now imagined her to be. But he saw no astonishment, no outrage, written on her face. There was only a last, desperate flicker of anger, then surprise, and finally, as her red-rimmed eyes fell away from his defiant stare, what he could only assume was shame. "And it was also you," Tam continued, his voice now brittle with condemnation, "who nearly got her killed by running a red light while shit-faced stoned." He rolled the plastic cover into a tight cylinder. "Yes, your ex-mother-in-law told me everything."

"I made some mistakes," she mumbled, at last.

"*Mistakes*? Letting your kid stay up too late or eat half-a-box of cookies is a mistake. Driving around with her while you're messed up is ... well, it's a damn crime. You give me this big lecture about my bad behavior—" He sputtered to a pause as words momentarily failed him. "You're not just a bad mother, you're a damn hypocrite on top of that," he continued, his voice oozing disdain. "You and your stupid blue book."

The fire returned to her eyes. "A *hypocrite*? I'm not sure what qualifies as a hypocrite in your book, but let me tell you what else I did for my daughter. I quit the dancing gig, even though I was making a thousand bucks a week. Then I went through two months of rehab hell. You think kickin' a daily six-pack habit is tough? Try an all-day crank jones. Meth eats you alive, Tam. It takes you over and makes you forget everyone you love. But I used all the money I had left to get cleaned up. And I did it, every single hurtin' minute of it, for Brandy. And I'm *still* doing it for her. When I got out, I wanted a hit every hour of every day. I probably always will. But I've stayed clean. I swapped crank for chewing gum, and I even gave that up for you. You don't know what hell I've gone through, so don't judge me, Tam Malonee." She threw another clump of clothes into the suitcase. "And, for your information, the blue book isn't just some stupid prop. I carry it with me for a reason. It reminds me what I have to do every single day."

"You also lied to me about Mark," Tam said. Madison's heart-wrenching explanation had purged his voice of the judgmental tone. "You said he abused Brandy and he clearly hasn't."

"You don't think keeping a little girl away from her mother is abuse?"

Tam snorted. "Not if her mom's endangering her."

"Don't you think that making a child hate her own mother is abusive?"

Tam shrugged. "I don't know, Madison, but I don't think that ever happened."

"Oh, and how would you know that?"

"I asked Brandy, that's how. She clearly doesn't hate you. She just thinks you're sick."

She shot him a fierce look and ducked into the bathroom. She appeared a moment later with a hairdryer, two plastic bottles, and a cosmetics bag. She threw the dryer and bottles angrily into her suitcase.

Tam said, "If you want to regain custody, you should get an attorney—"

"Like the attorney you got when you got served with divorce papers? Oh, wait. That's right—you opted instead to get drunk, tear up your father-in-law's office, and steal a car." She snorted. "Who did you say the hypocrite was, again?"

Tam's face reddened. He met her defiant stare silently for a long while, finally said: "I've changed, Madison."

"Oh, yeah, right. Since when?"

He squeezed the doll and plastic bag and stared down at the toes of his boots. "Since I've been with you."

She tossed the cosmetics bag into the suitcase and didn't reply.

"I'm not kidding, Madison. I've really changed. For the first time in my life, I thought—" His eyes rose to briefly meet hers. "I mean, I've always done the wrong thing, the easiest thing, the thing that got me what I wanted right then. But today … I don't know. I think the last couple of days have changed me. Today I realized I cared about doing the right thing—the best thing for the kid. *Your* kid, I might add." He tossed the blanket bag onto the floor. "I knew it wasn't exactly what I wanted, it sure as hell wasn't what you wanted. But it was the right thing to do."

"Well, it wasn't," she muttered. "And thanks a lot for not caring what I think about the situation."

"I do care, Mad. It's just that taking Brandy would have ended up horrible for everybody. You don't want to have to live on the run. You don't want *Brandy* to have to live on the run. Believe me, that's no life for anybody, much less a six-year-old kid." He paused. "Let me earn some money, we'll get a lawyer—"

"I've already told you—no lawyer will help me."

"I don't agree." He tossed the doll into the suitcase.

"What's that for?"

"You can give it back to Brandy when y'all meet at the lawyer's office."

"Tam, you're not in touch with reality," she said. She slammed the suitcase's top shell and secured the locks. "After all this mess today, no judge would ever—"

"Nobody should even suspect you're involved."

"You talked to Mark's mom, for crying out loud!"

"I told her that I was just some random kidnapper-for-hire."

"Then why did she say all that stuff about my past?"

He shrugged. "When she said she thought you were behind it, I assured her that you weren't. Then I asked her why she had such a problem with you." he shrugged. "You know. Just to throw her off the track. It was never my intention to, you know—" He stared down at the dirty shag carpet. "—to pry into—"

"Brandy doesn't know you were bringing her to me?"

"No way, Madison. Give me a little credit."

"Well, it doesn't make any difference. I gave up on the legal system a long time ago, Tam. It's all about money and connections, and, as you can plainly see, I ain't got none."

"I don't believe—"

"Whatever." She yanked the suitcase off the bed and pushed past him into the main room. "It doesn't matter anymore what anybody believes."

"Madison—"

"It doesn't matter, Tam," she snapped. "Don't you see that now? It's over with."

"Okay, fine. You played me like a chump and didn't get what you wanted, so it's over."

She set her jaw and glared at him.

"You knew all along that your supposed friend in Pensacola was having her baby and wouldn't be around to help." He gave a short, derisive laugh. "Man. You sucked me right in, got me to execute your little plan. And, yes, it was *your* plan. You knew the whole time exactly what you were gonna do. You just got me to think I was a partner in it." He slowly shook his head. "Sucked me dry, then tossed me in the trash like an empty beer can."

She shifted the suitcase from one hand to the other. "You're partially right," she said. "Yeah, I got you to help me get my daughter back. And isn't it awful? Here you thought you were playing *me* and it got turned around on you."

Tam rubbed his face and didn't reply.

"But you're wrong about one thing. I was *not* gonna throw you away like a beer can. I truly believed that, after Brandy was here, you and I—" She paused as her voice cracked. "I'm leaving because you betrayed me, Tam. Because you judged me, then betrayed me. There ain't no other way to say it."

He walked to the sofa and sank into its thin cushions. Elvis sauntered over to him and lay his head on his right thigh. "Well, I guess that's that, then." He reached into his pocket, got the Fury's keys, tossed them to her.

"What's this?" she asked, dangling the keys from her left pinkie.

"By all rights, it's yours, anyway. I mean, we did swap the Honda for it."

"What are you gonna do?"

"Me? Not a damn thing. I'll ride this thing out, then paint some more, sell some stuff ..." He shrugged dismissively. "Hell, I don't know. It'll work out. I'm not worried."

"You can't stay here," she said after a long and uncomfortable silence. "The hurricane's supposed to land—"

"Fuck the hurricane. I'll be fine." He turned away, directing his purposefully blank stare at the ugly charcoal sky boiling outside the balcony doors.

"Tam, I'll give you a ride to wherever—"

"I said I'll be fine. See you."

She cleared her throat. "I'm gonna take Elvis, then. I ... *we* can't leave him here. He won't be safe. We promised to take care of him."

"I think everybody's blowing this storm a little out of proportion."

"That's just so typical. You know more about it than all the weather people."

Tam rubbed the dog between the ears and gave him a gentle push in Madison's direction. "Go with her, Elvis," he said. The dog set his paws on the floor, gave Tam one last doleful glance, padded toward the door.

Madison cleared her throat. "If you've got some money you can spare—"

He nodded toward a glass stuffed with paper money on the round dining table. "Take what you want," he said. "Just leave me enough for a six-pack."

She frowned. "Tam, you don't want to get started back—"

"Don't," he interrupted. "Don't *even*. It's my life and it's none of your business."

"I—"

"Just take the money, Mad. Take the money, the dog, the car, and anything else you want. Just spare me any more speeches about how my life could be better."

She gave him a long look, a penetrating expression that seemed to be equal shares pity and contempt. She turned away, plucked a wad of bills from the glass, and, with Elvis in the lead, walked out into the wind and rain.

CHAPTER 13

▼

SPINDRIFT II

Tam finished the eleventh frame, his hastily rendered interpretation of a grinning, rain-drenched Brandy, and wiped the tip of his brush with a wet paper towel. He angled the whole canvas toward the glass doors so as to best capture the scant available light. Squinting and holding the painted surface close to his face, he shook his head and frowned. As he'd feared, the panel's background story couldn't be found among the still-moist streaks of color. At least *he* saw nothing vaguely representative of the streaming storyboard that had played out in his mind as he'd worked. With a desperate urgency bordering on panic, he hastily examined the canvas's other ten frames. *Nothing.* He saw captions and colorful little pictures, but that was it. No message called out to him; he detected no obvious unifying theme, no emotional reagent exposing the canvas's dramatic substrate. His increasingly sober eye now recognized that his once imagined visionary project was, in reality, probably little more than a time-occupying diversion. *Something to do while waiting to be drowned.* He let the canvas fall away from his face as he sank back into the threadbare sofa cushions. Sweat poured from his brow, into his eyes, down the sides of his face. He scolded himself for wasting the last hours of his life on something that—assuming it was ever found—would never mean anything to anybody.

No, that's not true—Madison would get it.

He'd known that when he'd started the painting, he now admitted to himself—he'd known it all along. She'd been the project's inspiration; her phantom presence, her voice, her mercurial temperament had haunted every frame. But he again posed to himself the critical question: *What, exactly, is the point of it all?* Even if the painting miraculously survived the storm's landfall, Madison would never see it. She was long gone, probably already hundreds of miles away. He doubted she'd ever look back, or ever *want* to, for that matter. Nor could he blame her. St. Bart's—indeed, *that whole journey*—would forever represent only inconvenience, disappointment, and, ultimately, failure. And, although he doubted that she'd mourn him for long, now his ridiculous and totally unnecessary death, as well.

A strip of twisted, shorn metal crashed into the glass doors, snapping Tam into an upright posture. He watched with both fascination and horror as the strip smacked the balcony's balusters, oscillated violently, spiraled away into the late afternoon darkness. Still clutching the painted canvas, he got to his feet and moved tentatively to the spindrift-encrusted balcony doors. He stood a few feet back from the shuddering glass panels and wicked sweat from his eyes. His sense of dread heightened as he watched driven curtains of seawater flail the great condo tower's wind-stressed shrubbery. With no way of knowing for certain, he had every reason to believe that the storm's powerful eye wall was within an hour or so of the coast.

He backed away from the doors and noticed the blanket bag twisted at his feet. Heavy drops of sweat spattered the container's clear plastic shell as he bent to pick it up. He unzipped the bag and did his best to reverse the warping caused by his angry twisting. He recognized now that this simple object, this unadorned unit of protective packaging, had become—even more than his primers, paints, or brushes—his most important personal possession. Its thick plastic shell and more or less air- and watertight zip seal represented the painting's *only* chance for survival. Despite the fact that the final frame remained but a captioned, empty box, despite the fact that the painting would be meaningful only to Madison, he felt a powerful impulse to protect it. After all, even in his desperate isolation, he could never know for sure what fate had in store for him. For all he knew, that thing, that canvas testament to his brief interval as fate's obedient servant, might be the means to some veiled but nonetheless noble end. And, for all he knew (although he'd reluctantly jettisoned a vision of this occurrence from his mind), there was always the extraordinarily remote possibility that it might somehow find its way back to Madison.

His eyes danced from frame to painted frame for one last time. A leaden, almost unbearable sadness settled over him as his sense of impending loss deepened. It wasn't just Madison that he'd miss—there were other cherished subjects represented in those frames. Whether or not they were part of a plan to reshape his life, they had in fact done just that. One by one, these people and things streamed through his mind in a gauzy mental slideshow. There was his buoyant half-brother, Rocky. And Pete, the enigmatic hero. The extravagantly generous Mr. Babb; Elvis, the legendary dog; the ethereal rainbow dance; the innocent and spirited Brandy. A deep and audible sigh issued from the depths of his soul, a mournful sound infused with regret and desolation. He bowed his head to pray, but for what? He thought it absurd to ask to be spared, for he'd already been granted—and arrogantly rejected—the opportunity to escape Gregor's fury. Furthermore, he hadn't prayed in years—not to praise, nor beg forgiveness from, much less to petition the Almighty—and to make such a boon request now seemed, well, insulting almost to the point of blasphemy. Besides, hadn't he always known he was destined to die by drowning? Hadn't those almost-nightly dreams of sinking into icy depths portended his watery demise? He knew by then what the dream did *not* foretell—that he was meant to be the heroic man in the black shoes. No, he decided: It would not only be impious to pray for his survival, it would be also be futile.

So Tam asked for forgiveness. For his every destructive act and negligent lapse, for every person he'd hurt and then blamed for his own failings. Beginning with his poor mother. And then, in order of appearance in his disordered life, every friend he'd used or manipulated, every person and institution whose trust he'd betrayed. And he begged forgiveness for his behavior toward Lauren for, although she certainly had her vanities and idiosyncrasies, he knew that she *had* once loved him, at least until his selfishness, neglect, and abandonment had driven her away. And he included Madison in this petition, as well; although she felt betrayed by his final actions, he now believed that it had been his initial, self-interested complicity that may have sealed her fate as far as Brandy was concerned.

He slid the stiffening canvas into the plastic bag and tugged on the zipper. He gave a quick glance around the dark room and decided that he'd best protect the canvas by placing the bag beneath the sofa cushions.

That being accomplished, there was nothing left to do. Almost sober, the concept of being reincorporated in another dimension now seemed like complete stupidity.

Still he wasn't going to sit on the sofa and wait for the storm to rip the condo apart.

He placed a trembling hand on the glass door latch and gave a tug.

The wind-driven rain and debris struck his face like a thousand flying nails.

CHAPTER 14

▼

December 13

The name Arden, rendered in retro-reflective white lettering on the green high-way sign, jostled its way into Janelle Burke's awareness, briefly returning her to rubber-on-asphalt reality. Fully focused now on negotiating the vehicle-clotted interstate, she threaded her way through the traffic and steered the Lincoln onto the eastward-curving off-ramp. She had been on automatic pilot since heading north out of Montgomery two hours earlier. So engaged had her mind been that she had scarcely noticed the parade of gleaming Airstreams, the gradual transfor-mation of the landscape from squelchy bog to leaf-strewn foothill, the barge pass-ing beneath her on shimmering river water. For the time being, at least until she found her bearings in unfamiliar territory, she was keenly focused on her imme-diate task: locating the residence of one Roger Malonee.

The main reason for her being on the road was the lawsuit she'd filed in the state of Florida. It had been this proceeding that had dispatched her to court-houses and paneled conference rooms in quaint but alien Panhandle hamlets, now had her in northern Alabama, and clearly had the potential to propel her even further north, across yet another state line. To the average observer, it seemed a most unglamorous task, the type of itinerant fact-gathering mission that other similarly ascended trial attorneys often delegated to junior associates, para-legals, even retained investigators. But Janelle viewed her journey in quite differ-ent terms. To her, it plainly had more to do with resolution than litigation. In fact, the suit was all but settled, the parties having recently forged an independent peace outside the legal system. Her hours behind the wheel had given her time to think, time to spin individual threads from knotted spools of newly acquired information. More importantly, it had given her the opportunity to investigate two separate reports of miraculous occurrences.

Her quest had begun at the Mangrove Point section of St. Bartholomew. While she certainly had some forensic interest in the northern Gulf coast—the hurricane-related death there had been the lawsuit's major triggering event—her immediate attention was not on interviewing witnesses. Rather, it was her intention to *bear witness*: to both the fragility of human existence and the persistence of life and living. Too, these surviving places and things were critical elements in an important story that, by fate or chance, had touched—no, actually *merged into*—her own life. While she had begun registering her impressions of that fusion in periodic journal entries, she knew nothing would put flesh on her notional skeletons like actually *seeing* the damage Gregor had wrought. Now, even as she continued to process the gathered information, a vivid picture of the storm, its fury and its aftermath, was crystallizing in her mind. Even though the sky that December day had been the deepest blue and the winds unusually calm, she needed only look down that rubble-spoiled sweep of shoreline to imagine the storm's terrifying dimensions.

Certain local landmarks and treasures were embedded in her mind before she even arrived at Mangrove Point. Each of these—the boardwalk, the art gallery, and the remarkable painting enshrined therein—prompted her to think of Tam Malonee. In the beginning, this stubborn preoccupation had puzzled her. Why should her thoughts be so occupied with a man she barely knew, someone from another generation, another region, and, to be perfectly honest, a whole other *world*? Then it had occurred to her that she and Tam had been bound together all along by a length of silver twine. Of course, Don Pedro O'Malley had been—excepting her son and Marvin, her late husband—her best friend; Tam had only been his guest-for-a-day. But Pete would never have entrusted Tam with the Fury and the dog unless he was quite confident that he *knew* him. Meaning, of course, that he harbored no doubts about his fundamental character.

So now it was her turn to get to know Tam. It had been her hope that laying eyes on these surviving places and things would help her find answers to certain persistent questions about the man. Who exactly was he? Was he a genius or merely a talented fool? Regarding Brandy Monroe's abduction, had he been a hero, a villain, or just an ordinary man caught in an extraordinary—and unfortunate—circumstance? And, perhaps most importantly: Had he been a worthy custodian of Pete's treasured possessions? Even though Tam was long gone from St. Bartholomew, she felt the local objects of her sensory experience, from the resonance of the boardwalk's weathered redwood decking to the textured canvas of the panel painting, had helped connect her to him. Now, as the interstate hummed under the Lincoln's wheels, she concluded that her visit to Mangrove Point had fulfilled her expectations. Which was to say that, having actually experienced his paintings—particularly the hastily constructed portrait of Madison Monroe and the illustrated chronicle of his Southern adventure—she was certain of his artistic genius. And, having investigated the details of his last days in St. Bartholomew, she was almost as sure of his overriding sense of decency and fair play. And that was an important step for her in characterizing the true nature of the unfolded events.

Her mind retreated two days, highlighting the moment she had stepped from her car at Mangrove Point.

It had been a beautiful late-autumn day: cool and unusually still, the sun tracking its ever-sinking orbit in a perfect blue sky. She recalled that the only sounds had been the wash of the surf, the strident piping of seabirds, and the drone of a single plane as it bisected a canopy of feathery, crossed contrails. She recalled having walked the boardwalk and somberly surveying the eroded beach still strewn with clumps of seaweed, piles of debris. The dozens of tarp-roofed structural carcasses. And the helmet-clad construction crews arriving to displace departing cleanup teams. Visible reminders of the impermanence of life, the inevitability of change.

Not that she needed to be reminded.

Just three weeks earlier, she and Sam had buried Pete O'Malley. She already knew from previous burials that the loss of a beloved spawned the most virulent form of personal change. Pete's death, in fact, had weighed heavily in her decision to visit St. Bartholomew. In her mind, a bit of his spirit lingered over that sprawling arc of sand and loam. After all, he'd rescued Tam and Madison from peril and quite unwittingly aided in the execution of their abduction scheme. In addition, she'd learned that Pete and Elvis were the feature subjects in one of the frames of the painting. For better or worse, the two travelers had insinuated themselves into Pete's personal history. Which, as Kelsoe Babb had more than once reminded her, made them a part of her personal history, as well.

Kelsoe Babb. Her thoughts now turned to the gallery owner: tall and wide and unforgettably larger-than-life, with his Tom Wolfe ice-cream suit, flowing mane of white hair, and other Southern-planter affectations. He'd given her a quick tour of his compact gallery before the two of them settled into his sparsely furnished office for an hour-long conversation. She recalled having been mildly surprised by his appearance—the soft, thin voice and aristocratic Southern accent she had heard during their several long-distance phone conversations had fooled her into visually representing him as short and slight of build. And, while he certainly seemed knowledgeable, open, and gracious, she knew that a few telephone conversations couldn't give her the true measure of the man. However, after having had the opportunity to spend time with him, to peer beneath the veneer of perfunctory civility, she was now confident that Kelsoe Babb was also a good and decent human. After all, although he'd benefited economically from Tam's talent, he'd clearly given back to Tam and Madison far more than he'd received. He'd provided Tam with a place to work and the opportunity to make money. And he'd also done personal favors for the two travelers: loaning Tam his car and cash, even inviting them to his house for lunch. Like Pete, his generosity had helped them survive, even as it made possible the spurious enterprise of Brandy's abduction. Like Pete, he'd been victimized by the couple; like her husband, he'd reacted to the discovery of his material losses with understanding and compassion. Of course, Janelle now wanted to believe that Mr. Babb's kindness, like that of Pete and others before him, had been a thread relied on by Tam. To repair the damage he'd caused and, in the end, to mend his own hurting soul.

*   *   *   *

The letter, scrawled in pencil on three creased sheets of wide-ruled notebook paper, lay unfolded and curled upward on the Lincoln's passenger seat. Ever-prepared for any contingency, Janelle had removed the well-read pages from her purse before she'd even reached the Arden city limits. But she wouldn't actually need to refer to the directions appended by the author to the end of the last page. She had read every word of the missive, including the graphite smear of the scrawled directions, at least a dozen times. Besides, she spotted the distinctive vehicle as soon as she'd turned onto the Malonees' broad suburban street. Before she'd had a chance to check the numbers stenciled neatly on the curbs, before she'd counted the houses or looked for the itemized landmarks (including the custom-built wooden wheelchair ramp), she knew exactly where Roger Malonee lived. Her attention thus focused on the purple Fury, she nudged her own car down the street, ever oblivious of the grazing reindeer, snowmen, and Santas nestled in the dormant Bermuda lawns.

She guided the Lincoln to a stop at the curb just short of the Malonees' driveway. The Fury was parked at the end of the wide concrete pad behind a compact Honda and a red van. Never taking her eyes off the Plymouth, she switched off the Town Car's ignition and sighed. The entire right side of the car, from front fender to quarter panel, was pocked and dented. The roof had a massive indentation that ran from the right door to just past the center line. And although it had long since been repaired, Janelle was aware that the car had taken another, potentially lethal, hit—a four-foot-long chunk of siding had been impelled through the rear window into the passenger compartment. It was apparent even to as untrained an observer as Janelle that the car's finish was completely ruined. Her eyes misted over as she recalled the day Pete, in light-hearted complicity with her nephews, had applied coat after coat of the purple paint to the Fury's expansive body. *And now.* Now Pete was gone and the car, his greatest automotive treasure, was …

But no, she reminded herself, Pete hadn't seemed bothered in the least by the car's condition. The letter—it had actually been addressed to Pete—had set forth a full and satisfactory explanation for the vehicle's many unsightly blemishes. Each major impact had been catalogued and photographed, then linked to a separate commentary on the various "miracles" that had shielded driver and passenger alike. Pete had read the letter as many times as she, often while reclined in an Adirondack chair on his back deck with his beloved painting of Elvis propped in plain view. He'd never commented on the letter, although Janelle was sure she'd seen a blush of color in his sallow face, a glimmer in his lifeless eyes, even the slightest hint of a smile every time he read it. Nor did he have anything to say about the car, other than to once note—with obvious satisfaction—that it was "a freaking tank."

And of course, there were his last words. Uttered in a hoarse whisper through lips too parched to sip water, but curving one last time into that slight smile: "It *was* a miracle, you know."

For months she'd tried to distill those words into a profound but concise summary of his life, their friendship, or some other length of silver twine. But now she was quite sure that Pete was simply concurring with the letter writer's take on the Fury's occupants' extraordinary escape from Gregor. And who wouldn't agree that human and animal alike had been extremely fortunate?

But had there been anything *miraculous* about the sequence that saw the sturdy vehicle and its passengers removed from harm's way? Janelle had long believed that a "miracle" was an otherwise impossible event of biblical dimensions: water becoming wine, dead men rising and walking away, things of that nature. Unexpected, even extraordinary, developments resulting from human industry and diligence, while by no means common, fell far short of qualifying as miraculous. Didn't skilled medical professionals, using modern technology, bring people back from the dead, restore sight, and help the lame walk every single day?

Hadn't scientists plumbed unimaginable depths and hurled men safely through the black void of space? Her own improbable ascent from an austere childhood to leafy university campuses, study abroad, and a distinguished professional career had been attributed to hard work, the encouragement and support of many, and a trail blazed by many champions of social justice. Of course, she would be the first person to admit that a huge dose of good fortune had also figured into the equation. But was her life story *miraculous*? Until Pete's deathbed observation, she would never have thought to characterize it that way.

But the story of Gregor's survivors had given her new evidence to consider, even though the remarkable events described in the letter seemed more the product of human determination than divine intervention.

Madison Monroe, of course, had been that drama's principal player. And, as it developed, its director and author, as well. With darkness setting in and roadway obstacles appearing almost out of nowhere, she'd made the decision to encamp for the night at a makeshift shelter in a small town near the Florida-Alabama state line. The letter revealed that while there, huddled with a panting Elvis in the relative safety of the old gymnasium, Madison made the decision to get the Fury back on the road. It was just after daybreak on the day of Gregor's predicted landfall, and functionary and refugee alike begged her to reconsider. But she was determined, and there was nothing they could to do to stop her from leaving. And so she gathered up Elvis and went. The author then described how Madison had fought the wind, sporadic bursts of intense rain, and ever-increasing danger from airborne debris. Janelle could easily imagine the fear that must have gripped the woman as she steered the Plymouth into blinding sheets of rain and dangerous, high-velocity projectiles. But still she motored on, obviously driven by the same stubborn will that had powered her every vice and virtue.

Janelle picked up the letter and shuffled its well-worn sheets. There, in the middle of page two, the author described the first of the several reported miracles. She'd read the critical paragraph so many times that she almost knew it by heart:

> I never heard her come in. I was on the balcony, holding the railing with both hands. It was raining so hard it was hurting me. And the noise was so loud I couldn't have heard her if she was right next to me. But then I felt a hand on my arm. I was shocked, of course, because nobody was left within fifty miles of that place. But I turned and she was there. Madison, this angel, pulling me back in. It had to be a miracle. I think I just fell into her arms, I don't even remember what I did. Wait, yes I do. I cried like a little baby. And I held her and I wouldn't let her go.

She blotted a tear from her cheek. She could certainly understand why Tam might characterize his rescue as miraculous. From what he'd said elsewhere in the letter, he had never expected to see Madison again, much less be rescued by her. On the other hand, it *had* been Madison's determination and courage, her guilt, especially her love for the man that had made the improbable a *fait accompli*.

But Janelle was almost willing to concede that there might have been at least a *small* miracle underpinning the rest of their story.

The rest of their story. Janelle knew it well by now, having pieced it together from her phone conversations and meetings with Kelsoe Babb and Madison, as well as from Tam's letter. After leaving the creaking Surfsider, Tam had steered the Fury through foot-deep swells of water, around downed trees and power lines to Kelsoe Babb's house. After finding the property abandoned, Tam and Madison decided to break into the house to ride out the storm. Neither of them felt good about this decision—both had made prayerful promises to never again break the law—but, as Tam put it, they either had to "do it, or die somewhere in a flooded ditch." Indeed, with the Plymouth's gas tank nearly empty and the sustained winds approaching one hundred miles an hour, it would have been foolish to remain on the road. And when the piece of siding blasted through the car's rear window, their minds were made up for them. As it was, the Babb's house (which had lost both power and telephone service) had creaked and vibrated and even took a glancing blow from a falling oak tree. But the travelers rode out the worst of the storm there and, after the frightening winds began to abate, Tam "borrowed" eleven dollars in silver coins and a plastic grocery sack full of about-to-be-spoiled food and got back on the road.

Madison's most immediate concern through the whole ordeal had been Brandy's safety. She knew that the grandparents lived pretty far inland and had a decent storm cellar; if Brandy had ridden out the landfall there, she should have been safe. But then, she couldn't know for sure the girl's whereabouts during the storm. Although she had grossly misrepresented the nature and extent of Mark's maltreatment of Brandy, it was true that her ex was being treated for depression and clearly had withdrawn from the girl. If his unpredictable recent past was any indicator, there was really no telling where he and the girl might have gone.

But Tam, arguing that caller ID might have proven her to be nearby—and therefore a viable suspect in the abduction plot—had counseled Madison against calling to check on Brandy until they arrived back in Tennessee. When, eight hours later, she was finally able to get through to the grandparent's residence, she was greeted with a mix of news. First, and most importantly to Madison: Brandy was just fine. When Madison heard her voice, tears of joy poured from her eyes.

The girl told her mother about the horrible wind and about the nice man with the dog—despite what she'd been told by family and authorities, Brandy saw the abduction episode as an odd but otherwise enjoyable adventure. Madison got no sense that either Brandy or her grandmother suspected her of involvement in the plot. After mother and daughter had said good-byes, Brandy was shooed from the room, and Mrs. Monroe got on the line. In a hushed tone, the distraught woman informed a stunned Madison of the bad news: Mark was missing and presumed dead. Nobody had had any contact with him since early Friday morning, when, according to one observer, he was seen standing alone at the end of a surf-whipped pier. The search for storm victims continued even as they spoke, but the destruction in and around that stretch of the coast was so complete and widespread that it would take time to know for sure.

Two days later, Madison got the call confirming Mark Monroe's death.

From what Janelle could only assume was a deep wellspring that had fed a mother's desperate plot to abduct her own child, now came shock, sadness—for her grieving child—and later, genuine grief of her own. When Madison came to retain Janelle to file the petition for return of Brandy's custody, she'd displayed her own genuine distress over dealing Mark's grief-stricken parents one additional blow. Indeed, the Monroes' initial response to the petition gave every indication that they intended to fight the suit with all of their considerable resources and to the bitter end.

And then, just a week earlier, one more incredible thing had occurred. Madison Monroe, acting completely on her own, had bought a bus ticket to Azalea Spring and arrived, uninvited with suitcase in hand, on the Monroes' front porch. A few words guardedly exchanged through a sliver of doorway opening begat a less tense and more detailed conversation in the mansion's palatial atrium; soon she and Mrs. Monroe were tearfully embracing and awaiting Brandy's arrival home from school. The upshot of the reunion was an informally negotiated agreement that would allow Madison to take back legal custody of her daughter. By the terms of this arrangement—which was still tentative and subject to court approval, to be sure—Madison would move to Azalea Springs, take a job provided by the Monroes, make Brandy available for regular visits with her grandparents and make herself and her home available for periodic checks by designated authorities. Far from being put-off by Madison's separate and uncounseled negotiations, Janelle wished only to complete her witness interviews before drafting an official proposal for the Monroes' team of attorneys.

As for Tam, he had his own loose personal ends to attend. After a brief stop in Tennessee (where, after giving Robert temporary custody of the Fury, he reacquired the Alero), he had headed back to Michigan, fully prepared to "face the music" for his ridiculous crimes. Upon arriving in Minter Lake, however, he was astounded to learn that there had never been warrants issued for his arrest. Even more surprised was Norman J. Holdsworthy, who arrived at his Auto Corral office to find first the purloined Alero, then Tam Malonee, sober and apologetic and offering to "work off" his debt. Frozen momentarily like some gape-mouthed tiki, the flabbergasted Holdsworthy could only blather nonsensically until it finally occurred to him to order Tam from the premises. But then, in yet another vastly improbable turn of events, he stopped his ex-son-in-law just as he was walking off the lot and presented him with a proposal: If Tam was willing to detail cars (and perform other odd menial tasks) for four dollars an hour (Tam assured him that he was), he'd provide him with a tiny room and a small food allowance until his debt had been repaid. Thus engaged, the cloistered Tam Malonee worked eight-hour days and spent his evenings composing a list of people to whom he yet owed amends (Lauren was the first name), painting on available scraps of paper and canvas, and reading the "big book" he'd been given at his first AA meeting. Two months into this contract of barely voluntary servitude, Norman Holdsworthy called Tam into his office and released him from any further obligation.

And then, in yet another improbable turn of events, he offered Tam his old job. Tam politely declined, informing Holdsworthy that he'd be heading back south to "take care of some things." When asked about his ultimate destination, Tam had simply shrugged. Of course, he had a place already in mind. He didn't yet know its name or its precise location. Wherever it happened to be, there'd be sun and sea and room for his easel and sitting chair. He wouldn't worry about fancy accommodations or the acquisition of material things. All he'd need were his supplies and his clothes. After all, he already knew he could survive on next to nothing. And too, he wanted to be able to move quickly at the first sign of trouble in the storm latitudes.

Of course, as Tam had noted in his letter, he knew that he could have no further contact with Madison, at least not until the passage of time allowed circumstances to change and memories to decay. Additionally, he'd advised Madison to dispose of or destroy Brandy's Estelle doll. After all, it would be plain foolish to risk linking herself with the aborted abduction when custody of the girl was within reach.

And it was then that Janelle first began to accept that perhaps a miracle *had* occurred. Not a single episode of supernatural intervention, to be sure, but a process rendered miraculous by the sheer accretion of related improbable occurrences. Even Gregor, having done its worst along the coast, quickly became a provider of much needed rain to a drought-stricken Southeast. It was as if the three named storms—two human, one atmospheric—had been destined to collide; having done so, each transformed into someone or something useful.

Janelle got out of her car and began moving up the driveway. Toward the house where Tam and Elvis and their new family awaited her arrival. She paused briefly at the front of the Plymouth. She remained there a moment, staring at the battered hood and trying to imagine how proud Pete would have been at that moment. Everything had to have some use to Pete, and the Fury had been waiting its whole allegedly storied lifetime for the life-giving flight from Gregor. Her hand gently brushed the car's dented fender.

And with that touch she realized why she was there. Tam Malonee wasn't just an important witness to a custody case or the beneficiary of Pete's largesse. No, he *was* Pete, or at least the twenty-five-year-old version of the man. Both were geniuses, in their own ragged ways. Both were rebels. Both had raged against warty inner demons and won at least qualified victories. And, like the empty final frame of Tam's painting, they were both not so much unfinished as open-ended. Like the spindrift that Tam often referenced—not quite whole and not quite nothing, driven by the wind, free.

She smoothed back her hair and continued up the driveway.

978-0-595-41783-4
0-595-41783-3